STEVEN DEPAUL

Frequently Asked Questions

A Rock and Roll Confidential Mystery

For all my family, past and present

Contents

Acknowledgement

For all the great teachers and professors out there who help foster a love of learning.

1

Chapter 1

June 26, 2021 - 16 months into Covid.

The long-legged brunette in a knit mini dress breezed out of Zanzibar, gave the valet a ten and got into the bright red Tesla X that matched the soles of her Louboutin stilettos. She pulled away from the restaurant into the mix of cars crawling down Abbot Kinney Blvd.

In June of '21, traffic was back with a vengeance as the pandemic seemed to take a breather. With the vaccines widely available, the streets of Venice teemed with nightlife. Months of rainbow-colored quarantines were past and trendy restaurants like Gjelina and Zanzibar set up outdoor eating areas and had valets catching keys and big tips from baby-faced tech millionaires. Money was back on the street.

A black M6 Beamer, waxed like patent leather shoes, entered traffic behind the Tesla, heading towards the canals, the most exotic and expensive place to live in Venice. The original bungalows had long ago been replaced by massive homes on double lots.

A well-placed twenty to Leon at the valet stand bought a heads-up text that the Tesla driver was rolling.

Going over the Howland Canal bridge, the drivers took no notice of a woman in a hoodie and a black SF baseball cap talking on the phone. The Tesla turned into a short driveway and slid under the opening glass garage door. The Beamer stopped at the head of the alley and it's ;lights flashed.

An excited Mona Longworth came out of the garage and waved her friend over to park in the driveway. The garage door closed behind them as they made their way, high on weed and wine, to the cabana by the pool. It was a warm early summer night.

Standing on the bridge, Paloma Grant had taken photos of both cars, pretending to be on the phone. When the lights came on around the pool, she sent a text and a canoe pulled away from a small dock further up the canal. Her operative, Neely, paddled into position, balancing a beer on a cooler propped up in the boat.

Overhead, a small drone followed the canoe down the canal, its buzz covered by the city noise. Paloma started a real phone conversation, glancing at the second-floor window of an Airbnb across the canal. The curtains were opened slightly.

Inside, Neighbor Dave, the best electrician in Venice, sat on a couch with a joystick and an iPad in front of him, maneuvering the drone over the pool and cabana, while next to him, Ellis, Paloma's partner, worked the drone camera, snapping stills. The directional microphone concealed in Neely's canoe cooler was aimed at the public walk along the canal.

As the drone camera zoomed in on the thin billowing curtain drawn across the front of the cabana, Ellis switched it to thermal, tracing body heat. There was plenty. On the screen, a shimmering green silhouette of a woman, long hair and naked breasts quite defined, head thrown back, straddled her lover whose arms reached up to caress her body.

"That didn't take long," Dave said, matter of factly.

"Just like the movies, tearing at their clothes," Ellis replied, shaking his head.

"You got the guy's permission, yes?" Dave said.

"You bet. As the owner of the property, it's legal to take photos."

He texted Paloma to be sure she got the plate number on the Beamer. Still standing on the bridge, she tipped her SF cap to Neely as a sign that all was working.

After a few more minutes of vigorous lovemaking, the woman climbed off her lover and the two of them burst through the curtain to the deck. Ellis switched the camera back to normal view in time to see a naked Mona Longworth, hand in hand, smiling and laughing with a beautiful tall, trim, well-endowed redhead whose hair spilled over her shoulders. They slipped into the hot tub, a bottle of champagne waiting on ice.

"Crazy way to make a buck," Dave said. "Damn pretty women."

"Don't get me started," Ellis said, shaking his head.

"Skinny-dipping in a million-dollar pool," Dave replied.

Ellis nodded in agreement. "Another minute and we pack up and split. This will be plenty for the guy to see what his wife does while he's out of town."

Mona's husband, Glenn Longworth, worked tirelessly on financing for Banshee, his latest tech startup, traveling, meeting with VCs every week. When he sold his first company, he bought the house on the canal, two Teslas and married a horny woman he knew from college. At her request he also bought her the finest breasts in town. Lately, Mona was spending more time at the gym, while at home she seemed distracted, reading on her Kindle by the pool. Dinner was delivered, never cooked.

While attending a conference, Glenn's old friend suggested Glenn hire professionals to 'check' on Mona. His firend had heard about the exploits of Paloma and Ellis at the MoPop museum a year before, and had kept in touch with Ellis, the tour manager of the Earl's Court band, who made him a hero by bringing the band for an office visit and recommended him and the FAQ detective agency.

Climbing out of the hot tub, the women put on the white robes carefully laid out next to the champagne and excitedly went into the house. Whatever fun started at dinner seemed to have more to go. Mona appeared thrilled with the beautiful redhead.

Neighbor Dave landed the drone and Ellis sent out a "well done" group text. Everyone would meet back at Ellis' house on Electric Avenue. Covid-19 had shut down the concert business for over a year. As each month passed, there was no vision as to how the pandemic would play out or end. Road crews had scattered, finding work where they could. Neely, the stage manager for Earl's Court, had been doing odd jobs for the last year. Tonight, he was working for the FAQ detective agency, meaning his rock n' roll refugee friends Ellis and Paloma.

What a scary, crazy year it had been. The pandemic came on like a blizzard in March of 2020. The concert business slowed down to nothing. Ellis and Paloma had not taken it slow by any means. Two days after Paloma's mom, Lana, had invaded the house with her gun-wielding friend looking for emeralds and were arrested, as Ellis' head wound started to heal, they were in an Ojai bed-and-breakfast, mostly in bed, exploring each other's pleasures and the freedom of being together. Each confessed how they had navigated the past month of wanting to be together but not sure how to go about it. Ojai provided neutral territory for both, with no connection to the late Bob Grant, Paloma's dad and Ellis' mentor, inhibiting them.

Bob Grant, a legendary rock tour manager, had passed away on the beach, leaving an empty brokerage account and a balloon mortgage for his partner, Cindy and Paloma to deal with. Paloma enlisted Ellis to help her look for the missing money. They discovered that over a million dollars had been secretly lent to the Human Rights Collective Tour to pay for the daring rescue mission Grant was hired to lead, smuggling a human rights champion out of Africa in a large speaker cabinet. The money was never paid back, and after he died, the house that Paloma and Cindy lived in was facing foreclosure.

When they finally were able to reach leader of the Human Rights Collective Tour in Bolivia, he told them of emeralds stashed by smugglers and if they could find them it would speed up the repayment of the loan. Paloma deciphered clues her dad had left her on postcards he had sent before he died. With others in the hunt, Paloma and Ellis managed to recover the emeralds, with Paloma hanging off scaffolding to reach inside the speaker during a Jimi Hendrix Woodstock video at the MoPop museum and Ellis being rescued from the bad guys.

Upon his return from trying to secure human rights for Bolivian lithium miners, Father O'Conner approached his big donors to pay back Cindy and Paloma. He was met with tepid response since the Human Rights Collective tour was over and the big donors had moved on to other causes.

With foreclosure on the house closing in, Paloma and Cindy looked for a way to sell off the gems. Renting a suite at the Peninsula hotel, Paloma and Cindy arranged a display of the African emeralds on black velvet with high-tech lighting. Properly cleaned, the emeralds were knockouts. Eddy Dotoli, a rather imposing tall friend, hung around the suite as security.

They hit the jackpot when the third of the "invitation only" wealthy supporters of the Human Rights Collective purchased the entire lot of emeralds as a hedge against his other investments, which had taken a hit in the first months of the pandemic. The total take was 1.7 million dollars. Cash.

Cindy and Paloma were made whole; the balloon mortgage on the house paid off just in time with cash left over. True to their word, after deducting some reasonable expenses and the next year's taxes, they gave Father O'Connor a split of the rest of the money for the cause.

Because of Covid, Cindy had not renewed the lease on her vintage clothing store "Chill" in Malibu, even though the landlord made an attractive offer. Instead, she beefed up her website, which was the right choice at the right time as online sales boomed during the pandemic and "Chill" did well.

Ellis had asked Eddy Dotoli, 6'5" with huge hands, to guard Cindy and Paloma last year when thugs were looking for the emeralds. Eddy ran a motorcycle repair shop, and some would refer to him as a 'biker'. During that week Cindy discovered he loved to read books and was a great cook.

In the first months of the pandemic, Cindy and Eddy burned up FaceTime like a couple of high school kids, eventually deciding to quarantine together, cooking, talking about books and taking rides, Eddy on his vintage Indian Trailblazer, Cindy on Grant's Harley.

They took it slow at first, with Eddy staying in the casita where he had stayed last year, but soon he was invited to move in. Cindy had mourned Bob Grant, her partner of twenty years, and he was always in her heart, but Covid had moved lives on faster than expected.

During the first wave of pandemic shutdowns, Paloma split her time between Venice and Malibu, not wanting to leave Cindy alone. When Eddy returned to stay in the casita, Paloma moved some of her stuff to the guest room at Ellis' on Electric Avenue, spending most of her time with him. A weekly "distanced" outdoor Sunday dinner was instituted, with a rotating group of friends attending.

Like the rest of the world, rock n' roll touring people tried to find some equilibrium during the ever-changing pandemic. Some were more successful than others.

Earl's Court's manager, got two rounds of PPP money, but it wasn't enough. The band scattered to second homes away from LA. Ellis and the crew had no such options.

Of the Earl's Court crew, the Thorazine Kid worked on guitars, taking in repair jobs that musicians had put off, and supplemented his income with a run once a month to Lake Elsinore or Paso Robles and his marijuana connections. Even with legal pot shops everywhere, fifty percent of the business was still done the old-fashioned way. "Clean," a keyboard tech who also rode with the Compton Cowboys, had started driving for FedEx, where after a month his true talent was recognized and now, he was in logistics. Neely, without a stage to manage, had started working for his sometimes girlfriend Alena at a "ghost kitchen," started by three out-of-work tour caterers. They supplemented other restaurants' capacity for the boom in takeout orders. Eventually they posted their own "rock n' roll" specialty menu items with delivery services. "Eat like a rock star," the web page said. The dishes were named after musicians they had cooked for, like a virtual celebrity deli.

As the crazy days of closures dragged on, Paloma and Ellis started to kick around ideas about how they could work together and not be on tour. Would those touring jobs come back? Would the vaccines shorten that time? Finding the emeralds before the bad guys was exciting, the small hairline scar on Ellis' scalp a souvenir of that time. Cindy *had* compared them to private eyes, Paloma said, so why not explore the idea.

On the Los Angeles County website, they discovered a large hurdle: it would take thousands of hours for them to get their own PI license. More research showed they could work for a licensed agency if they didn't 'present themselves' as private investigators. One day, over a slice, they mentioned their plan to a friend who worked at Abbot's Pizza. He said he knew a PI, his landlord Duffy, and offered to introduce them. The office was upstairs.

The O'Donoghue Detective Agency had been in the offices on Abbot Kinney for decades, when it was still called Washington Blvd. Duffy O'Donoghue was seventy-two and semi-retired, not chasing work anymore. In its prime, the Agency did a lot of divorces and undercover stuff when business partners had suspicions. When Venice was still run-down, with shopping carts littering the muddy canals, Duffy had the foresight to purchase several buildings on and around Abbot Kinney Boulevard. Now with it being the "hippest street in America," the rents they commanded made Duffy rich. He worked because he liked to.

A few inches under six feet, pudgy with a shock of white hair, he was old-school, wearing short-sleeve Oxford shirts, pants with cuffs and slip-on loafers. He bemoaned the loss of the Pacific Dining Car and other places like it for business lunches and used "dated" terms for women that were throwbacks to the Sinatra Rat Pack, whose oversized black and white poster adorned one wall in the office. The office was a 1960s-time capsule, with worn furniture, irreplaceable wood trim and linoleum. Duffy had connections with both the LAPD and the County Sheriffs. He also played cards with lawyers and judges, sometimes separately.

It turned out he was eager to hear what Ellis and Paloma had to say.

Laying out their proposal over a calzone and beers they brought upstairs, Ellis spoke about targeting the music business to expand the client base of the agency. Paloma explained their long-term connections with bands, managers, and agents. Duffy warmed to the idea. He liked rock music, and like most people thought it would be cool to hang out backstage sometime.

Then there was the kicker. Silicon Beach.

Ellis said there was nothing better for business than young tech millionaires misbehaving, of which more were minted every day. The influx of tech startups and companies like Google and Snap in the last ten years pumped money and mischief into this coastal part of Los Angeles, from Santa Monica to Venice and the Marina. The office on Abbot Kinney was sitting on the epicenter.

Paloma and Ellis offered to pay rent for office space and a percentage of what they brought in for a little equity. Duffy said forget it, "I own the building," so they settled on twenty-five percent of fees they brought in and ten percent equity position.

Duffy figured there was nothing to lose, so an agreement was established to work under his county PI license.

"You can't be called associates without the hours though. It's a lot of hours," Duffy reminded them.

"We thought about that. How about interns?" Ellis suggested.

"Like college kids? Pretty funny. Well, you're not on my payroll, so why not?"

The last part of the presentation was a branding decision to change the name of the agency. Paloma assured him that they recognized the O'Donoghue Agency was a respected name in town, but now they needed a name that would resonate with savvy, younger and richer clients.

Duffy, a proud man, flinched a little at that idea, but his current business was with clients who already knew him. He only advertised with the local weekly paper because they did a profile piece occasionally and they gave him merch, like coffee mugs and water bottles.

Paloma presented the name, showing Duffy a mockup of his window with a new name painted on it in similar gold and black letters.

FAQ.

Frequently Asked Questions.

It was a ubiquitous link on most web pages, universally recognized. After all, they were in the mystery business, and didn't every situation have its own set of Frequently Asked Questions?

Duffy leaned back, smiled, and said he liked it; it gave him digital cred. Besides, his house in Cabo was almost finished and he didn't really plan on spending that much time in the office once winter came.

"We'll print up some intern cards to make it official," Duffy said, reaching out is hand.

They had fallen into a perfect situation. Walk to work and pizza downstairs.

2

Chapter 2

June 27

Glenn Longworth was due to arrive at the FAQ office in an hour. There were desks along the windows, a seating area of a couch, coffee table and a few chairs and a glassed-in back office that now housed stacks of file boxes.

Ellis was editing the drone photos on his laptop for the presentation Paloma was putting together at her desk, next to Duffy's. The riot of tchotchkes littering his desk was a contrast to hers, with only a dashboard surfing hula girl and a small photo of her dad and Cindy.

"Quite a looker," Duffy said, rocking a little, looking over Ellis' shoulder as he edited the drone photos. "I saw a video like this once, something like 'Big jugs in hot tubs.'"

Paloma shook her head. "Duffy, you sound like a sixteen-year-old. Change it up."

"Oh yeah, sorry. I still have to get used to having you guys around."

Ellis shrugged and continued to put photos into a slideshow bin.

"So how are you going to tell him?" Duffy asked as he grabbed his checkered sports coat. "Some small talk, a few benign pix and then drop the bomb? You know, maybe Paloma should take the bomb part. Might be easier hearing it from a woman."

"Makes sense?" Ellis said, looking for agreement from Paloma. She nodded ever so slightly.

"You got a retainer from this guy, right?" Duffy probed. "Some of these young guys have no honor."

"Already in the account. Referred by someone we know," Paloma replied.

Duffy looked at his cell phone.

"I'm off. Client dinner at Chez Jay by the pier. See you in a day or so. Always on call if you need my help," he said, walking out the door.

"Gotta love him," Paloma said. "Otherwise, I would murder him. He needs to evolve."

"It's funny, him being in Venice all these years, you'd think he would have soaked in the ways and means of the counterculture ten times already. However, is this not the perfect arrangement for us? We even have pizza downstairs."

"The little things in life," she said, standing behind him, putting her arms around his chest. He turned around and kissed her.

The pandemic had created terrible hardships for some, inconvenience for others and opportunity for a few. Ellis hammered his savings to pay his mortgage, but at least he had savings. Six months of PPP money from the Earl's Court band had helped, until it ran out. In the last few months, they made just enough money working at FAQ to pay their bills, Paloma insisting she kick in some rent from the money Grant had left her. But like everyone else, if you stayed away from Amazon, there really wasn't much to spend money on other than food and rent.

Showing up fashionably fifteen minutes late, Glenn Long-worth, a Carnegie Mellon grad, slumped down on the couch, complaining about no valet parking. Dressed in a gray Mack Weldon T-shirt and expensive raw denim jeans, his short, skinny frame was swallowed up by the multiple couch cushions. He was about thirty years old and already worth north of forty million dollars. Ellis thought he looked like a ferret.

"Okay, so is she banging someone? The pool guy? Mikey someone from the gym?" he said aggressively, trying to sound street.

Calmly, Ellis started the report. "She was observed leaving Zanzibar in the Tesla, followed by another car, winding up at your house."

Paloma showed the photos of the cars making the turn into the alley she had taken from the bridge.

"They then entered through the garage, and we picked them up behind the pool house curtain."

A sequential slide show of drone photos started playing on the wall TV, first approaching, and establishing the house, then zooming in and switching to the infrared heat display. He could see the defined breasts, long hair and arms reaching up to caress a body rocking back and forth.

"I knew it. She loves that cowgirl thing. You think DMV would give me a license plate for her that says 'SLUT'?" he said, spitting out the word.

Paloma took over from Ellis for the reveal.

"Name is Michael. Trying to find an address."

The slide show switched back to normal view and two naked women joyously burst through the curtain and slipped into the hot tub.

"Wait a minute, that's a woman. Michael is a woman? She's getting off with a woman? Aw man, this sucks."

He jumped up and started to pace.

Paloma and Ellis shared a look. This was the part of the job they hated. Seeing some guy freaking out when his suspicions are confirmed, in pain when you provide the proof.

"Wait. Keep going, I want to see this. What are they talking about?" he said, leaning forward.

"We couldn't record them. Your permission to take photos on your property is as far as it goes."

"Yeah, but you guys recorded them on the sly, right? Were they talking about me?"

"No, we didn't record," Paloma said, trying to hide her disgust. "We're sorry to confirm your suspicions, Glenn. We'll send copies of our file, with a full set of photos, to you and your lawyer in the morning."

Longworth looked surprised. "Lawyer? Why would I send these to my lawyer?"

"They would be part of your divorce proceedings?" Ellis said.

"Divorce? No way. I'm not giving her half. Prenup only covers what I had from the first company, before we got married. This next round of financing and the possibility of a SPAC buyout, that could mean zillions. Nope. I know what she did now, so we are going to work this out. This is like an experimental fling, in college. Everyone had those, right?" he said, looking at Paloma.

Ellis looked at Paloma, her head tilted a little sideways

restraining herself. She had no patience for guys like this. It was the downside of the new job. Ellis hoped she wouldn't hit him.

Longworth clocked her negative reaction and dealt with it the only way he knew. He took two envelopes out of his pocket, looked at the writing on the front and slid one across the coffee table, nodding to them both.

"Send the photos and report to my office. There's some extra in there for a good job," he said, tapping the envelope. "Call it a performance bonus. I heard you were dependable. Hey, the next time Earl's Court plays, any chance of getting some passes like he got? Anywhere in the west, I'll NetJet to the show."

Ellis half-nodded. "With Covid, who knows?" he said.

"Well, keep me in mind. I have signed posters and an Eddie Van Halen guitar in the living room," he said as a parting comment, hoping it impressed them. They heard him go down the stairs.

"I wonder what Mona's life is gonna be like now. Does he confront her? Do they have wild makeup sex? Does he invite Michael?" Paloma asked, shaking her head as she put a file in her backpack.

"Funny. Hard to read that guy. He doesn't want to divorce her because it will cost too much? He would still be left with 'half a zillion.' Wouldn't mean living in a shack."

"I hate these kinds of cases. I don't like being in people's lives. Too messy," she said. "Chicken enchiladas at the Talpa? Hama sushi?"

"Trader Joe's stir fry at home?" Ellis said, laughing.

"C'mon, we just got a 'performance' bonus," she said, waving the check. "We can treat ourselves a little."

"I guess I'm missing the per diem from the road. The Talpa

it is. Cadillac margaritas. Let's bolt."

After more than a year of various quarantine restrictions, going to dinner and eating outside at a restaurant felt special. A few of their favorite places had gone under, and those that didn't were slow to reopen with full service. Outdoor dining was now allowed everywhere, on the sidewalk and in parking areas. They chose the sidewalk. Paloma loved the Talpa, family-owned for many decades and the enchiladas were fantastic.

Over dinner they talked about bands that were talking about makeup shows for last year's postponements. Paloma kidded Ellis about getting the urge to go on the road. His skills as a tour manager made him in demand. He would be offered more than one tour. Being known as one of "Grant's guys" didn't hurt.

But the FAQ agency was partially theirs. And he was madly in love with Paloma. They had grown so close so fast, a bottled-up, awkward past had exploded in the present. Ellis had met Paloma's dad, Bob Grant, when a Falcons tour played at his university and Ellis was on the student crew. He had helped Grant take down the rigging in the roof, impressing him. Not many college students wanted to be up on the catwalk in a large arena. The invitation to come out to California after he graduated was a surprise. Spending a few weeks at Grant's home in Malibu, being exposed to the Los Angeles rock scene, he was thrilled when Grant offered him a touring job.

Paloma was a wild child then, a sixteen-year-old surfer living in the casita out back. The attraction he felt at that time was overridden by her being sixteen and Grant's daughter. Spending a lot of time with her as an adult during the quest for the African jewels stoked the heat that brought them together.

Over the enchiladas, Paloma marveled at Duffy, such a throwback, one-of-a-kind guy. He knew the business, the right people and they learned from him. Duffy had asked around about Ellis and heard that the guy was legit and took rock n' roll bands around the world. Someone told him Paloma, because off her late dad, was rock "royalty," whatever that meant.

As they left the Talpa through the bar to the back parking area, Ellis' phone chirped. He didn't recognize the number, so he didn't answer. Spam was getting worse with endless offers from desperate hotels and car warranties. Were time-shares next? The phone started chirping a second time, the same number, so he answered it as he stood next to Paloma's 528i BMW for the ride back to Venice.

"Ellis? This is Robby Benny, from RimShot and 'The Most.' I work for Tommy Ralston."

Ralston was the vocalist and lead guitar player for the metal band RimShot, with millions of album sales and streams. "The Most" was his softball team that played in the Hollywood entertainment league. Ellis played for a team called the Hoovers 2.0.

"Oh hey, sure. Second base, right? How are you guys doing during all this pandemic stuff?"

"All good. Tommy heard you and Grant's daughter were working for some detective agency. How's that going?"

"Yeah, Paloma. All good. FAQ Agency. You know, no concerts. We got bored."

"I hear it. You guys' free tomorrow morning? Tommy would like to meet with both of you, at his place. Ten o'clock work? I'll text you the address and the gate code."

"Sure, anything more you want to tell me first?" Ellis replied.

"Ah, I'll let Tommy tell it. Okay?"

"Sure. See you there."

Climbing into the BMW, Ellis looked over at Paloma as she started the car.

"Who?" she said.

"Robby Benny. Interesting call."

"What?"

"Tommy Ralston of RimShot wants to meet with us."

"When?"

"Tomorrow morning."

"Where?"

"His house."

"Why?"

"Stop doing that," he said, laughing at her.

"Who?" she replied, smiling.

"Ralston Ten o'clock tomorrow morning. Probably offer me a job. Benny is texting the address."

"Well, my calendar is clear," she said, not looking at her phone and starting the car.

"And how about your calendar for tonight? That clear too?" he asked.

"You bet. Why, you need to get on the schedule?" she said, throwing the BMW into third gear, ripping west on Pico Boulevard towards Venice.

3

Chapter 3

June 28

The sun was peeking into their tiny Venice backyard when Paloma returned from an early morning surf. Ellis had a breakfast of fruit and coffee, laid out on the table. Balancing a laptop on his knee, he was scrolling through the promised Ring video footage that came in late last night. The video was a wide angle meant to focus on who might be at the door. The street was twenty feet in the background.

"Got anything?" Paloma said as she slid her surfboard against the fence.

"Not great quality, just getting to the time we want. First I went to where I see Willem enter the frame and run down the street, then backed up. Hopefully his time estimate was correct, and we will see the guys or a car before and after, although it is a two-way street so we might see nada," Ellis said, jockeying the arrow buttons for fast forward and reverse. There was a red sedan, a FedEx truck and a white van coming along the street around 1:42 pm. They saw no people walking down the street.

They slowly advanced the video and there was nothing until about 2:09 when a flurry of cars and a pickup came by, followed by the same white van as earlier. Ellis stopped the video.

"What is it with us and white vans? Those little creepy ticket scalpers get out of jail yet?"

"No idea, but that isn't their van. Roll it back. It's newer. More pronounced front end, no window on the side. Can't make out a driver," Paloma said, pointing to an image. "What is that on the back door? Some kind of logo?"

"Looks like a smudge. Too far away."

They watched as Willem entered the frame, frantically moving from car to car, looking in driveways. He appeared desperate. Gary went in the other direction, out of the camera range.

Ellis put the laptop on the table and said they needed the Thorazine Kid to enhance the logo with Photoshop.

"We probably need to learn how to use that program someday."

"Yes, but for now we have the Kid. And it gives us a chance to get him out of his guitar cave and into the office. I'm sure we can entice him with pizza."

"Call him. It's the only clue we have in the eighteen hours on the case."

"It's 7:45. Let him sleep a while," Ellis said.

Paloma looked at Ellis, put down her cup, started to unzip her wet suit and led him into the house. Another great way to start the morning. In the arms of someone you love.

The coffee got cold.

Duffy was puttering around the office, listening to the jazz trumpet of Blue Mitchell on the local Venice radio station, 99.1, when they arrived. He was dressed up, wearing a patterned sport coat and a vibrant Gary Garcia designed tie. You could smell his cologne down the stairs.

"Hot lunch date?" Paloma teased, looking him up and down.

"These are my 'going to court' clothes. Take note, young ones. I have to testify in a store employee theft case. Watched this guy and his cohorts for two days filling out false credit applications. How's by you?"

"We're on the hunt for a stolen guitar. Pretty rare. The rocker it belongs to agreed to double the rate," she said.

"Nice. Any band I know? The Killers? Green Day?"

"You listen to those bands?" Ellis asked, surprised.

"Oh yeah. More too. Marjorie, my former assistant, took me to lots of concerts before she got married and left."

"Ever heard of RimShot? Tommy Ralston, their lead guitarist, it's his guitar."

Both Paloma and Ellis decided to leave out the George Harrison part for now.

"Never heard of them. They any good? Well, keep tapping that rock n' roll gold mine," he said with a big smile on his way out. "Later."

Calling music stores and pawn shops was the kind of grunt work that was not the glamorous side of being a PI. Tedious conversations with salesmen/musicians, awake too early, trying to upsell guitars, had Paloma pacing back and forth in the office as she spoke to them. The more calls they made, the more refined their questions became, shortening the calls.

No vintage Country Gentleman was for sale or had been offered. Nothing new had shown up on eBay or Craigslist. Ellis spoke to Raymond at Raymond's Rare Guitars and half explained a version of the situation. His place was perfect to hear about a guitar like that.

And then Benny called.

Paloma answered and he immediately asked to talk to Ellis. Some guys had problems with smart, assertive women. She put him on speaker.

"Update. You know anything?" he asked.

"Hey, hello to you too. Spoke with Willem about how it went down, and we are looking at a Ring camera recording of the street where the shop is."

"And?"

"And we are hoping we can develop a lead from that. We need to talk with Gary." Ellis said, waiting for a reaction.

"You know how long Gary has worked for Tommy, right? They go way back," Benny said.

"Great, we need to talk with him. Today. How about our office in Venice?"

There was silence, then a muffled voice as though he put the phone against his clothes.

"He'll be here at our office. Say two o'clock. We are making a music video tomorrow, so it's all hands-on deck. 9200 Sunset. Use my name with the guard in the lobby," he said gruffly. Maybe Ralston was in the background chewing him out.

"Got it, see you there."

Paloma's fuse was lit. These guys were sexist assholes, and she wanted no part of them. She was compromising herself for money, and that felt like shit.

"I know what you're going to say."

"Do ya?"

"Yes. They're everything you think and probably more. Not the kind of people we want to be associated with, professionally or otherwise. Let's find the guitar, take the money, and be rid of them," Ellis said.

"Ralston shouldn't be allowed to own such a famous guitar. Did you see Cindy's face watching those old clips of the Beatles? Gotta be millions of women feel the same way."

"I agree, but this is what we do. You want me to take this case solo? Happy to do it," Ellis said.

"C'mon, man, let me vent a little. It's healthy."

The Thorazine Kid rolled in around eleven, a Falcons backpack over his shoulder. He had boxes of tour swag from over the decades in his garage, but this one he used. Maybe because the logo was cool and small.

After bro hugs with Ellis and Paloma, he looked around, saw the giant Rat Pack photo on the wall, the beat-up wooden trim and desks and commented on the office.

"Love what you haven't done with the place. This a sixties time capsule or something?"

"You haven't met Duffy, our patron," Paloma replied.

"Throwback, huh?" the Kid said.

"Fascinating," Paloma said and left it at that.

The Kid pulled his laptop out and set up next to Ellis. Inserting the SD card, he brought up the video and Paloma read off the time code they wanted him to work with. He pulled a still and enlarged it, commenting on the "video noise."

"Wide-angle camera, front focused and the van is moving. Not what I call the best parameters. Give me an hour and a mushroom-olive pizza. They cooking downstairs yet? I need breakfast," he said, hunching over the keyboard.

Paloma and Ellis shared a look, her eyes widening as her head tilted slightly forward. Ellis got the message and called downstairs, ordered the pizza, and said he would be down to pick it up.

Halfway through his meal, the Kid had enlarged and sharpened the focus on the van. The logo looked like a military patch with a crossed brush and nozzle. Above it was the fuzzy words "Detail Ho!" A quick Google search found a mobile car detailing service with that name and logo, an address, and a phone number.

Leaning back in the chair, the Kid said, "Maybe they clean your car and salute."

"Amazing," Paloma said, leaning on the desk to get a closer look. "I gotta learn how to use this program."

"But you got me," the Kid said.

"You'll be gone on the third tour bus out of town once concerts start back up," she said, jokingly, but not.

"We're going to talk to Ralston's guy, Gary. You'd recognize him from The Most. He's never more than five feet away from Ralston."

"One of *those* guys, huh?"

"You got it. Then we check out Detail Ho! and have a chat," Ellis said.

"I'm taking the leftovers," the Kid said, pointing to the pizza and closing the laptop. I have a nasty fret job on a vintage Fender Jazzmaster waiting for me.

Driving down the once glorious, always famous Sunset Strip to the RimShot office, you would pass some of the clubs that would be in the history of rock n' roll forever. The Roxy, the Rainbow and the granddaddy of them all, The Whiskey. Owned by Elmer Valentine and later, partner Lou Adler, The Whiskey served as a launching ground for bands of the 60s, like The Doors, Love, The Birds, Buffalo Springfield, and many others.

Johnny Rivers of "Secret Agent Man" fame ripped it up as the house band for a while.

One momentous night at the Whiskey, in the sixties, with dancers packed in, Elmer sent his cigarette girl, Patty, up to a platform above the dance floor to DJ between sets. A few nights later he added two dancers, twenty feet above the dance floor in an old glassed-in security area from when the space had been a bank, creating the "Go Go Girl." Patty added the white boots and fringed tops, and the iconic look was soon found on TV and in clubs around the world.

The Whiskey was also involved with the Sunset Strip Police Riots in 1966. The City of West Hollywood forced The Whiskey to change its name to the more puritanical "Whisk" and rescinded the "youth permits" that allowed eighteen- to twenty-one-year-olds who could not be served alcohol, into the clubs. The local government of the mid-60s had bowed to the wishes of a few large land developers who hoped to turn the funky Sunset strip into a row of high rises.

Trying to clean up the area, a 10 pm curfew was tried. The streets stayed crowded, with teenagers sporting the new "hippie" look, the curfew was ignored, and the police got into it for a few nights. In the spirit of the civil rights movement, large groups sat down in the middle of the street by the Pandora's Box club. After the curfew, Los Angele police in riot gear and batons were called in to clear everyone out. What ensued was called a police riot by some.

Some historians say this was another turning point in the culture wars that were to come. The new wave challenged the old guard. One week later the Buffalo Springfield recorded a song about that protest, "For What It's Worth," which soon was also adopted as an anti-war anthem. The next year, 1967, was the "summer of love in San Francisco," hippies were everywhere, and the establishment grudgingly accepted their presence, though the culture war would continue through the Vietnam War.

At the end of the strip, where the last of giant billboards and eclectic architecture gives way to the huge homes and lawns of Beverly Hills start, the 9200 office building looms like a bookend, holding everything in place. With a commanding view of the western basin of Los Angeles below, the building is full of entertainment companies, with the private Soho House club in the penthouse.

"Jeez, they better validate this parking ticket. What a rip-off!" Paloma said as they rode up in the elevator.

"Expensed to Ralston, remember?" Ellis said.

"Just can't get used to the rates in the real world, I guess. I thought the beach was expensive."

The elevator opened on the ninth floor, RimShot's management office. Floor-to-ceiling glass walls with a killer view south. Modern design gave the office a very cold austere look, nothing like the shaggy band that roamed the stage hammering out rock n' roll songs at a deafening volume. It was no accident that the office was on the same floor as the Ford Models Agency.

The receptionist had them wait on the couch while she rang back.

"Nice office. Maybe someday we will have a view like this," Ellis said.

"You don't think our digs are homey, in Venice? Walk to work, pizza downstairs? This is kinda Beverly Hills-y," she replied.

"Beverly Hills is twenty yards that way," he said, pointing away with his thumb.

"Here you are," Benny said, walking over quickly and shaking hands. "C'mon this way."

Benny led them down a hallway. They passed a kitchen/lounge and a conference room where a group of shaggy videographers were being led through storyboards of tomorrow's video shoot. They entered an office that was the exact opposite of the waiting room. The shades were drawn, oriental carpet, thick leather furniture, a clutter of posters and silver records on the walls. From the posed photos all around it was a no-brainer that this office belonged to Ralston.

"When you sell twenty million records, I guess you get your own office," Paloma said under her breath.

Standing behind the desk was Gary Edison, bearded with an angular face, less than six feet and well fed. Wearing jeans and a vintage RimShot T-shirt, he reached over the desk to introduce himself then sat down. Sitting behind the desk was body language that said to Paloma he needed a layer of protection, like crossing your arms during an uncomfortable conversation. Benny sat down near the window, and they were on the small couch.

"Hoovers, right?" Gary said, making small talk, referring to the softball team. "Tommy hired you to help find the guitar. Benny here says you want to hear from me what went down at Willem's place."

"That's right. Just trying to get as much information as we can. Whatever you have might help us find the guys."

"What about Willem? He was standing right there."

"We spoke with him yesterday." Ellis let it stand at that.

"Sure. Okay, like I told Tommy and Benny here. I went over there with the guitar. Willem works on Tommy's guitars. He had an acoustic guitar laid out on the counter, showing some guy the repair, he had done. I think it was a Martin," he said, trying to impress them. "I leaned the guitar case against the counter, waiting on them to finish. Phone chirped and I stepped away to talk, over by those guitars he rents. Tommy's green Maserati was in the shop, and I needed to be sure that it was ready cause Tommy and Maggie wanted to drive it to some premier in Westwood."

"What about the two guys who came in with the other guitar? Your description would really help confirm what Willem saw," Paloma said.

"The guys come in. About my height, in black jeans and T-shirts. One was real skinny and pale as all get out. Either had what we call 'arena tan' or maybe a druggie. The other guy was a Mexican. Kinda ashy complexion. Coulda been a druggie too."

"Mexican? How do you mean?" Paloma asked.

"You know, brown skin and black hair, plump," he replied with a shrug. "Anyway, their guitar case looked like a million others. Must have placed it down next to mine. While I was asking about the car, I think I heard Willem say something like it would be a while cause I was next. Then they left. Weren't in the place more than a couple of minutes."

"What happened when you discovered you had the wrong guitar?" Ellis proceeded.

"I put the case up on the counter and opened it for Willem. We looked at it and it was not the Country Gentleman. We bolted out of there and ran down the driveway, almost knocked over the guy with the Martin. We split up and checked cars and driveways down the street to see if they were still around. Man, I was sick to my stomach. I know that guitar. Couldn't believe Willem let them walk out with it."

Throwing Willem under the bus. Paloma refrained from shooting a look at Ellis. Benny was watching them, not Gary, his running buddy.

"Who else knew that you would be taking the guitar to the shop?" Ellis asked.

"Good question. I called from the lounge. People in and out all the time."

"You tell anyone?" Paloma inquired.

"Of course. Tommy and Benny," he replied, getting a bit hot. "Look, I've been with Tommy for twelve years. On the road and at home, I'm always doing stuff for him. Do I wish that I didn't have to deal with the car and the video tomorrow at the same time I was bringing the guitar in? You bet. But I don't want anybody looking sideways at me over this. I hope you find the fuckin' guys, believe me." He sounded like he wanted ten minutes alone when they did.

Gary and Benny stood up, signaling the meeting was over. Ellis thanked them for the help and gave Gary an FAQ card, in case he thought of anything else. Walking out, Benny made a friendly remark about Neely almost taking Ralston's head off at the last softball game before the pandemic. A rematch was coming.

And now the Hoovers had a ringer. Eddy.

They drove out of the garage, Paloma handing off the parking ticket that the receptionist had put little stickers on. Heading west on Sunset, always a fun drive in the BMW, massive Beverly Hills mansions now flanked the road.

"You know what my dad used to call guys like Gary?" Paloma said, downshifting into a sweeping curve near UCLA.

"OFOW, right?"

"Yup. Old Friends on Welfare. He's the guy that's been around so long they don't know what to do with him, so he picks up cars at the shop and drops off guitars. A gopher with some title of personal road manager on tour not to be confused with the real road manager," she said. "Ready to lay the blame off on Willem. Or some Mexican. I'm always surprised that some people haven't evolved. Hard to say if he was involved or just can't hit a curveball."

"Then there is the money he could get for that guitar, even splitting it with the thieves. Gary might feel underpaid."

"Having Benny in the room altered the dynamic."

"I glanced at Benny when you asked who else knew he was going to bring the guitar in. Didn't flinch when Gary named him and Tommy," Ellis said.

"Felt like he wrote Gary off a long time ago. Who else might know?"

"Well, if you are on the phone in a bullpen, anyone can hear your conversation. You saw the kitchen/lounge we walked passed up there. People all over."

"Or Gary could have been talking about it in a bar. He comes off as that kinda guy who needs people to know he's important."

Tupac's "California Love" came on blasting. What better song to drive west on Sunset?

"You good to check out the van? The New Upsetters are gonna sound check early in Malibu," Paloma said, turning on to the 405. "It's time to shake off the rust and play a few sets."

"Looking forward to it. No problem, I got it covered."

"You're just gonna drive by and see if the van is there, right? No adventure?" she said.

"I'll check out the address on maps and see if it is a house or an office. The company could have more than one van."

"That would complicate things," she noted, downshifting the BMW as they went into a wide curve.

Neely was leaning against his car in front of the FAQ office when they arrived.

"If I make one more 'Petty's chicken enchilada' plate or 'Torch's famous' sausage and peppers, I'm gonna puke," he said, referring to the ghost kitchen where he was helping Alena. "I need to get back on the road, let a tour bus rolling down the highway rock me to sleep."

"Hey to you too," Ellis said as he led the way upstairs.

"At least you guys are out and about, a little adventure once in a while," Neely said. "I mean, you did a job in Yucca Valley. I've been AWOL. Always west of Lincoln."

"Things are loosening up. Bands are gonna be making up last year's shows. Heck, RimShot is shooting a video at Culver tomorrow."

"Hate those guys. I did flatten Ralston with that line drive," he remembered fondly. Ellis nodded. "Wait, you hanging around with them? Aw man, evil empire."

"Nope, just a small investigative job," Paloma added.

"He's a crook, right? Or he's bangin' a hot influencer and the Victoria's Secret model found out and is pissed?" Neely observed pop culture lately through magazine covers while waiting on the long pandemic lines at Ralphs supermarket.

"Nothing like that. Just a case of something he lost and we gotta find it," she added, looking at Ellis. Her eyes slid over to Neely. Ellis looked back and shrugged.

"Neely, if you're not busy, Paloma's off to Malibu for her sound check and I have to check out a van before I head up.

Want to come?"

"You bet. What's the case? Victoria's Secret models?"

Detail Ho! was in Blair Hills, a small neighborhood that backed up to the Inglewood oil fields, where slow-moving pumps worked day and night, bringing up the last remaining barrels. The Victory Motel showdown scene in the movie *L.A. Confidential* had been filmed there.

Turning off the recently named Obama Boulevard, Ellis drove down the short streets, passing small industrial buildings and then into the neighborhood of older, tightly packed houses. Wind out of the west made the whole neighborhood smell like creosote-dipped telephone poles.

"There's the house," Ellis said as he pulled up across the street. In the driveway was a plain white van with the logo matching the screen grab Ellis had on his phone. He had only given Neely scant information about what he was looking for. He had however mentioned the description of a skinny guy and a brown-skinned guy he was hoping to talk to.

Hooking up a hose on the side of the van was a bearded guy who could pass for one of Eddy's biker pals. Big and beefy, tattoos scattered over his arms, wearing a "digi" camo shirt and a ball cap.

"Doesn't quite fit the description, huh?" Neely said.

"Gotta check it out anyway," Ellis replied, resigned.

They casually approached, crossing the street. The big guy gave them a side eye and continued working.

"Hey, you do car detailing?" Ellis said.

"That's what it says," he said, pointing to the logo, voice flat.

"My name is Ellis. I'm investigating a theft on Monday.

Maybe you can help me."

The guy looked them over, walking slowly down the driveway. Ellis handed him his FAQ card.

"Doubt it," he said, barely looking at the card.

"Were you on the 4200 block of Camino Paso around two o'clock on Monday?"

"What the fuck's it to you?" he said, immediately hostile.

"Well, we were hoping you may have seen something that could help us."

"I'll help you across the street into your fuckin' car," he replied.

Neely instinctively stepped a few paces to one side of Ellis, spreading out the ground the guy would have to cover if things got hot. Neely looked all hippy-floppy but was a guy you wanted with you if there was trouble.

"Hey, no offense. We're just trying to help someone find what was stolen. You see, we saw your van on a doorbell video and hoped you could help," Ellis said, trying to keep things cool.

"I hate those fuckin' things," he said, looking over his shoulder at the house. "Okay, look. I got a *sick friend* over on that street and once in a while I check in, see how things are. You know what I mean, right?"

Ellis and Neely nodded. The guy was having a "nooner."

"So, you have my van, on this video. Not good. Isn't there some kind of privacy law about filming me?"

"The intent of the doorbell was not to film you, just whoever comes to the door. Your van was in the background," Ellis explained.

The guy looked them over, then looked back at his house again.

"If the video ever sees the light of day or my old lady finds out, I promise I will come to your office and fuck you up," he said, waving the business card. "You feel me?"

"Final thing. You see a couple of guys on the sidewalk as you drove off? Maybe carrying a guitar case?"

"No, now fuck off," he said, walking back up the driveway.

Returning to the car, Neely said that going by the "Indian in the star" logo on the hat and the tats, the guy had been US Army, Second Infantry. Growing up in Tucson, Neely hung out with a guy at the Circle K who had the same hat.

"Doubtful he would hang with some junkie-looking guys dressed in black. Unless he was their dealer," Neely pondered.

"I sure didn't get that hit. Seems like wasted time."

"So c'mon, give me the skinny on what we are looking for? A guitar?"

They stopped for sushi before picking up the Kid and Neighbor Dave. Ellis filled Neely in on Ralston, the guitar, and the search.

"Harrison was a fuckin' Beatle! The guitar is part of Rock history, like McCartney's Hofner bass. And 750K+, that's huge dollars. Either it's A, not a mistake or B, the two guys are the luckiest people in town. I'd go with A, "guitars for a million, Alex", not a mistake. Now that I solved your case you can buy me dinner."

"How did you solve my case?" Ellis asked.

"I gave you the options. Gotta be one of those."

"Neely, we know the options; it's the specifics we don't know, and I just spent part of today finding out I'm back where I started from."

"Well, even if it's not Victoria's Secret models you have to let me work it, cause that ghost kitchen is making me crazy."

Of all the accommodations that were made for Covid, the move outdoors for dining and entertainment was a rare win. Especially in Southern California. Restaurants took over the curb lanes, parking lots and sidewalks for seating. This summer the atmosphere in Santa Monica and Venice was social life trying to return to normal from the pandemic. Everyone hoped this craziness was tapering off.

In Malibu, just across the PCH from the Pacific, there was a pop-up music venue called The Lot, an outdoor parking lot behind an empty insurance office, with some picket fencing, Astroturf, tables and chairs and a small stage. Strings of lights created a festive atmosphere, and a few food trucks provided pizza and tacos.

The New Upsetters, the latest edition of the band Paloma had been singing with for years, had added the Malibu Horns, creating a large powerhouse retro R&B dance band. As they ripped through their first set, the dance area in front of the stage was packed, Paloma sharing the vocals on R&B hits like "Tell Mama" and "Mustang Sally." People loved to dance to the old soul tunes.

Neighbor Dave, Ellis, Neely and The Thorazine Kid, arriving quite stoned and late, found a table off to one side, grabbing pizza and beers from the trucks. These guys, who worked for famous musicians, were blown away at how talented Paloma was as a singer and her poise on stage as a band leader. She rarely talked about it. Ellis remembered the first time he saw her on stage before the pandemic, performing a sensual version of "Walk on Gilded Splinters." The crowd had gone nuts. Ellis was entranced.

In between songs, the conversation at the table centered on old rock drummers, The Who, and how outrageous and explosive the great Keith Moon was.

"Played the drums like another lead instrument while he kept incredible time," Neely declared.

"There's a concert video where Moon has headphones, gaffer taped to his head. Gotta love that," Dave added. "He influenced another madman, Ginger Baker of Cream."

"Did you see that documentary? Baker attacks the guy making the film in the opening three minutes," The Kid said, roaring.

"I hate to tell you this, Kid, but Peter Townsend, trying to be louder than Entwistle on bass, had Jim Marshall put two cabinets on top of each other, creating the 'Marshall stack' before he switched to HiWatt amps," Ellis said. "I heard it on this podcast Paloma listens to."

"Well, keep that to yourself."

After a Curtis Mayfield medley, the New Upsetters took a break. Paloma came over to the table and looked at the goofy smiling faces.

"You guys are blitzed," she asked. "Who drove?"

A row of BYOB tequila shots was on the table. She helped herself and sat next to Ellis.

"You got my text?" he said. "The van was a bust. Some ex-army guy having a nooner with his other girl. Kinda back to square one."

"Well, we'll split up tomorrow and hit some of the clubs that have reopened. A pale, skinny guy dressed in black shouldn't be too hard," she said, lifting another tequila shot.

The guys exploded in laughter.

"Only half the musicians in town," Neely added.

"So, what guitar did they leave behind?" Dave asked, still laughing.

Paloma and Ellis looked at each other.

"Shit, we never looked at it. We're idiots. I'll text Willem and let him know we're coming first up in the morning." she said, shaking her head.

"Rookie mistake," Neely said, taking another hit on a vape pen.

Ellis leaned into her. "We've got a lot to learn doing this detective work."

"Rookie mistake for sure. We jumped ahead of ourselves, checking out the neighbors. Willem still has to have the other guitar, right?"

"Well, if he doesn't, the suspicion arrow will bounce his way for sure."

The New Upsetters powered through their second set and the dance floor was packed, finishing up with "Standin' on Shaky Ground" and Jackie Wilson's "Higher and Higher."

The emotional release in the crowd was palpable, people dancing outdoors in the night, together, having a blast. Was this the beginning of the end of Covid, just in time for summer?

4

Chapter 4

June 29

In the early morning summer light, Paloma sat on her board waiting as the swells moved in. Everyone was getting solid rides, although it might be challenging for the surf schools that took over part of Santa Monica beach later in the morning. The water helped clear her head after the mighty Paso Robles Red and tequila shots last night. She thought the band had played well, the Malibu horns 'brought it', big and brassy.

Ellis was still asleep when she returned. Creeping into the bedroom, she leaned over him and gently shook some water from her hair, whispering that if he woke up, he would see a real live mermaid. He suddenly grabbed her, and they rolled around on the bed laughing. Being together had proved so comfortable, and if dealing with idiots and creeps on the job was what it took, for now, so be it.

A half hour later, padding barefoot into the kitchen, Ellis turned on his phone and saw a message from Benny, saying

Ralston wanted to see them this afternoon at the video shoot at Culver Studios. He would leave their names at the gate.

"Jeez, what's it been, a day? Two? And he wants to see us."

"Music video, huh. Lots of spandex and big boobs," she said, starting the coffee maker.

"Oh yeah?"

"I saw them live at UCSB. It was not a casually dressed crowd. Can't wait," she said sarcastically, reaching for her cowgirl coffee mug.

They had left a message for Willem telling him to expect them at nine, before he opened. Stopping at Lodge Bakery, they picked up a few things to bring him and a loaf of the incredible seeded country bread to bring home. Lodge had made it through the worst of Covid, first closing, then opening limited hours with sidewalk service only. The whole grain breads they made were world class, as were some of their sweeter treats.

Willem was waiting, pacing in the driveway outside the shop entrance. The stress was starting to show. Gary had probably called and rattled him after their interview, continuing to shed any kind of responsibility for the theft.

Turning on the lights, he led them into the shop, going behind the counter to get the switched guitar. Today, the smell of glue and varnish was overwhelming. Willem opened the case, they saw the guitar was a beat-up Epiphone Casino, much thinner than a Country Gentleman. John Lennon played one like it at the last Beatles performance on the roof. Willem lifted the guitar to show them and see the serial number.

"Probably about ten years old. Not taken care of at all," he said, first looking at it, then laying it down on the counter.

"The neck is off, and the fretboard is filthy with dead skin cells. It's been refinished, poorly."

Going to his computer, he pulled up a photo of a Country Gentleman and showed them the similarity of body style and size, though the Country Gentleman was fatter.

"We can rule out a mistake," Ellis said. "They walked in here to make the switch. If somebody says, 'Hey, you got the wrong guitar,' they apologize for the mistake. No foul."

"I'm sorry. I should have shown you this guitar when you first came here. I was still in shock about the whole thing," Willem said.

"No, we should have asked. Our bad," Paloma stated, taking responsibility.

Ellis studied the guitar. Not in the best shape for sure. The refinishing job to natural wood looked a little rough. He turned the guitar around and found a worn sticker on the back. Paloma took a photo of it and texted it to the Thorazine Kid for enhancement, then of the guitar. Ellis opened the small storage area inside of the case and found a few picks and spare E and B strings, still coiled in their paper sleeves. As he picked them up, a paper ticket fell out into the case. It was from the Golden Gopher, an old dive bar downtown.

"A drink ticket," Ellis said, examining it. "Most clubs limit how many free drinks the bands have and in some places that's all they get paid. Didn't know the Gopher started having music. We should go down there and look around. You too, Willem, since you saw the guys best."

He looked from Ellis to Paloma and back.

"Me? I don't go downtown."

"You'll love it. New stores and restaurants all over the place. Even a Whole Foods," Paloma added.

"Yeah, but I don't go downtown. Or to clubs. Take Gary what's his name."

Willem was their first choice to go to the Gopher. He got the best look and had skin in the game. Gary might prove too volatile in an alcohol-fueled environment.

"Willem, look at me," Paloma continued. "You want to maybe have a chance to get the guitar back and not have Ralston take your shop away?"

He nodded and his shoulders sagged. He lived in the front, worked in the back. His was a solitary life, days spent repairing fine wooden stringed instruments. This interruption of his routine was taking its toll.

"We're going to check the bands that have played there. Pick you up around eight-thirty," Ellis said as they started to leave.

"Isn't eight-thirty late to be going downtown?" he said.

They didn't want to tell him that it was early for the clubs.

"Don't worry, you'll be with us. In and out. We can navigate the scene for you. Gonna get you a disguise. Fake glasses and a stingy brimmed fedora? You got any old jeans, like what you might wear digging in the garden?"

"I don't do that, but yes I have some old clothes," Willem said sadly.

"Good. We stand a chance of short-circuiting this thing if they show up tonight," Paloma said. "You're in good hands."

Returning to the FAQ office, they found Duffy, feet up on his desk, in an animated phone call. Remnants of a pecan roll were on his shirt.

On the drive over, Paloma again questioned why Ralston was not bringing in the police. Not wanting anyone to know about the guitar and claiming that he would be made a fool of if it was known it had been stolen? That didn't add up. Ellis replied, "So are the ways of rich people," rock stars or otherwise. They get wrapped up in their world of fame and adulation. Sometimes their actions don't add up. Still, it bothered her.

Duffy ended his call, and they brought him up to speed on what was happening, admitting to not having looked at the switched guitar the first time.

"Hey, you're still the new kids. Can't know all of it yet. Don't fret."

He agreed that the Golden Gopher lead was solid.

"Well, we just picked up another case. Glenn Longworth, CEO of . . . Banshee Systems, some tech firm," he said, looking at his small notebook. "He said he worked with us before. Repeat business. Well done. Anyway, he wants our help. Seems like they develop 'apps' and someone got inside their server, don't know what that is or how, and then there is something called ransomware. Thinks one of his lead engineers messed up. So, you go in there with the good cop/bad cop thing, maybe bring in a silent friend to watch."

"Silent friend?" Ellis asked.

"Yeah, you two don't come off as the schoolyard bullies. Bring a big guy to sit in the corner. Know anyone?"

Eddy came to mind.

"Why do I know this name, Longworth?"

"He's the guy who had us watching his wife. In the hot tub."

"Oh, with the redhead. Yeah, we want to work with him. Pays on time," Duffy said, covering his real interest of more possible surveillance photos.

"He's sending an email with all the deets. I'll forward it to you, and we can start the interviews. The office is down near the old Howard Hughes hangar and all those apartments they put up in the swamp."

"The Googleplex?" Ellis added.

"I guess," Duffy said tentatively. He looked at them. "Probably you two should take the first round. I'm not currently conversant in all that app and Google stuff.

Benny texted, asking them to be at the video shoot early to meet with Ralston. That sounded like "not fun," Paloma said. She had unresolved issues with Gary. The interview had ended too soon, with questions remaining. Now that they felt it wasn't a mistaken guitar switch, she had doubts about his being distracted in the small workshop. Maybe the guy was an oiler or a stoner.

"You know anything about tech companies and code writing? I hope all the deets give us something to help with the interviews. We should research this Banshee System company before we go to the Gopher tonight, you know, get a sense of what they do," Ellis said.

"Oh good. I thought we were going to have to hit the gym and bulk up."

RimShot had booked the largest soundstage at Culver Studios to shoot their music video. It was one of the older movie lots in town, right in the vibrant downtown Culver City.

Across the street stands the Culver Hotel, a hundred-year-old landmark that had once housed famous movie stars. Locals know it as the hotel where over a hundred little people who played the Munchkins in *The Wizard of Oz* were put up during filming, sometimes three to a bed. Many of them had never seen another little person in their lives, so they built community fast. The tales of their marathon parties were legendary.

The guard at the studio gate directed them to park next to a huge soundstage at the back of the lot. A large video control room truck, smaller trailers and a craft service tent were lined up on one side. A dozen statuesque women, tall with long blown out hair, a mandatory part of any RimShot video, were being escorted from the makeup trailer by a few PAs.

Ellis and Paloma walked through the giant loading door alongside two vintage '50s convertible cars being pushed inside, Ellis giving a nod to a few of the local stagehands he knew. The concert stage was set up along the back wall, with RimShot's full production set of amps, drum risers and backdrop. Overhead, chrome trusses with banks of lights had been raised. There were cameras on cranes, tracks, and remote mounts all around. It was a busy scene.

Five large dressing room trailers with "pop-out" sides were in two lines along the opposite wall, creating a little village courtyard area for the band and their entourage.

Benny found them watching the last of the four convertibles being pushed into place, giving them each a laminated pass to wear. He excused himself and rushed off, saying Ralston was arriving and he would meet with them shortly.

Looking around at all the activity setting everything up, Paloma turned to Ellis.

"Missing it? All the pieces coming into place?" she said.

"It's a little weird watching other people do it, and I'd be lying if I didn't say I missed it a little, but I'm good. You know they're going to play the same song twenty-five times, right?"

"Doesn't stay too fresh, huh?"

"Nope. You get the good takes of the whole band, then the closeups and special effects shots. Looks like the line of convertibles will be used for cutaways. See there's also a green screen rigged up high that will be lowered for who knows what."

Paloma looked at him.

"Don't miss it. Really," he said innocently.

There was a commotion at the door, and they turned to see Ralston, dressed in black leather pants and an official Kirk Gibson #23 Dodger uniform shirt. He was a huge Dodgers fan. Maggie was on his arm and a group of support people and friends headed to the camper village, Benny leading the way. Gary was in the crowd, carrying large leather saddlebags over his shoulder and a guitar case in the other. He was not pleased to see them.

Benny returned and said that when Ralston settled in, he would send for them.

After Benny left, Paloma declared, "You mean he will summon us? Bullshit. Seeing those women outside in spandex leggings and crop tops reminds me of what kind of audience these guys appeal to."

"You said you went to one of their shows," he said.

"In college, yeah," she said and looked at him. "Bet you wanna know what I was wearing."

He did, but that would wait for later.

One by one the band members arrived with their own mini mobs until the lounge area outside of the trailer area was well populated with people drinking and smoking liberally in the early afternoon. Covid felt a long way away. The bass player looked like he had been up for a few days and was especially loud.

Just after Paloma said, "Glad we friggin' got here early," Benny signaled them over and escorted them to Ralston's trailer as Gary watched from one of the courtyard couches. In the trailer the smell of patchouli oil was overwhelming and gauzy colored material covered all the lamps, giving it a "club" type atmosphere. Ralston was now in his performing clothes, all black offset by colorful scarves, silver rings, and plenty of bare chest. Maggie was curled up on a couch, half listening, looking at an iPad while he was finishing up a conversation with a woman who must be the video director.

"So, stage shots, slo-mo's, then we move each of you down to a convertible with the girls and get a bunch of cutaways in front of the green screen. The storyboards will be next to camera, but we will follow you. You need me, just talk and I will hear you in the truck."

She left and a man entered, dressed in expensive black clothing.

"This is Marc Soloff, Tommy's financial manager," Benny said. "These are the two looking for the guitar. Ellis and Paloma." Soloff was a solid six feet, a mop of curly black hair, early five o'clock shadow, sunglasses hanging from a V-neck T-shirt. Early Lindsey Buckingham look.

"What ya got?" is the first thing Ralston said. Why bother with "hello, thanks for coming down"? He looked over to Soloff. "These are the ones who found Charley Hines' sister in Yucca Valley."

"This guitar thing is bullshit," Soloff said. He looked them up and down.

"Are you sure you're up to it? I hear you're new."

He turned to Ralston.

"I could get some guys on this in an hour."

Paloma looked at Soloff. Twenty-something words out of his mouth and she didn't like him.

"Nice to meet you," Ellis said, diplomatically extending a hand. "We told Tommy he should bring the police in on this. It still would be a good idea. If you want to replace us, that's your choice."

"No, you're on it," Ralston said, seeing Maggie looking at him from the corner.

"No fucking cops though," Soloff said, echoing Ralston from their earlier meeting. "You just find them, and we'll take it from there."

Soloff was quite aggressive for a financial manager. Most were happy reviewing the concert financial settlement and then watching the show from the side of the stage.

"Either we are working it, or someone else is. Not both," Ellis said.

Paloma couldn't resist. "You really think news about this would hurt you and RimShot?"

"Don't let that concern you," Ralston added in his usual dismissive tone. "So, what do you know?"

"We have a few things we are following up on," Paloma added.

"What's that?" Soloff said, looking Paloma up and down.

"We have checked out the guitar that was swapped, and it is close enough to the Country Gentleman in shape that we believe this was intentional, not a mistake. It was a good plan, because if Willem or Gary had said anything, the guys could have said 'oops, sorry' and walked out with the guitar they came in with."

"We are looking at video doorbell footage that might help us with seeing the guys in a car drive by," Paloma added.

"That should be easy, CCTV stuff," Soloff said, nodding to please Ralston.

She looked at him. "And we are going to check out a few clubs where these bands play."

"Gary should help you out ID the guys," Ralston said.

Paloma doubted that Gary could or would help. He was trying to survive this thing by laying the blame on Willem, who was their best bet.

"We're taking Willem first. We'll shoot you a photo on the spot if he sees the guys," Ellis said.

"You mentioned Maggie's cousin who represented you at the auction. I know it was two years ago, but it would be great to talk to him about who else was bidding, maybe who got pissed off getting outbid." Paloma wondered if Paul was part of the setup.

"Paul, yeah sure," Ralston said, looking to Maggie for approval. "Where is he staying, Mags?"

"I'm not sure," she replied lazily.

"Someone in my office will check the records," Soloff chimed in.

"Maybe in the valley? I own entire cul-de-sacs of houses out there," Ralston boasted. "Tell him to come into the office tomorrow to talk to these guys."

"Great. To recap. We are following our leads and video. We will check in with Benny and keep you in the loop. You will get Paul into your office," Paloma stated.

"You should stick around and watch," Maggie chimed in. "The band is really hot," she said with a smile, jumping up to hug Ralston from behind, her hands all over his bare chest. "Smokin' hot."

Recorded RimShot music started to blare from the stage, power chords and cannon-like drums. They walked across the cavernous soundstage to the exit. The twelve dancers in spandex, now wearing very high heels, were working with the choreographer. As the RimShot hit song "Bet You Like My Ride" blasted through the sound system and giant fans were turned on to blow their long hair, the dancers moved around and through the convertibles, crawling on all fours over the cars, draping themselves across the hoods, pawing and licking the faces of the stand-ins for the band.

"C'mon, you miss it," Paloma said as they walked to the car.

"So, what the fuck was that?" Paloma asked as they drove off the lot. "We are working the case so he can command us to come see him? A waste. Next time tell him to use the phone."

"Kinda felt like he wanted to show off for Soloff," Ellis added.

"Ralston's a creep. And Soloff, he watched too many episodes of *Entourage* and *The Sopranos*."

"I still don't get the thing about not reporting it to the police. The bad publicity aspect. What am I missing?"

"Well, we're in it up to our hips, so let's find this famous guitar and be rid of him."

Driving back to Electric Avenue, they called Longworth to set up a visit. His office said he would be back in the morning, and they should come first thing. Then they moved on to figure a plan for tonight, should Willem ID the guys, should the thieves be dumb enough to hang around the Gopher. If they were amateurs, they might.

The older stores and restaurants in downtown LA backed onto a common hallway or alley. They could brace a guy in the bar, hustle him out back and try for answers, while calling in help if necessary. That would mean hiring Neely or Leon for the evening, parked nearby.

From the time they picked up Willem, Paloma sensed the evening going south. Giving him a hat and an old black T-shirt to wear made him uncomfortable. On the drive, he was silent, as though going to the hospital to lose a kidney.

The Golden Gopher was a dive bar in downtown LA that had been fixed up to become a trendy dive bar, with the revitalization of the area over the last decade. Rummy bars that had been barely hanging on were reinvented as hangouts for a younger, hipster, richer crowd who populated the new condos that were going up all around it.

They paid the cover and led Willem, who was taking halting steps, through the door. It was early, so they found two seats at the bar, Paloma sitting with him while Ellis made his way to another side of the room by the performers' area to watch and wait as the place started to fill up. After ordering two beers, Paloma showed Willem how he could look in the mirror behind the bar for the guys and still have his back to them. He was sweating and the music hadn't started yet.

The dress theme of the night appeared to be various faded shades of black, so Willem fit right in. Not surprisingly, there were several thin, pasty-skinned guys in skinny, ripped jeans, all fitting the earlier description. Willem recognized none of them. A woman with dyed black hair and tatted-up arms sat down next to Willem and tried to make small talk. Paloma, on the other side of him, could smell the cigarettes and sweat coming off her. Willem looked over at her and just gave a slight motion with his hand, telling her he wasn't interested.

Near the side of the small stage, Ellis looked and listened where tonight's band hung out. He was hoping someone had a big mouth and bragged on what they had done or seen. No such luck. He listened to endless conversations about how fucked up someone had been the night before, whose old lady was now screwing who and how trying to make a living as a musician during Covid sucked.

Going back to the bathrooms, he found the doors were covered with stickers. Everything from BLM, ads for pot stores, bands, religious symbols, and telephone numbers for who knows what. One sticker caught his eye. It was the same iridescent green as the one on the back of the switched guitar, but newer and in better shape. It was a scarab beetle, no writing on it. He took a photo with his phone. The sticker should be new since it wasn't covered over with others. The Gopher had been closed off and on for the duration of the pandemic.

Tonight's band, "Quix Fix," got up on the tiny stage in the back where a pool table had been and began their assault of the audience with three, maybe four chord pop songs. Out-of-tune guitars and a vocalist who could only be described as not promising did get the crowd of friends bouncing around in front of the stage. Willem started to shake slightly. This was way out of his comfort zone. Paloma saw he was no longer glancing at the mirror, just staring down at the bar. She looked over to Ellis and gave a head nod to come over.

"Our friend is not enjoying himself. Kinda shut down once the music started."

"It's still early. We need at least another hour, or maybe two," Ellis shouted over the music.

"Look at the guy, he'll be in a coma by then."

"How about a walk to the bathroom and back?"

"Sure but try not approaching the bandstand to get there."

Ellis went over to Willem and started to lead him to the bathroom. Again, the halting steps of a man about to be executed. And then he just stopped. A complete and total shutdown.

"Plan B," Ellis shouted to Paloma, guiding Willem towards the exit.

Ten minutes later they were in the BMW parked on 7th street with a view of the neon-bathed entrance to the Gopher. Willem was in the front seat next to Paloma, watching people come in and out. At this distance, with the shelter of the car, he was recovering.

"I told you that I don't do well in clubs," Willem emphasized, shaking his head.

"You weren't kidding," Ellis said from the back, eyes rolling.

They sat as people came and went. There was an ever-changing group smoking in front, none of which registered with Willem.

"I really don't remember them that well," he said. "They were only in the shop for a few minutes, and I was involved with the other customer and his guitar. Maybe Gary remembers better. We should probably go."

"A little while longer?" asked Paloma. "Kinda important given it's our only lead."

"Just a little more," he replied.

Ellis sat in the back seat with his phone, searching on Google for the scarab sticker, learning all kinds of ancient and religious references but none that applied.

"Sit tight; I'm going inside for a minute," he said, opening the car door. He looked back and gave Paloma a slight nod through the window.

Making his way over to the now-crowded bar, Ellis hailed one of the well-tattooed women in a black tank top serving drinks. She had eye mascara that went up on the ends for that faux Cleopatra look but none of the attitude he might have expected. He showed her the photo of the scarab sticker.

"Oh yeah, Dung Beetle. They played right after we opened. Not great, but they sang on key, had plenty of friends who drank and left primo tips. Rich kids. May have been a few fake IDs," she said with a shrug.

"Would the manager have info on them? I'm looking to hire a band for a party in Venice."

"He leaves early. The bands are paid either in cash or we give them each a few drinks," she said, reaching under the counter, then showing Ellis the same type of drink ticket they had found in the guitar case. "Call tomorrow after one," she said flatly.

Ellis said thanks and put a twenty down on the bar. Never know if he needed to come back. It was Ralston's money.

Getting back into the BMW, he told Paloma what he had learned, while checking his iPhone to see if "Dung Beetle" had a website or Instagram like most bands.

"Might as well split," he said.

Willem gave out a loud sigh and sank back into the seat.

"Dung Beetle," Paloma said, putting the BMW in gear. "How'd I miss that name for my band?"

After making sure Willem got in his home and had the lights on, they stopped to meet Neely for a drink at The Brig, a Venice fixture for decades, now featuring a Kogi food truck in the parking lot. Neely had sat in his car for three hours by the Golden Gopher alley on standby if they needed him. The place was crowded.

Carrying drinks to the outside seating area, Ellis brought him up to speed on Dung Beetle.

"I'll ask around about them tomorrow cause otherwise it's 'chile relleno and fish tacos' at the kitchen."

"Doesn't Alena rely on you to be there?" Paloma asked.

"Nah, she just wants to keep me busy. And look at my fabulous body," he said to the expected laughs.

"Okay. We're on a new case in the morning, then hoping to meet with this guy who bearded for Ralston at the auction. We need to find this band, Dung Beetle," Ellis said as he showed Neely the sticker and air-dropped it to his phone.

"You got it," Neely said, bobbing his head up and down. "Gonna go all Scooby-Doo on this and find the Dung."

5

Chapter 5

June 30

Ellis joined Paloma for sunrise at the beach. He did his swim workout, then watched her surf. With undeniable skills, she made it look effortless. The other surfers respected the real thing. And she was fearless.

That openness to "whatever" was the second thing Ellis had noticed about her when he had stayed at Grant's house years ago. The first was that she was knockout beautiful, but as she was Grant's daughter, nothing was going to happen. He marveled at the light she brought into a room.

Showering off at home, Paloma asked what you wear to a tech firm. Ellis, thinking of JenBloc last year, said T-shirt and jeans if you want to fit in, or embellish to your heart's content. Ellis wore his typical Hawaiian and jeans. Paloma put on a rare Condors T-shirt from her stash. The deep blue made her eyes stand out.

The sleek Banshee offices were off Washington Blvd. in an

area of old industrial warehouses that had been renovated by the new "Silicon Beach" businesses. The whole Westside of Los Angeles felt like one big redevelopment project, with apartment buildings going up on every other block and the traffic that came with it.

Longworth greeted them, making it seem to those in the office like it was the first time. Trays of lunch were being delivered and he offered them to hang around and eat when they were finished. Back in his office, he explained the threat. Someone had gotten "ransomware" into their server, with the threat to encrypt data files, leading to a complete shutdown that would make the apps they created useless if a payment was not negotiated.

His IT people had told him that the hack had bypassed the "honeypots," which were fake file depositories that would enable detection of the attack. Only the three lead engineers knew about these. He needed to find out who it was, now, while trying to figure out the encryption code the hackers had used.

"My engineers say they weren't hacked, yet somehow the malware got into our system," he said, shaking his head in disbelief. "The hackers said they will contact us in twenty-four hours with a ransom price, and if we don't pay, our apps will start to lose their functionality," he said, showing them the envelope and note. Old school.

"We have been presenting to investors for our next funding round. If there are problems with the apps, it's torpedoes in the water. We're sunk. It has to be a leak or sabotage."

Paloma asked him to explain the funding process, if it was reported in the press, then about the people who worked for the company.

"This is a major funding round. I have been in Austin and

Denver since I last saw you." He was silent for a few seconds. "These lead programmers are different than you might be used to. Pretty lively bunch."

They weren't "used to" any programmers. They would "wing it" after trying to write questions on note cards last night. He led them into the back part of the warehouse, the "coder cave." Unlike the sleek front offices, it looked like they had moved a week ago. Cardboard boxes were strewn about the main room with stacks of monitors on a conference table pushed against one wall. Blue internet cables ran along the floor into smaller rooms, some set up with gray cubicles, others had closed doors and windows news papered over. Well-ventilated EMC server cases hummed along a glassed-in back room, giving the room an ozone odor competing with moldy take-out boxes scattered everywhere.

"Anybody leave or get fired, who might hold a grudge?" Ellis asked.

"In tech, people move around all the time, usually getting recruited at a higher salary with more stock options. No one readily comes to mind."

Ellis and Paloma heard shouting.

"Die, fuckin' zombie scum!"

"No prisoners!"

In two of the back rooms, large wrap-around monitors were stacked high on the desks. Sitting in red and black gaming chairs, two guys wearing headphones over backwards baseball caps were blasting opponents in some online video game, shouting, and cursing as the action progressed.

"Don't look too stressed to me," she said, "considering you've been hacked."

"They're taking a break. Gets their creative juices flowing,"

Longworth explained.

"I bet," Paloma said.

"Great coders. Once in the groove they can go for days."

"I saw the cases of Red Bull in the corner."

Longworth studied them. He had more to say. "There's even talk about a SPAC."

"What's that?" Ellis asked.

"It's a 'special purpose acquisition company.' SPAC. A pile of money is raised by a company with the intention of buying or merging with another company, yet to be named. We could cash out much quicker than expected that way, including these guys."

"Wait, you want to cash out?"

"If the price is right, everyone wants to cash out. I'd probably have to stay for a year or two, then move on to the next big thing."

"Next big thing, huh?" Paloma asked.

"If the apps shut down, it's public in an instant. You have to help get a handle on this, soon. Our clock is running."

"Here we are. Have your ninja turtles shut down so we can interview them," Paloma said.

The lead engineers, Marik and Rusty had vanquished their opponents and were rolling out in their gaming chairs, comparing notes on their victory, and pounding fists. Both men obviously worked out and had a frat boy relationship with each other frequented by boasts and put-downs.

A glance at their background files had shown that Marik had come to a small college in Worcester, Massachusetts, directly from the Emirates to be a video game major, then on to California, where he totally embrace the SoCal lifestyle, sporting shorts and Adidas flops. Rusty came off as a total California frat boy surfer, although Paloma doubted he surfed much, even with the bleached blonde hair. He had grown up in working-class Downey and gone to Long Beach State.

"You so cut him up, dude," Marik said, shades reversed on his head, spinning around in his chair.

"Whomped him, yeah," Rusty replied, holding out his fist for a bump. "We should play those guys again. Where are they? Finland? Up late."

"Or early. You know, I do my best work up late," Marik said, smiling, addressing Paloma.

"You're a hound. Who was the hot stuff in the Porsche the other night?"

"Great ride, dude. You should ditch your sorry-ass Mustang or at least get that new electric one."

Longworth introduced them, explaining that security checks had been done.

They slowed down and Ellis introduced Paloma. Rusty nodded, looking her up and down. She tilted her head ever so slightly, signaling Ellis to continue reviewing how the ransomware got into the system. Marik and Rusty had enough stock options for this to matter.

"We crushed that code for those apps during the pandemic. It was epic. I was micro dosing for weeks," Marik said. "Maybe someone broke in here, or those dweebs in the office downloaded some porn while connected to the main server."

"Alarm and security cameras don't back that up. Did you do all your work here?" Ellis asked.

"There are cameras?" Marik said, looking around.

"We did shifts," Rusty said. "Worked on my tan in the backyard. Everything from home is RSA encrypted. For all of us. That's standard safe, bro."

Marik nodded agreement. "Don't worry, we'll have this malware figured out before they slow us down."

Then, bursting through the office door came Riina Hernitz, a thin, athletic, six-foot-tall woman in a leather vest, no shirt, with a shock of spiky white hair, holding up both hands like Rocky.

"In the house!" she exclaimed with a beaming wide grin. "Pushed my code in while you morons were blasting some geeks in Finland."

"You go through a case of Monster last night?" Rusty asked.

"Nah, little greenie micro dose. Love it," she said, all smiles with perfect white teeth.

Longworth introduced her to Paloma and Ellis, explaining what they were doing. She too had enough stock options for it to matter. He left them to it.

Riina grabbed a chair and sat down next to Marik, throwing an elbow into his arm. She pulled a few Monster cans out of her shoulder bag and offered them to Paloma and Ellis, who politely declined, before popping one open for herself.

"It's all hands-on deck with this malware. We'll figure out the key. No one is better than us," she shouted, hands raised again. She liked to do that.

Ellis awkwardly looked at his note cards and asked them to explain their procedures over the last few months, if their laptops had been left unattended, if there were any car break-ins or any situation where something weird may have happened. Paloma played her questions to the fact that she knew very little about what they did. Rusty spoke to her patronizingly about encrypted communications with the company, trying to use big words that would require her to ask what they meant.

When they seemed a bit more relaxed and at ease, Ellis asked about living situations. And roommates.

"Mine moved out during the pandemic. Went to live with his girlfriend in Encino. He was already remote during the day and said it was 'too lively' late at night. Sorry, that's when I work the best," Marik said, punching Rusty's arm for the double meaning. "I turned his room into a gym so I could have the garage back for my Porsche. Now that Equinox and Riva are open again, I can get back to my routine."

"Pump it up, pump it up," Rusty chimed in.

"Never had a roommate for more than a night or two," Riina said proudly. "I use 'em then I lose 'em." She exuded self-confidence.

Rusty explained how his condo was not to be shared, but he did have conquests spending the night. He boasted about the underground clubs that popped up in rented houses during the pandemic, where everyone was eager to mingle ignoring the restrictions.

"It's like fishing in a stocked pond. Blondes, cougars, spinners. Everyone was ready to party hard. Helped blow off some steam after mobbing for a few weeks."

"Mobbing?" Ellis asked, unfamiliar with the term.

"Yeah, we all jump on the same stack. We did that virtually for a while, then said fuck Covid and got together at Marik's for a few runs. Had food delivered and the kid next door was good for errands."

Paloma got their attention.

"Well, the hack and the ransom might turn your stock options into drawing paper, so I suggest you all 'mob' that idea and think real hard about how the code got in."

Finishing up before noon, Ellis said they would be back. Now they needed to do a deep background dive on the coders. Driving out, Ellis checked his messages. Benny had forwarded a text from Paul, saying he couldn't meet them at the RimShot office because an infected toe meant he couldn't drive. Could they go out to Chatsworth? He gave them the address.

"Chatsworth? At noon on a weekday? Aw, with traffic back we're gonna get slammed on the 405. Both ways. Grab some lunch and hit the road?"

Any day, the I-405 over "the hill" into the San Fernando Valley can resemble a slow-moving parking lot. A decade ago, the state spent eight years adding a carpool lane in each direction only to see it full the day it opened. There were so many Priuses they wound up taking the carpool stickers away from them. Now the lanes were full of Tesla's.

Ellis played a Spotify playlist of RimShot tunes. Heavy guitar power chords, screaming vocals and the cannon-like drums. One song ran into another, similar structure, similar sound assaulting the senses.

At the turn for Highway 118, Paloma held up her hand and said, "No mas."

"I thought you would be reliving the concert you went to at UCSB."

She looked at him.

"C'mon, what were you wearing?" Ellis prodded.

"Still thinking about that, huh?" She looked over at him, raising her eyebrows. "What was I wearing . . .?" Paloma left it hanging.

"Like the dancers we saw, right?" Ellis said.

"You'd like that, would you?" she replied.

"Uh, yes," he said.

"You're thinking spandex? Crop top? Hair blown out?"

Ellis tried not to drool.

"Dude, I was working crew at that show. Levi's, a long-sleeve T-shirt and had work gloves stuffed in my back pocket. Sorry to burst your bubble." There was a pause. Paloma looked over.

"But for you, I'll see what I can pull together."

Ellis smiled.

She downshifted and slid the powerful BMW over to the DeSoto ramp into Chatsworth, not far from the stony hills where the Lone Ranger and countless westerns were filmed before the scrub land grew up into houses. In the '50s, the singing cowboy Roy Rogers and his wife Dale Evans lived there, a remote suburb of Los Angeles, separated by miles of orange groves.

Weaving through the curved streets of mid-century modern homes mixed in with midi mansions, they found the cul-de-sac where Paul lived. Climbing out of the car, they were assaulted by heat, at least 25 degrees hotter than it had been in Venice forty minutes earlier. And windy.

Paul greeted them at the door, a little too quickly. The shades on the window were moving, as though he had been watching for their arrival. Unshaven, hair high and tight, he filled out his green Adidas tracksuit with arms and chest he obviously worked on. Barefoot with a large purple wrap bandage on his right big toe, he greeted them with his cell phone held to his ear, one finger raised in the air.

"C'mon in. Just give me a minute," he said, going back to talking fast on the phone, limping, and leading them through the sparsely furnished house, doors to most rooms closed.

"We gonna make this deal or not? . . . Huh? I told you; you

will love these . . .. Uh huh . . . Uh huh. . .. You know, I'm concerned you're not taking me seriously. . .. Okay. Okay. This time tomorrow. No later. Hit me up then," he said.

"Hey, have a seat. Sorry, this toe is causing me plenty of grief," he said. "Something bit me, and it got infected. Scorpion maybe? Out here in this godforsaken place. Hard to drive with this. Want anything to drink?" He spoke fast, going over to a small drink setup on a desk by the window, pouring himself a Spindrift seltzer.

Paul limped back and settled into the couch with a sigh.

"Maggie said you had some questions. The George Harrison guitar really got stolen? What the fuck was Gary doing?"

"We are interested in the auction, when you represented Ralston and bought the guitar."

"Well, it was over two years ago, but shoot."

"Do you remember who else was bidding on the guitar?" Paloma asked.

"Hmm. Well, it was a pretty formal deal, you know, big room, paddles with numbers, no names. I wore a suit and a tie. A lot of people there, probably five or six people bid on the guitar. One was on a speaker phone." He seemed proud to remember that.

"Did you talk to any of them while you were there, or get a sense if there were any sore losers?"

"Nah, not like that. Seemed like a couple of rich collectors, you know, maybe some new money. I think one guy ran a guitar store somewhere," Paul recalled.

"What else was up for auction that day?"

"Uh, I came in late. Let me see. Maybe some Frank Zappa things, a solid chrome drum set, I mean the tom-tom weighed like thirty pounds, famous movie star stuff and uh, some *Star*

Wars thing. A white helmet," he said, elevating his bandaged foot on the coffee table.

"Pretty expensive guitar. Anybody look at you sideways when you raised your paddle?"

"What's that mean? I was shaved and wore a suit. Looked like the businessman I am," he shot back, defensively.

"No, I mean like you were taking something away from them."

"Didn't notice. I was focused, man. My mission was to get the guitar and I got it. Tommy gave me an amount he would be willing to spend. I probably saved him about a hundred grand!" Paul bragged, bullshit proud of himself.

"So how does it work, once you're winning bid is accepted?" Ellis asked.

"Uh, one of the assistants took me to the office and we did the paperwork and the money transfer. They took fuckin' ten percent on top. What a business."

"Did you use your account?"

"Seven-fifty plus? You kidding? I had all the bank account and routing information on my phone. The money was transferred from Marc's office to the auction house. They used the touring company account so it wouldn't be traced," he said. "Although by then it didn't matter. We got the guitar without someone bidding up the price because it was Tommy."

"And that's why you were the beard? So no one knew it was Ralston bidding."

"Yeah, I guess some people resent rich rock stars and want to make them pay more. People do it all the time. The seller could have had his own beard."

"You recall talking with anyone? Maybe after?"

"I probably spoke to one or two people. Congrats on getting

the guitar. Chit-chat Beatles stuff. I'm a social guy but I didn't say anything about Tommy."

"This is a little sensitive, Paul," Paloma said, leaning in. "In the last two years, did you mention this to anyone? Maybe just in passing conversation?"

Paul took his foot off the table.

"What the fuck you saying? I didn't tell anyone. Nada. Are you looking to pin this on me? No way. Seems like Gary's the guy who fucked up. Big time." He said, standing up, obviously hostile to Gary. "I'm Maggie's cousin, remember that."

He was pissed. Or it was a great show.

"Paul, you understand we are *working for* Tommy and trying to find the guitar, right? We're not accusing you of anything. Your help is important to us," Ellis stated. "The more information we have, the better. We appreciate what you have told us."

"Yeah, okay," he said hesitantly as he led them out. "Tommy really wants to play the guitar, at the benefit. Have you seen the lineup? Gonna be a great show."

Paloma nodded and gave him an FAQ card and said he should call if he remembered anything else that might be important. Paul seemed to have cooled down from his outburst as he let them out.

Walking through the outdoor blast furnace again to get to the car, Paloma commented on the sparse furnishing in the house.

"Maybe he just moved in. Or had a wife who cleaned him out," Ellis said.

"Well, being the *cousin* of the *wife* of a famous rock star certainly appeals to him," Paloma commented.

They turned the car around in the cul-de-sac.

"I bet land is cheap out here with this heat," Ellis said, looking at a few of the empty lots.

"It's still LA. Nothing's cheap. Out here you turn the AC on in April and turn it off in December," Paloma said.

Making a U-turn and heading down the street, Ellis said, "Look in the rearview and tell me if that black Escalade turns around."

She shot Ellis a look then checked the rearview.

"Uh, brake light and blinker, aaaaand, turning around. We have friends?"

"Not sure. Two guys sitting in a car, one looking at his phone a little too high up. Probably taking photos or a video. Paul was looking through the curtain at them when we arrived, then again when he went to the desk to get a drink and as we walked back to the car."

"Wow, you've been taking lessons from Duffy?"

Ellis shook his head. "These guys follow us from Venice?"

"Or they knew we were coming and were waiting."

"I'm not liking that. What do you think?"

"Ralston? Soloff? Cops?" Paul called Soloff by his first name, like they were pals. Maybe called him to work out his story, since he wasn't meeting us at the RimShot office? Soloff did imply he wanted his guys working this, maybe to follow us and pick up on our leads?"

"Well, I hope this guy in the Escalade knows how to drive. Hang on," Paloma said as she downshifted, made a quick left and the big engine roared to life. The Escalade barely made the turn and followed. She made a right into a back alley and sped along, dodging a few misplaced trash cans. The Escalade was losing ground when she flew out of the alley, caught a yellow light, and made a quick four-lane suicide slide across a busy

DeSoto Boulevard.

She picked her way through more side streets and alleys, heel and toe driving, figuring she would go like this all the way down to the 101, maybe Coldwater Canyon for an alternate way back to Venice. Pulling up in another alley, they waited for the Escalade to pass by. Nothing. She then pulled into the busy lot at the Tally-Ho liquor store for cover. After ten minutes, Ellis got out and did a once-around look. No sign of the SUV.

"What the fuck was that?" Paloma asked.

"Beats me, but we're being followed."

They cut over to Coldwater Canyon as an alternate route to the Westside. The traffic wasn't terrible, so Paloma enjoyed driving the BMW on the winding roads over the hill.

Ellis had Paul pegged as a lowlife LA hustler. You find them all over Hollywood and the music scene, trying to taste the nectar of success. Hanging around trendy clubs, dropping names, glomming onto whatever tentacle of fame they can associate with. Talk up some deal for weeks, trying to get people to invest, that is so close to getting done, then blame someone when it doesn't and move on to the next.

Since Maggie hooked up with Ralston three years ago, Paul had promoted that relationship anywhere he could, even though he rarely saw them. He was a *distant* cousin. When RimShot played a concert in or near Los Angeles, he was on the phone to Benny, then Maggie, for tickets and backstage passes to promote himself as a connected guy, collecting favors along the way.

Paloma landed on Soloff for the guys following them, as he seemed eager to impress Ralston.

"Remember what he said at the video shoot. You find them and my guys will take care of them. Maybe those are his guys.

He wants to be the hero."

"That's a real stretch," he said. "We have no idea who they are."

Ellis wanted to let everything settle down until tomorrow. Sometimes Paloma would go with her gut a little too much. Antagonizing Soloff would be counterproductive at this point. Finding the guitar was proving hard enough without them having to look over their shoulder.

Neely's online search for Dung Beetle found the past schedule of bands at the Golden Gopher and a gig in the valley from two years ago, but nothing else. It was strange that no Facebook page or Instagram appeared under that name, but in LA, bands came and went quickly. He knew a band, the Park Strangers who also appeared under the name Murakami and Horse Face, depending on where they were booked.

The manager of the Gopher, said a guy from Dung Beetle walked in off the street and played a few songs on his phone, not unusual. He told him they could play for drinks the first time and see how many friends and fans showed up and how much they spent. This type of arrangement was not uncommon at small clubs in Los Angeles. The manager hadn't kept the phone contact, but said he met with Ben something, not fitting the junkie description that Willem and Gary provided.

Most local bands didn't have the money to hire a real rehearsal hall, instead using a parent's garage or school's small theater. But since Ellis said the bartender had described them as rich kids, Neely checked in with places he knew. A few laughs at the name, but no luck. He also texted friends who knew the club music scene to see if anyone had heard of them. Responses again were comic and pun filled but not fruitful.

On a hunch that rockers who wore black usually got inked up, Neely mapped out five tattoo parlors around Venice and Mar Vista. From what Ellis had told him, the guys who stole the guitar didn't have any noticeable tats, but to Neely it was a given. At the third place, Ink Monkeze, a tattoo artist recognized the Scarab sticker and showed him the same on the bathroom door, half covered with a BLM sticker. That dated it to more than a year old.

"Yeah, I look at it every day when I go to the john," she said.

"Remember the guy or guys? Any kind of records I might look at?" he said.

"We're a cash business. You know what I mean?"

Neely understood. Cash business, scraping to get by, not wanting to get slammed with taxes. He put down a twenty. In the end he hoped it was Ralston's money.

"You know, I think Dina may have hooked up with one of those guys," she said, picking up the bill.

"Dina working today?" Neely asked, in his best charming voice.

"You looking for a tattoo?" she replied with a smile.

"How about I just give you another twenty?" Neely said, handing over another bill.

She smiled at him again. Her arms were covered down to her fingers in a very intricate design of dragons and beasts. Looking at the ink on her exposed cleavage, he could only imagine what lurked beneath her shirt. Amazing 3-D effect, if that was possible.

"She quit. Cooks sometimes at the Grandview market over on Venice. Tell her Mai-Lin says hi. Sure you don't want a nice serpent on your back?"

"Gonna pass on the serpent, but thanks for the info," he said, heading out the door.

Neely called over to the Grandview. Dina would be cooking the dinner shift.

Driving back to the office, fighting traffic for the first time in a year, Ellis and Paloma drove down Abbot Kinney. Leon was setting up the valet station on the sidewalk in front of Zanzibar. He waved them over and leaned into the passenger window.

"Business is crazy back. Had to get one of my cousins to help out," he said.

"And the traffic. What's with all these red lights?" Paloma joked.

"Someone called it the great reopening the other night. So many people out on the street again. Big tipping too. Feels like the old days. Almost."

"Right?"

"Hey, that killer redhead was back, with a guy this time. All over him waiting for the cars. Someone in line said they should get a room."

"Sure it was her?" Paloma said.

"Hey, I never forget a face.

"Was she driving the black beamer?"

"Yeah. It's a rental, by the way. The guy was trying to get her to go to his place. One of those streets north of Montana." North of Montana was the very upscale part of Santa Monica, large houses on large lots.

Valet parking attendants were invisible to most people, preoccupied with coming or going. Confidences and secrets were shared during the wait for the car, inhibitions lowered, and tongues loosened by wine or weed.

"Thanks, man," Ellis said, giving him a fist bump. "Come

by the office when you can."

"You bet," Leon said as he went back to setting up.

Walking up the stairs to the office, Paloma wondered about Michael, the redhead, stunningly beautiful with a killer body, seemingly making the rounds in Venice. Longworth thought she worked at a gym. Made sense. It would be a natural place for people who were working out in skintight clothing to hook up. If Mona was unhappy in her marriage, or just looking for a thrill, the gym seemed like the perfect hookup spot.

Never much of a joiner or a group person, Paloma would rather surf.

Pacing back and forth in the office, Paloma was pissed. Had they been followed? She already disliked Ralston, and after meeting Soloff she felt the same about him. Were these "his guys"? When you have an office, it isn't hard for someone to wait and follow you.

Someone else was looking for the guitar.

Ellis read Neely's texts, about the scarab sticker at a tattoo place in Venice and a lead on someone who may have hooked up with someone in that band. Paloma remarked that Neely was trying to stay out of the ghost kitchen as long as he could. She was on a roll. Checking tomorrow's calendar, they had more work to do at Banshee. But Paloma was determined to confront Soloff at his office the next morning. She would try to get back for the interviews.

"We're gonna look really stupid if they weren't his guys," Ellis said. "And if not, who are they?"

"Well, we're gonna be pretty stupid if they are. And let's say they're not, it's a shot across the bow for Soloff to stay out of the way."

"You met him once and you're convicting him."

"Hey, I'm not going to tell him to fuck off or anything."

"Gee, that's good. If you're going to go, you should probably let Benny know, keeping all lines of communication open so he's not blindsided."

"Nope. He would probably get in the middle of it. If we are going to work for Ralston, this guy can't be in the way. Otherwise, we hand in our bill and move on."

"Paloma, please don't blow it up. I really want us, FAQ, to find this guitar. More than burnishing our reputation, now I want to find it because it is important. You said it yourself, the way Cindy and millions of people felt watching those *Ed Sullivan* performances. This guitar is a piece of music history. We're gonna get it back, even if it is for Ralston."

"Nice speech. Should I call you coach?"

He looked at her, trying to reel her back.

"Who would have sold that guitar anyway? How'd they get it?"

"Great question. There was that story about Ringo selling it for an animal charity, but the auction house wouldn't say. I'm hoping it wasn't some nameless Dutch company that does business through the Seychelles," Ellis replied.

"They have those, huh?"

"Yeah, lots of dark money floating around in accounts all over the world, untaxed, just waiting to be spent on something cool, like a Picasso or a famous guitar."

He looked at her. "Why don't you call him instead of going over there?"

Duffy wandered to the office, whistling, chipper as always. They recounted their meeting with the coders. He reminded them that they should have spoken to each one separately and had a big guy sitting in the corner to smack the back of their heads once in a while.

"You can't do that anymore, Duffy," Ellis explained.

"Well then you need to pour salt on the eggplant and slowly ease it out of them. My well-established gut tells me someone in that wild bunch fucked up. Whatever happened to people sitting at their desks nine-to-five?" he asked.

"Long ago and far away," Paloma replied. "But I think you're right. This is a wild bunch. I looked up some of their profiles online. Some friends call them 'Bro-grammers.'"

"Bro?" Duffy asked.

"Like frat house 'Bros.'"

Duffy was not getting it.

"One definition I found was 'white, party-loving, egotistical, sexist males.' Marik isn't white, but he fits all the other categories. Rusty is totally in the pocket and Riina could be the Xena warrior of the female bros."

"Oh," Duffy said. "Dudes and . . .."

"Good catch, Duffy," Paloma said.

"Pretty funny. Sorry, I don't know more about tech stuff. Kinda out of my league. They gave us a decent retainer. Why not bring in a specialist? How about that black guy with the drone? He knows about this stuff?"

"The black guy? C'mon, Duffy."

"Yeah, sorry. Forgot his name."

"He's Neighbor Dave. Yeah, he's helping us," Ellis said.

"Neighbor Dave?" Duffy looked perplexed.

"His name is Dave, and he lives next door. First time I met him he said, 'Hi, I'm your neighbor, Dave.' It stuck."

"Oh yeah, that is simple," Duffy said, slightly rocking back and forth. "Let's see then. I have a Neighbor Tree Lark to the left and a Neighbor Genesis in the little blue house," he said, nodding, quite satisfied that he got it.

Paloma looked at him.

"Hey, you know, it's Venice," he said with a shrug.

In the late afternoon light, the Venice sky was dull orange, a result of forest fires hundreds of miles to the north, the smoke smarting your eyes. Ellis and Paloma sat on the porch, chilling with a shared pre-roll. Her new friend Prewash, was resting in her lap, enjoying getting lazily scratched behind his ears.

Cindy and Eddy pulled up on his motorcycle, after bringing some clothes down to a friend's vintage store. They always helped each other out.

"We were in the hood and thought we'd stop by, maybe grab a bite. Bad time?" Cindy said, taking off her helmet.

"You kidding? Great time," Paloma replied, moving in for a hug. She was always happy to be with Cindy, who raised her. Her real mother had addiction problems that never really got solved and now was serving two to five years for attempted robbery and assault where a gun was used. "You can have your own pre-roll." Same households shared during the pandemic.

Ellis dragged a few kitchen chairs out to the porch and Eddy lit up. Paloma needed to forget about Soloff for a while, so she asked Cindy about her website. The spirituality surge during the pandemic was great for business. The singing bowls had been especially in demand but stretched her overseas supplier, so Cindy found a guy in Santa Fe who made them in his small foundry. Vintage clothing also took an uptick as people spent time cleaning out their closets and had money to buy stuff cheap.

Eddy's shop on the PCH was so busy he was looking for

another mechanic to work for him. This new location, with his proud Trailblazer parked out front, brought in a different clientele than he was used to.

"You wouldn't believe these folks, decked out in expensive Vanson leathers from back in 'Fall Rivah,'" he said, stressing his Massachusetts south shore accent.

"They run these massive companies and hedge funds, but they still have time to yak about old bikes. I should have office hours," Eddy said, taking a hit on the joint. "

Neighbor Dave called over for Prewash and they invited him to join them at the Murtosa Cafe for dinner. Ellis hoped Joaquim could accommodate them with his outdoor seating. Restaurants all over town had taken over the parking lane with a variety of makeshift cafe-style dining enclosures, creating a new, exciting vibe along the streets. A rare upside of the pandemic.

Walking down to the cafe, Dave was bringing Eddy up to date on his drone, while Cindy and Paloma held hands and laughed about wiping down all the food at the start of the pandemic. Ellis feasted on watching his friends.

Joaquim welcomed them warmly, Ellis introducing Cindy and Eddy. A chorizo plate with bread and cheese materialized immediately, and a cold bottle of Portuguese Vinho Verde followed. Paloma regaled everyone with the story of the RimShot video rehearsal with the girls crawling over the cars while they waited for the Bacalhau a Gomes de Sa, an excellent codfish casserole with hardboiled eggs and black olives. As it got dark, strings of lights came on overhead giving the entire block a festive atmosphere.

The wine flowed freely. Leaning forward on the table, Eddy asked if anyone knew about the Bohemian Grove, explaining that one of his new very rich customers said that he had been invited.

"So, in northern California, there is a kind of summer camp for super rich types, you know mostly old money, in a grove of redwoods, like three thousand acres, owned by the Bohemian Club of San Francisco. Been there for over a hundred years. Kinda like a semi-secret society that people know about. Republican presidents, members of government, celebs too. Guys from the Grateful Dead, even that guy Kissinger went there. All men. Probably mostly white too," he continued.

Nods around the table for him to continue.

"They split up into different tent camps, each with a theme, kinda like tribes. Of course, they aren't really roughing it since the place comes with cooks and valets. The lumberjack look is in, you know, red checked wool shirts and stuff. And get this, there are some nighttime Pagan rituals."

"That's totally off the hook," Neighbor Dave said.

"Sounds like a bunch of creepy rich guys who need therapy," Cindy replied.

"I found an article written by a reporter who infiltrated their tight security and spent a few days there. Talked about daily camp activity, a lot of drinking, rituals, speakers to make it sound like a cultural retreat and nighttime plays presented by different tribes in an outdoor log amphitheater. Sounds like college hijinks. I'll send you the link."

"The money they spend on security to keep it private. Imagine how some of that money could help people," Ellis chimed in.

They all agreed.

"Another hedge fund guy who rides an old cherry BSA, mentioned that he was invited but wouldn't go. Not for him.

He said, 'I'm not Republican enough for that place' and that he had enough camp as a kid. Even if it was in a beautiful stand of redwoods."

Eddy reached for a piece of bread.

"Well, like I said, my new shop has so many customers who want to talk about motorcycles I can't get a lot of work done. Dave, how are you with a wrench?"

After dinner, Cindy and Eddy said their goodbyes. One of the local kids had been admiring the cherry red Trailblazer, so Eddy placed him up on the seat, handed him the helmet to hold and Paloma took a photo before they left. She sent it to his mom down the street.

Neely pulled up to the house, all excited.

"Couldn't wait till tomorrow. On the trail of the Dung," he exclaimed, arms flapping in excitement. "Get this, so the same beetle sticker was on the bathroom door at a tattoo parlor on Lincoln. Must have been there a while 'cause it was partly covered with a BLM sticker and the tattoo artist wanted to put a serpent on my back and told me to see a cook at the Grandview Market on Venice who used to work with her who went out with one of the guys in the band. Follow?"

"I think you texted me some of this," Ellis replied, Paloma standing next to him in wonder over the burst of whatever that was.

"We need to go and see if this woman, Dina, is working tonight, which happens to be bluegrass night. We gotta go speak to her."

Ellis agreed.

Paloma decided to stay back and hang with a few of the Venice surfer girls. She had been having a deep think on what, if anything, should go down at Soloff's tomorrow. Ellis was not for it, not wanting to blow up FAQ by offending a guy who was well connected in the music business. She recognized that the evidence was thin to none that it was his guys in the Escalade. But she couldn't let it go.

The Grandview Market on Venice Blvd. was an eclectic throwback to the 1950s. Wooden barrel roof, high walls with large tin logo signs of airlines that long ago had been merged out of existence. A few short aisles had wire racks with essential food items, but the focus was a lunch counter and a table area where food was served, from breakfast through dinner. A limited liquor license allowed them to set up a wine bar and serve craft beers. A few years before Covid they started bringing in live music.

Neely was all turned around at how time had stood still during the year-plus that the Covid virus had ravaged the country and the quarantines had made his daily orbit very small. From traveling all over the country on tour, working concerts for fifteen thousand people a night to a few friends smoking pot in his backyard in Mar Vista, maybe hitting the beach at Ocean Park. The vaccines had loosened things up for now, but he doubted that it was over, as he kept hearing some Delta variant on the rise in India. Covid strains never stayed put for long.

The Ballona Blue Grass Boys were well into their set when Ellis and Neely found two seats at the counter. Dina was thin, fit, with long, dark hair, wearing a tank top that showed off a panorama of tattoos that swept from her shoulder down her arm. Multicolored birds in trees in the jungle seemed to be the theme. Her green eyes had a twinkle to them.

Neely ordered a burger and fries, Ellis a beer. Watching her work at the grill, Neely liked the economy of motion she had prepping the plate. The ghost kitchen had given him a new appreciation for how everything got laid out to be most productive. Making one hundred tacos took planning. On tour, it was the same thing, just with much larger pieces, like amps and drums.

Striking up a conversation, Neely mentioned that Mai-Lin had offered him a great serpent tattoo that he had turned down, but after seeing her ink, he was having second thoughts. She brought the beers, then the burger and fries. Neely continued to chat her up between orders, the acoustic music low enough that he didn't have to shout. She seemed to be enjoying him. Ellis saw that Neely was enjoying her. When he asked her about working here, Dina told him it was an in-between job, that her passion was making chocolate, with dreams of her own "bean to bar" store someday. Neely almost made a stupid remark about tattoos and chocolate but stopped himself.

Getting around to Dung Beetle, Neely mentioned that he had caught the end of their set at the Gopher and how hard it was to find them for a gig. When he pointed out their sticker while contemplating the serpent tattoo, Mai-Lin had said Dina may have gone out with one of them.

She studied him. "They're around, I guess. UCLA and USC, I think. Probably done by now. Yeah, I went out with Ben for a while before the Covid. In high school they were called the Cool Jerks. Brentwood School rich kids. Outrageous smoke, drove really nice cars and went to great parties, so I hung out with them," she said, sounding earnest and open.

"You know where he lives by any chance?" Ellis inquired.

"Never went to his parents' place. Dorm rooms or off-campus apartments. He changed cell phones and ghosted me so, you know, I moved on," she said matter-of-factly. Neely had a hard time imagining any man in his right mind ghosting Dina. Ellis and Neely shared looks. It was a little progress. The Ballona Bluegrass Boys ended their set with "Rocky Top," a bluegrass classic.

As he was finishing the last of his burger and thinking about ordering another just to hang out, Dina turned from the grill and said she remembered dropping off some amps at a storage and office place where they rehearsed in Santa Monica, on their way from a gig to the dorm. She told them where it was and commented on his fancy Porsche SUV. She was impressed by fine things. Neely was impressed by her.

6

Chapter 6

July 1

The surfing report was bleak, so Paloma stayed in bed, then heated a tortilla on the burner and some coffee for breakfast. Ellis had rolled in from the Grandview Market and faded quickly. Vinho Verde and IPA would do that, so she let him sleep.

She had made up her mind to talk to Soloff about the guys in Chatsworth despite Ellis' protestations that they had no proof. He noted the stubborn part of her personality might hurt their business.

Paloma felt that a good defense was sometimes a strong offense. She had watched a lot of football with her dad as a girl.

Driving through Westwood Village to Soloff's office, Paloma noted all the empty storefronts, some existing long before the pandemic hit. With forty thousand UCLA students, and a huge hospital staff just up the street, the lack of a vital retail district was a decades-old concern. Before the pandemic, restaurants prevailed and office space had been nearly filled.

Longtime residents still blamed a "rampage" through the village thirty years ago by crowds who couldn't get into an early screening of *New Jack City* that took the bloom off the Westwood rose. But that was a very long time ago.

Soloff's office space was near the top of a remodeled office tower that had once housed Monty's steakhouse, a longtime westside entertainment hangout. Most people knew it by the huge neon sign atop the building, seen from the freeway. Many of the offices in the building were occupied by companies involved in the entertainment industry. Agents, managers, production companies and the accounting firms that served them.

An assistant walked Paloma down the interior corridor, passing a bullpen of "Covid" empty cubicles on one side and a few casually dressed account executives in glassed-in, windowed offices wearing phone headsets, pacing back and forth, or tossing balls in the air while they talked. This was a large operation, probably also had people working remotely as so many businesses were. The cubicles reminded of her summer college internships and of the jobs she was about to interview for when the pandemic broke out. She doubted the reward outweighed the soul-crushing cubicle she would have to work in.

Paloma was a surfer, and now a detective. Kinda.

Soloff's office was anything but corporate. Persian carpets on the floor with thick curtains, that, unlike Ralston's, were mercifully open, letting in the rare June morning sunlight. One wall was devoted to framed photos of Soloff with celebrities, probably clients. Artifacts and masks from Africa and South America covered another wall and table.

There was no desk. He did business in a wood and leather Eames chair, his feet up on the ottoman, with a phone headset, iPad and an unlit cigar flicking up and down in his hand. Soloff rose to meet her.

"What a pleasant surprise. Good news about the guitar?" he said, smiling and extending his hand. He motioned her to sit in one of the guest chairs.

"Following a number of leads."

"That doesn't sound encouraging. Every day that passes, that guitar could be moving farther away."

"Really? You know something?"

"No, just a way of speech. Have you spoken with Tommy again?"

"Nope, nothing to tell him. We talked with Paul, in Chatsworth, but you already know that."

"You went to Chatsworth?" Soloff asked. He seemed surprised.

"Said he couldn't come into the office. The toe thing was pretty good."

"Toe thing?"

"The infected toe? Let's just say Paul's limp was kinda inconsistent. So, who were the guys waiting outside his place? The ones who followed us?"

"Wait. You're being followed? By whom?"

"Your guys," she said, looking for his reaction.

"Not my guys," Soloff replied, shaking his head slightly.

"Well, they can't drive for shit. Look, if you think we are going about this the wrong way, tell Ralston to cut us a check and go to the police, like we have been saying all along."

Soloff took a few seconds. His nose resting on his steepled hands in front of his face. He considered her, then waved his hand.

"Sounds like Paul didn't want to go to the office. He's had run-ins with Benny at RimShot concerts. Something about his guests winding up in the band dressing room instead of the lounge with the wrong pass. Stuff like that. I'm sketchy on the specifics. Anyway, I don't know about the toe and had no guys follow you there or anywhere. However, we are prepared to give you help if you need it. Tommy wants his guitar back," he said, sounding concerned.

"Not your guys, huh?"

"If there were 'guys,' they were not working for me or Tommy."

Paloma held back from saying they are idiots to be so obvious.

"Keep them and anyone else off us or we walk."

Soloff held up his hand like taking an oath in court.

"Not my guys, I swear," he said with a thin smile, enjoying playing with her.

He took his feet down from the leather ottoman and leaned forward.

"You know, I met your dad once."

"Really?"

"Yeah. I was just starting out in the mailroom of BJR. One day the main partner sent me to meet Bob Grant outside that rehearsal place, SIR in Hollywood, with an envelope. Ten thousand in cash. More money than I had ever seen in my life. I was so nervous. It was the day after the British Racing Green concert in Anaheim. Legendary now. They trashed a whole truckload of rental gear. He was there to settle up the damage. Their fans talked about it for years. Only rock n' roll I guess," he said with a laugh.

Paloma knew the story but was silent and unimpressed. She

got up to leave, her mission accomplished.

"Hey, are you busy tonight or tomorrow night? We could talk more over dinner," he said, rising from his Eames chair.

She tilted her head a bit to one side. He didn't know or care if she and Ellis lived together.

"Not gonna happen," she replied.

"It's not like I'm the client. I just pay Tommy's bills," he said, hands out and open. "You're amazing, a beautiful woman whom I would *really* like to get to know."

"Sorry, not gonna happen," she said, turning to leave.

"Maybe lunch? I'm a member of Soho House at 9200 Sunset, the building Tommy is in. You'd love it. Lots of celebs. Terrific view," he continued, nodding his head hopefully.

"Nope. Just keep your hounds in their cages or we walk," she said heading out the door.

"I wish you hadn't gone over there."

Paloma was pacing back and forth. Ellis, sitting at his desk, was pissed off and amused at the same time. The FAQ agency didn't need Soloff against them. Duffy sat, remarkably silent. He could read the room.

"He hit on me. I went up to his office to tell him to lay off and he freakin' hit on me. Guy's gotta be fifty."

"He's a dick, but now he'll think we're rank amateurs."

"Not when we find the guitar."

Ellis considered how far to go with this and changed course.

"So they weren't his guys?"

"He says they weren't his guys. A few times."

"We believe him?"

"Who knows? A lot of bullshit with him. Seemed like he was preoccupied thinking about me."

"I'm always thinking about that."

"Stop it, it's not funny."

"You wanted to hit him, right?"

"Wouldn't ever."

"Ever?"

"Maybe with one of the friggin' African masks he has hanging all over his office. Just for practice," she replied.

Watching them while on hold, Duffy's head was going back and forth like at a tennis match.

She told them about making up a fake story about the toe and Soloff explaining about Paul probably not wanting to go into the office because of Benny. That story she could believe because Paul came off as a real fuckup.

"I like your style—FAQ all the way," Duffy said, pumping his fist.

"Paul is one of those Hollywood hustler guys you see in the movies. Like a greasy James Woods character, looking for a deal he can glom onto. There is something off with these guys. I don't trust him," Paloma stated.

"You think Paul is involved with stealing the guitar?" Ellis asked.

"His superstar moment was getting the guitar at auction, right?"

"Maybe getting it stolen, then finding it, raises his status with Ralston and Benny."

"Exactly," she said.

"Hey," Duffy said, hanging up the phone. "Two things. Muriel, an old friend at the hall of records, is pulling the deeds and permits you wanted." He thumbed through his pocket notebook. "And that plate you gave me from the car in Chatsworth? Leased to some LLC. Thought it might be a county car."

"County?"

"Yeah, LA County Sheriff's."

"As in stakeout?"

"Wouldn't be surprised."

"Sheriffs drive Escalades?" Paloma asked.

"Well, thinking about it, sometimes they use rental cars to really confuse the bad guys. Imagine being pulled over by a Volvo wagon with a roof rack," he said.

"I see your point," Ellis replied.

"Paul's running something out of that place," Paloma said. "Remember how little furniture there was? Maybe he doesn't really live there."

"Makes sense," Duffy added. "I've seen fencing or dealing setups at houses for sale. You know, a room full of TV boxes."

Paloma looked at Ellis. "Okay, so maybe Soloff didn't have guys following us. My bad," she said with a shrug.

Ellis smiled, knowing better than to say I told you so.

After Paloma had left, Soloff paced around his office, then picked up his headset and called Paul.

"Hey, what's happening?" Paul answered eagerly.

"What's happening is you're a moron."

"What do you mean?"

"You brought those two investigators out to your place? Something about your toe?"

"Man, I was up on the hillside behind the house, and something bit me. Must have been a scorpion or the like. Got all swollen and infected. I went to the minute clinic on DeSoto, and the doctor gave me some antibiotics and pain meds. Hurt like all get out. I haven't been driving."

"Did you stop to remember I said don't bring people out to the house? Do you have any furniture in there yet?"

"Yeah, I got some," he lied. "You know it takes a while to find the right stuff, and during Covid, well, everything is slowed down."

"Okay, I want you to listen. No more people come out there, got it? If they want to talk to you again, you come into the office."

Soloff had put him in the house as a favor to Maggie, at almost no rent, costing Ralston some of the monthly income these real estate investments brought in. Keeping the place occupied, even with a low life, distant cousin was important during Covid. Whatever Paul was into, he didn't want to know.

What Paul *was* into was fencing and selling very expensive watches. Men's and women's. Audemars Piguet, Patek Philippe, Antoine Preziuso. Teaming up with a few friends, he fenced ultra-high-end merchandise, stolen from luxury homes from Beverly Hills to Hidden Hills by a group of young thieves who called themselves the "Buckmen" in some of their less cryptic social media posts. Wearing Bozo masks and large puffy jackets to hide their bodies, they defied modern anti-burglary tech with brazen efficiency.

The "Buckmen" styled themselves after the "Bling Ring," who had become famous in the aughts for ripping off the homes of Paris Hilton, Megan Fox, Lindsay Lohan, and others who would forget to set their alarms or even lock their doors when going out for a night of well-publicized clubbing. Eventually they turned on each other and were busted. National media had a field day with them, and their story led to two movies being made about them, one directed by Sofia Coppola.

There was no shortage of customers, young and old, looking

for a deal or the thrill of buying something "under the table." Some of these watches, when new, sold for upwards to 100k or more. He knew a jeweler in Koreatown who did magic with serial numbers that made it hard to determine the origin of the watches.

His partner Rick, a washed-out airline pilot, trained some B and C level actors who made enough money to afford the Hollywood nightlife. To be seen around town at hot night spots, getting photos posted on Twitter and Instagram was all part of the publicity machine that led to being cast in films and TV. The ones who liked to flash an expensive watch on their wrist were good customers. Some wanted more than one. Paul said, "Hey, we should rent them."

One afternoon after drinking in Paul's barely furnished house, Rick proposed they steal the watches back, which triggered riotous laughter.

Like so many "players" on the make in Hollywood, Paul was a big score kinda guy, hoping his next "deal" would be the big one. Then he would have the money to stretch out Hollywood style, with an office and assistants, looking over projects brought to him. He was thirty-two and tired of being on the outside of the action. Splitting the watch money was making it take longer than he wanted.

Last month, on the way back from delivering watches in Palm Springs, he pulled into the reopened Morongo Casino with a large wad of cash, figuring he could quickly amplify his part of the earnings. After reading online about the "Martindale" roulette strategy, he saw a sure way to double or triple his money.

Martindale proposes you bet on red or black, the same amount when you win and double down when you lose. Paul figured he could be in and out in thirty minutes. It might have been the double bourbons at two in the afternoon, the woman rocking yoga pants and spilling out of a loose silk top gambling next to him, or that he didn't know what the fuck he was doing that kept him from executing his plan. He lost forty-seven thousand in three hours.

"Fuckin' red and black were dodging my chips," he told one of his pals. "Guy next to me said he had never seen anything like it. I'm sticking to blackjack."

Longworth wanted them to recheck the brogrammers' homes, ASAP.

Paloma listened to the recording of the group interview, trying to formulate questions she knew little about. They knew the coders were jamming on a possible workaround for the ransomware, set to go off in a few days. Who was playing both sides? They brought Neighbor Dave along to eyeball the electronics.

In the fifties, Marina del Rey had risen from a Pacific Ocean swamp into a huge seaside development with apartment and hotel towers. Rows of townhouses ringed the man-made harbor, where almost five thousand boats made it one of the largest marinas in America. Only a few minutes from LAX, it was originally a place where flight attendants would share apartments, as did pilots. The "shagging" was legendary.

Marik rented one of the Marina's townhouses, with world-class views of the Pacific. His sun-filled living room and kitchen were very well put together, as though done by a designer. Lead coders made that kind of money. He was not thrilled to have them in his home but acted the host and offered them something to drink, then led them back to the second bedroom "code cave," definitely untouched by any designer.

Electronic equipment dangled off shelves from colored wires, monitors were stacked on cardboard boxes, the work desk so cluttered it would be hard to know the color of the surface. Posters of Metallica and 50 Cent were on the closet doors. The incredible view was covered with curtains, shut tight.

"Do you mind if Dave runs a few tests on the network?"

"Go nuts. Everything is encrypted up the wazoo," he said as Dave got out his test gear.

"Some cables run through the garage. Just don't pull the power cord." He thought it was funny.

"You really left the Emirates and came to Worcester, Massachusetts? The first time in America?"

"Yeah. I needed to try something else. My family wouldn't dream of leaving, but I saw Becker College had this great gaming major. It spoke to me. I hear the program is being absorbed by Clark University in Worcester. It's a pretty good school."

"I had a pal who said winter in Worcester was the worst. Especially after where you come from."

"It was rough but lent itself to cuddling up with some babe on those cold dark nights. I got used to it."

"Marik," Ellis said as they walked back into the kitchen. "Has anyone you didn't know spent time here alone? Like overnight guests?" Ellis asked, assuming that some of the rave parties resulted in Marik 'scoring' with a woman.

"Kinda personal, isn't it?" he said, arms crossed on his chest.

Paloma and Ellis said nothing.

"Sure, I've met some people who spent a night or two. Nothing serious though. Of course, I never left them alone."

"Anyone who might be considered tech savvy?"

Marik thought for a minute. "Not really. Real estate agents, flight attendants, influencers. No one in tech."

"Plumber, handyman in the house alone? Cable guy?"

"Ditched cable last year. All streaming now."

Dave came into the living room, a slight shake of his head signaling he found nothing. He headed out to check the common cable connection from the pole.

Ellis led. "Marik, you know how all this works a whole lot better than me. What are we missing?"

"You should be looking at some of those front office twerps. They don't get us engineers, and they're not getting nearly as many stock options as we are. Not by a long shot. We're the ones who have the most to lose here if Banshee goes down."

"Would they know how to insert malware into the system?" Ellis asked.

"Uh, not without help. They're a bunch of morons. Someone probably found a thumb drive on the street and was dumb enough to plug it in to see what was on it."

"Would that show up somewhere?"

"Not if it was well done, which it obviously was."

Coders saw themselves as of a higher caste. Dave came back with nothing.

"You think you're close to a work-around for the malware?"

"Of course. We're the best."

Riina welcomed them in but wasn't any more forthcoming than Marik. Her condo was in a large, modern building near Santa Monica beach. Neighbor Dave checked the main Spectrum cable lines coming into the building before going to her condo and her "coding cave," which was as neat as the rest of the place. While showing Paloma around her spotless apartment,

Riina also disparaged the loyalty of people in the front office, saying that the coders *were* the company.

"This is my third startup, and it's always the same us and them mentality. The office drones can't get their heads around us going all out in work and play."

"Where did you learn to code?" Paloma asked as Riina offered her a cup of tea while Dave checked the system.

"Well, I grew up in Estonia, with one American parent, so I spoke English well. We always skied in the Alps and when the University of Denver offered a six-foot Estonian female a scholarship, I went for it. Lots of tech jobs in Denver that you never hear about. Started coding as an intern on the side to pay for my lift tickets."

"How'd you wind up at Banshee?"

"In tech they say you don't leave the company; you leave the manager. Well, I had the opposite experience where I followed my manager to beautiful southern California and realized it was where I was meant to be. I have the beach for volleyball, and I can drive up to Mammoth to ski."

"I saw you guys liked the pop-up rave scene during Covid."

"I love dancing to loud music. Great way to blow off steam."

"Ever get sick with Covid there?"

"You know, once those vaccines came along in February, I embraced them and hopefully the immunity they bring. So far so good. You should come to one. Wild scene."

"Thanks. I surf. Keeps my head straight," Paloma replied.

Riina studied her. A very self-assured woman like herself. She nodded agreement and approval.

"I'd love to try that sometime. Not a big sport in Estonia."

"If you have the balance to ski, you're halfway there."

Neighbor Dave had packed up his test gear and gave Paloma

a nod.

"Thanks for your help. We'll keep you in the loop."

"Sure, you know where to find me," Riina said, giving a sweeping gesture of the condo.

Calls to Rusty went to voicemail. The Banshee office said they thought he might have gone to a conference in Las Vegas and should be back in a day or so. They had not made his travel arrangements.

Ellis kept up his daily search of websites and music stores to see if by some slim chance the guitar had surfaced. Paloma checked more public social media pages of the "Brogrammers" and ran background checks using a website FAQ subscribed to. This was more of the "not glamorous" part of being a PI.

Neely came bounding into the office, arms flapping, all excited.

"I was thinking. It's Friday."

Ellis looked at him in wonder.

"I mean because it's Friday we should go sit on the storage place Dina mentioned. Local bands have gigs on Fridays and Saturdays, right? Maybe somebody shows, to pick up gear."

Duffy turned to Neely. "Stake out. Don't drink too much coffee so you don't have to pee."

"How about snacks?" Neely said.

"Chocolate, okay. No chips—they make you thirsty," he said and turned to answer the phone.

"You go over there with Neely," Paloma said. I'll do the deep dive on the 'brogrammers

"Brogrammers?" Neely said.

"Let's go. I'll explain on the way over."

Parked by the twenty or so "workplace" garages that formed a U-shape around a central courtyard, Neely and Ellis waited over two hours. If Dung Beetle had a weekend gig, and they still used the space Dina described, maybe they would pick up their gear. Neely had looked into the units that had windows trying to see any band gear, but most were covered with shades or paper. A guy who fixed furniture was loading two chairs out of his unit into a pickup, so Ellis went over and asked him about a band working out of here. He pointed to a roll down in the middle of the alley, said the band sucked, and drove off. A girl carrying a saxophone case entered a music studio next door. For Neely this was way better than making chile rellenos and endless fish tacos at the ghost kitchen.

Listening to podcasts made the wait bearable, as Malcolm Gladwell explained why french fries at McDonald's taste terribly different from the ones he cherished as a boy. Something about beef tallow. After a while a silver Jaguar SUV drove into the alley and pulled up near the door the furniture guy had pointed to.

"That qualifies as a fancy car alright," Neely said.

A youngish guy, early twenties, dressed down but expensive, got out of the car in a cloud of smoke. He opened the hatchback and they saw a small amp already in there. That looked promising.

"C'mon, lucky door number seven," Neely said, leaning over, trying to guide him to the locker. The guy took a key on a lanyard from around his neck and went over to door 7. Neely pumped his fist and whispered "yes!". Sitting low in the car, they waited until the garage-type door was opened. There was band gear inside.

"We have a winner," Ellis said, as they got out of the car and walked over.

"Hey, Ben?" he called out as they approached.

The guy looked at him, his eyes red and hooded. He was blitzed.

"I saw you at the Gopher the other week." Ellis replied, extending a hand.

"Uh, I'm Daniel. Ben has longer dark hair," he said.

"Oh sorry. But you're with Dung Beetle, right? Dina told me you guys practiced here sometime. Ripped it *up* that night."

"Yeah? Thanks," he said, trying to focus on two guys just materializing out of nowhere.

"Listen, my buddy wound up with a guitar that has a Dung Beetle sticker on it. Trying to find out more about it, you know, checking that it wasn't stolen or something. A tan Epiphone Casino, like a Gibson 335 copy."

"Natural wood with a sticker on the back?"

"Uh, yeah. Kinda worn, faded," Ellis said.

"I hope your friend didn't pay too much for it. That guitar was refinished to look like John Lennon's. You know, on the roof, the last Beatles concert? Not a great job. The neck was kinda messed up, too. Benji got that guitar for his bar mitzvah, before he got the Strat. I think he swapped it for a bag of killer Kush a few months ago," Daniel recounted. "His parents were pissed."

"A guy named Barker, right?" Neely said quickly, making up a name.

"Barker? No, it was Evan. He used to be at Crossroads. He liked it because of the John Lennon on the roof thing. I heard he's been rehearsing with Camel Smile lately," he said, now more at ease and on a stoner roll.

"Evan have a last name?"

"Garvin, maybe? I think."

Neely was thrilled at how stoned and chatty Daniel was, standing next to his Jag, in a storage alley at dusk, talking to two strangers who just walked over out of nowhere. Last year, looking for a guy, he had struck out at many Santa Monica funky motels. He figured sometimes you get lucky, so he would ride this wave the best he could. He was enjoying the private eye stuff.

As they helped load the amps into the Jag, Daniel described Evan. He sounded like the guy they were looking for, but Daniel wasn't sure of where he lived. He thought one of his parents might have a house on one of the Helena Drives in Brentwood, of which for some reason, there were eighteen. Marilyn Monroe had died in her house on one of them. He didn't know where they rehearsed.

Back in the car, a quick online check for Evan showed many people with that surname in Brentwood and but no photos of him on Google. Living with a stepparent was common and it wasn't uncommon for wealthy parents to hire companies to scrub all their kids' incriminating online posts before they applied to college.

He found a generic Camel Smile website with a crane image that said, "under construction." However, a banner flying from the crane said the band would be playing at a burlesque bikini bar in Hollywood, Jumbo's Clown Room,

On the way back to the office, Neely lit up a pre-roll to celebrate.

Drilling down into the public pages of the brogrammers' social media accounts, Paloma confirmed they were graduates of Becker College, Long Beach State and U. Denver. There were plenty of photos, working out, wearing VR goggles or hard at work blasting a computer gamer. There were also photos of wild parties, with revelers dancing in crowds by huge lit-up pools at some mansions in the hills.

The underground party scene during the worst of Covid had been quite active. In large Airbnb rentals or old industrial rave sites, if you wanted to party during the pandemic, you could, as promoters kept the scene alive. Like whack-a-mole, when the LAPD shut one down, two more would pop up. It appeared that Marik, Rusty, and Riina hung together and hadn't missed much fun.

Paloma decided to make a photo layout, just like on TV detective shows, for each case on the large whiteboard near Duffy's giant Rat Pack photo. Maybe this did help think about the case. On one side she put up photos she printed out from the stolen Harrison guitar case, with names on sticky notes underneath. Ralston wasn't hard to find, though a photo when he wasn't wincing over his guitar was rare. She found Benny and Gary on a team photo of "The Most" softball team online, Willem's from his website. She wondered if she should include Soloff. He was a dick. She found a photo of him backstage at a Kendrick Lamar concert.

For now, silhouettes would have to do for the two guys who swapped out the guitar.

On the Banshee side, she found a photo of Longworth and his wife Mona from some charity benefit. On public pages, selfies of Rusty with bikini-topped women hanging on his bare chest, nighttime shades and a backwards baseball cap, Corona in hand. There was Marik smiling on a chaise lounge with a large cigar in his mouth and a woman on his lap, Riina—at six feet tall, she stood out with her snow-white hair, vest with no shirt, dancing with a clutch of sweaty revelers at some house with Spanish architecture around a large lit-up swimming pool.

These people posted a lot of photos, the most recent taken at some rave that reminded her of a place she had been in, a Hayden Tract warehouse in Culver City, an industrial district that had rapidly been redeveloped. So many people crowded together; no wonder Covid had been so bad. Had she missed all the fun trying to stay safe? Guys in the photos were shirtless, girls who loved to say "yeah" or something like that, so their mouths were open at the camera. This place looked like a real nightclub with stage lights and a video screen behind the DJ.

In a few of the photos they were all together, Rusty, Marik and Rinna, dancing in a sweaty group, having a great time. They seemed tight. What if they were all in on the hack, taking a quick cash out to move on to the next startup? Lead programmers were always being recruited.

Or were they just having a good time at the raves?

Paloma had finished printing out the Dung Beetle logo for her board when the guys came stumbling into the office, having gone deep into the "victory" pre-roll.

"Up top," Ellis said, holding up his hand for a high five. Paloma indulged him. "We got really lucky! The girl Dina that Neely found at the market, you know the one who used to work at the tattoo parlor, she was right about where Dung Beetle keeps their band gear."

Neely jumped on the narrative. "We were hangin' there for a while and this guy pulled in driving a Jaguar SUV to pick up some amps. Gotta be eighty grand."

Ellis continues, "A Jag! Guy couldn't be more than twenty-two. We walk up and ask if he's Ben and he says no, his name is Daniel. The guy is totally baked and just starts talking to us. Says another guy in the band is Ben. Called him Benji."

"And get this, says Benji got the guitar that was switched at Willem's for his bar mitzvah. A few months ago, he traded it for a bag of weed," Neely said, way too loud.

Paloma just stared at them. They were on a roll; why slow them down?

"Then this guy, Daniel—man was he stoned—tells us a guy named Evan Garvin is the one traded the weed for the guitar," Ellis added. "And he plays in a band called Camel Smile."

"Damn. Another name I missed for my band." Paloma shook her head and looked at them. "You guys are baked."

"And so," Ellis continued, "we find out this band is playing a gig. Where?" And now Ellis and Neely said in unison, "Jumbo's Clown Room!"

"We're all going," Ellis proclaimed, smiling a bit too much from the smoke.

"Hold up. Duffy in a bikini bar? Uh, don't tell him. You sure they have live bands at a strip club?"

"That's what the website says. We called to confirm."

"Gee, I can't wait," she said, shaking her head in amazement.

From everything she knew about Jumbo's Clown Room, it was not a place she wanted to spend more than thirty seconds. Rows of drunk guys shouting and throwing dollar bills at women in tiny underwear was not part of her playlist.

"You 'clowns' done? Now I have a few things for you to ponder. Going through the brogrammers' social media photos, you'd think there hadn't been a pandemic with all the parties. Come see."

They walked over to her photo wall.

"Wow, just like TV," Neely exclaimed, taking it in.

Ellis looked at the wall, then at Paloma.

"Impressive. Just like the big kids, huh?"

"Yup" is all she said.

Neely studied the party photos.

"This has been going on during the pandemic? No wonder so many people got sick last winter."

Hoping that the ghost kitchen was closed, Neely collected his backpack to split. He found a note underneath that Duffy had left earlier. He handed it to Ellis. 'Call Longworth'. They did and it went to voicemail.

They closed the office and drove down to the beach as the crowds thinned out after a long, glorious day. With beers in brown paper bags, they crossed the vast Venice beach and sat above the high tide line for the last of the sun. The waves were small, but a few boogie boarders were having fun. Paloma couldn't help but watch.

"What are you up to on that podcast? The history of rock in five hundred songs?" Ellis asked.

"Yeah, now in the early sixties. I'm up to 'He's a Rebel' by the Crystals, who sometimes were also the Blossoms singing as the Crystals. The guy explains how the Blossoms sang background on most hit singles of the day, worked with Phil Spector, and how their own songs were released under different groups' names. The rights and residuals, as unfortunately it usually was then, were a mess," Paloma said.

"I found a clip of the Blossoms, Fanita, Jeannie and Darlene, singing 'Nighttime is the Right Time' with the Righteous Brothers from some old black and white *Shindig* TV show, that is 'take-it-to-church' awesome."

Ellis nodded and put his arm around her.

"My dad always loved 'Uptown' by the Crystals. You know,

wall of sound, castanets. He said it was a song about the common man. A working man."

"Yeah, one of the first," she replied.

The ocean waves went quiet for a few seconds, and so did the conversation as they watched the sea.

"What are we doing?" Ellis asked.

"Sitting on Venice beach having an illegal beer at sunset?"

"No, I mean us. FAQ. Is this really what we want to do?"

"You mean some of our clients are jerks?"

"Lately," Ellis replied.

"Hey, partner, we said we would give it a year, remember?"

"Well, you did agree while sick with Covid and slept for three days."

She knew the pull to go back on tour would be there like the tides, with the vaccines and tours started going out. Ellis, like her dad, loved what he did, and that meant being on the road.

"Working for rock bands was my dream. Grant opened so many doors for me. In ten years, I have gone all over the world. Great hotels, livin' large. Per diem. Big fun. But I really like being home. With you."

"Don't think about me. I'm not going anywhere," she said, putting a hand on his cheek. "Finding this guitar will pick up your spirits. You said it would do great things for FAQ's reputation. Ralston came to us because we found the Hines kid out in Yucca Valley. When we find George friggin' Harrison's guitar, we'll have to hire Leon plus, dare I say this, Neely to keep up with business."

"Neely? He's a road rat who won't stay long once tours start going out. He will have something before he makes his ten-thousandth taco."

Again silence. A few larger wave sets crashed on the beach,

sending a spray up that caught the late afternoon light. Paloma loved being in and by the water. She could never live anywhere inland.

"I already had a relationship that ended because I was on the road too much."

"Hey, remember the world I grew up in? I was on the road as a teenager while you were still in college. I grew up with a dad who was away more than he was home some years."

Ellis nodded. Grant was a great friend. He must have been a great dad.

"Sure I like coffee on the porch on Sunday morning, but I say we should do what we like." Paloma had grown up a surfer with relaxed parents. She was a free spirit.

Ellis pushed his beer into the sand and pulled her close. She leaned into it. They had made the decision to start FAQ during the hardest of times, the dark and scary days of Covid when everyone was wiping down their groceries and washing their hands twenty times a day. Being together, so close, so fast, during the lockdowns, the future plans they laid out changed daily. Paloma would throw out an idea and they would research it and bat it around for days, then Ellis would present an idea and they would do it again.

"Is our thing a Covid thing?" Ellis asked.

"A Covid thing?"

"There was a story in the *Times* about people who were thrown together during the quarantine. I have a college friend who had just moved into a studio apartment in Cambridge with his girlfriend. They spent six months in four hundred square feet. As soon as the restrictions were lifted, she moved to Colorado. Without the quarantine, would we have stayed together past the first sex-crazed months?" he asked.

"Well, that *was* fun," she said, looking at him with a smile. "Dude, I want you to remember something. I'd been kinda crushing on you since I was sixteen. We weren't going to burn out in eight weeks."

"Oh that. Well, I'm glad you're not sixteen now."

"Ain't that right?" she said, pulling him down on the sand. "Learned a lot since then."

"Oh? About what?"

"You're funny."

The fog stayed offshore. Venice nighttime streets were again crowded with tourists and locals. The shops that remained in business after the first year of Covid were clawing their way back to paying the rent on time. The pent-up need to be out and about crashed like waves over the beach community.

They had reached Longworth as he was returning from the Bay area, freaking out that they hadn't made progress. Paloma brought him up to speed, though she wished she had more. She asked him if there were other people, those in the office they should be looking at. He said no, which was frustrating.

Neighbor Dave had cooked some fried plantains with red beans and rice to go with Paloma's miso salmon. They sat in the small yard, drinking a new local hazy IPA.

The plates were full, and the beers were cold as they sat under the twinkle lights that rimmed the yard. Paloma shared a story of her only brush with the Navy.

"I was helping my dad's crew build a stage in San Diego on an aircraft carrier at that naval base," Paloma said.

"Been there," Dave shared, nodding his head.

"Yeah, the *Abraham Lincoln*. As we get the base layer of the stage scaffolding down, we use big-ass screw jacks to get everything level before we build up. Our Navy liaison asks what we're doing, so Grant explains. The guy gets this weird look on his face, says get your level, then starts talking into his radio. A minute later we feel a shudder and then the whole damn ship starts to slowly tilt, centering the bubble on the level. The guy had this huge grin; he could see Grant appreciated the incredible engineering feat going on below."

"Pretty neat trick, huh? Dave said. "When they are launching or retrieving planes at sea, it can get pretty rough. They shift the ballast around to different chambers. That allows them to help level the deck for landing."

"Yup, the guy just had to show it off. So damn cool. Of course, he was backstage for the show, and we put him in the wings stage right. It was a Tom Petty concert. Guy turned into a total fanboy and sweated right through his uniform."

Dave then turned the conversation to the present.

"So I was asking a friend what are the simplest or easiest ways to hack into a home Wi-Fi network," Dave said.

"Having the password helps," Ellis said to the expected laughter.

Yes," Dave continued. Once you have that, there are a variety of things you can use."

Everyone nodded.

"Otherwise, it depends on the level of encryption being used, and access to the hardware. Like if the servers were compromised."

"The boss says there were no events recorded by the security system, cameras or the code logger."

"That might localize the breach," Dave asked.

Dave proceeded to lay out various ways of getting into the system, mentioning items like "sniffers" and a salad of acronyms: WEP, WNIC, MAC. Then he added other simple ways like responding to a fake phone message from an "IT" associate, plugging in a thumb drive found on the street to see what's on it, letting a "RAT" trojan horse or keylogger program to load or even a fake repairman left alone inserting a device into the back of a router.

Ellis took notes so they could formulate new questions for the brogrammers and know a little of what they were talking about. From everything they had heard in the interviews, someone was compromised, knowingly or not. Checking the homes had turned up nothing obvious.

"My pal said you have serious stones to use the Stingray phone device last year. That thing's got felony written all over it."

"Well, it was a wild one-hour of phone numbers whizzing by on the screen, but we learned a lot. The robust reception was wild," Ellis replied, holding his hands wide apart.

"In the Navy, our country trained us to do many things. Once I knew the Stingray worked, I gave it back. Kinda like Kryptonite. You don't want it around."

Paloma was quiet and looked around the table. She knew the Stingray was illegal, but Ellis had downplayed it. The tone of Dave's remarks raised her understanding of what they had done for her and Cindy trying to find the missing emeralds. She looked at him and Dave with wonder, appreciation, and love.

7

Chapter 7

July 2

Ellis got to Trader Joes at 8:00 am when it opened. During the worst of the pandemic there would be long lines to get in the store, so Paloma had started making their list to fit the pattern of the one-way aisles so whoever did the shopping got to the register in less than ten minutes.

Now, with the unpredictable hours at FAQ, frozen prepared foods from TJ's became their go-to. Shrimp pot stickers, mushroom risotto, and peas, throw in whatever, had replaced some of the fun meals they had been cooking.

A tortilla on the burner was Paloma's usual morning break-fast routine, starting when she was young, and her addict mom Lana had little food in the house. Lana was usually passed out in a sleeping bag on the couch in the morning, so Paloma had to fend for herself. As with most things, she found the more butter the better.

Today she feasted on fresh berries and yogurt, topped off

with homemade granola Eddy had made. Fruit in California was always available and fresh. She missed that on tour.

Ellis was putting away the groceries when Paloma came out of the shower. The morning light behind her created a glow around her head. He was mesmerized. Covid had been so dark and scary, with endless stories of sickness and death before the vaccines, that seeing her beauty warmed him. Of the many things he was thankful for, finding her at exactly the time in his life when he could have a stay-at-home relationship was a super slot machine jackpot, all gold apples.

"What?" she said, seeing him staring at her. "Still have shampoo in my hair? Seed in my teeth?"

"Nope, just savoring the image of you with incredible morning light."

"Aw, that's nice. Did they have those tiny ice-cream cones again?"

Supply chain problems plagued consumers at all levels of the economy, even ice cream.

"Got 'em. Bought two. I'll make room in the freezer," he said, opening the door. During the pandemic's early days of empty store shelves, Ellis had purchased whatever he could and filled the freezer, as well as boxes under the guest bed filled with canned goods, thanks to no more room in the pantry. Paloma joked that "someone" was going to have to eat all the bags of pasta and rice, plus the cans of salmon and black beans he had purchased, giving Ellis a hard time; she knew they could be donated to the Westside Food Bank.

Entering the FAQ office, they found Duffy standing in front of the photo wall, his head moving back and forth.

"You made this?"

Paloma nodded yes.

"It's great, just like TV. They do this on *Vera*, my favorite detective show. Ever watch it? The photo board always helps her nab the bad guys. A British show, you know, with the accents."

"Yeah, with more than one case I thought it might help us focus".

"This the rocker guy whose guitar was stolen?" Duffy said, pointing to Ralston's stage photo of him posing and grimacing during a guitar solo.

"Yeah, how'd you guess?" Paloma said dryly.

"Don't forget the little lines," Duffy said, pointing to all the photos.

"Little lines?" Ellis asked.

"Yeah, the little lines, you know, to establish relationships. They always help Vera solve the case," he said.

"If only we had Vera's help on this," Paloma added.

8

Chapter 8

July 2 - Evening

There is no easy way to get from Venice to Jumbo's Clown Room on a Saturday night, but Neely begged for the "full ride," so they cut up to La Brea to cruise along the infamous part of Hollywood Boulevard, with Grauman's Chinese theater, the stars on the Walk of Fame, the superhero freak show at Highland. Lit up like Vegas, the sidewalks were once again packed with tourists who waited over a year to march down this distorted Disney-esque landscape, past the touts for Ripley's or the Wax Museum, the souvenir shops with three T-shirts for ten dollars and divey restaurants and bars.

In front of the Hollywood and Highland center were the usual cast of superhero characters, photo op for twenty bucks and get the El Capitan theater or the *Jimmy Kimmel Live* marquee in the background. Tourists from Nebraska to Asia to Europe clustered around sidewalk stars, cameras held high.

"Full house tonight," Neely shouted, his head half out the

window as they crawled along in packed gawker traffic. "Two Deadpool's, a Batman, a who-the-fuck-is-that, a fat Batman, two Spidermen, some kind of Elvis and a nice first-generation Wonder Woman, showing a lot of skin."

Ellis drove the BMW east, passing the famous Musso and Frank restaurant.

"That's Duffy's kinda place," Paloma said.

"Never been," Ellis replied.

"Really? It's pricey but we gotta go sometime. Red leather booths, lots of wood. Ancient waiters. Famous for their martinis and blue cheese iceberg salads. Real rat pack kinda joint," she said. "Way overpriced."

"Definitely not Jumbo's Clown Room," Neely added, now passing a stripper supply store, four T-shirts for ten bucks, the Pantages theater and the Frolic Room bar.

They continued on the Boulevard, past the 101 freeway, to the residential, much less touristy part of Hollywood, where they found Jumbo's Clown Room in a strip mall shared by a pet supply store and a few Asian restaurants. The front windows were bricked up. The parking lot was full, so Ellis cruised the side street looking for a nonresident sticker spot.

They paid the cover and entered the dark club. Red walls, mirrors, red seats. Bad clown illustrations everywhere. Loud rap music shook the room as the crowd whooped and hollered, dollar bills raining on the small stage where a woman in a Pillsbury Doughboy outfit was light-footing around the pole as another girl in a barely there bikini awkwardly tried to unzip the oversized costume.

Emerging from the costume was Cara, in a lacy, strappy, one-piece something, doing her set on and around the pole. More dollar bills flew through the air as she set to twerking the front row, allowing the occasional slap on her butt.

Finding an open place to lean at the bar, it was beers all around. The crowd was more Camp Pendleton marines and girls' night out than skinny rockers. To the left of the stage band gear was set up in a corner. No band in sight.

Cara's song ended as she picked up the dollars that covered the stage.

"One of a kind, this place," Ellis said.

"I sure hope so," said Paloma. "The clown art is like some horror movie."

"Twerking. How does she do that? How does someone have that kind of muscle control?" Neely wondered out loud.

Paloma just stared at him; Ellis knew better than to answer.

"No" was all she said.

Ellis leaned over to the pink-haired bartender and asked about Camel Smile. She replied they better be back in a few minutes because there was a break after the next dancer. There was only room for the girls backstage. Perfect, Ellis thought, they would be hanging around, easy to approach and scope out. A high top with a laminated clown face on it opened up so they moved over.

New thumping rap music came on and Lea Tune came out in a black microkini, stacked patent leather platform boots with striped knee socks sticking out of the top.

She was eating a slice of pizza.

Strutting around the stage, she leaned back on the pole, suggestively arching her head back, teasing the pointy edge of the pizza into her mouth, slowly sliding down to the ground. As she shifted her legs to a more "welcoming" position, a shower of bills started to cover the stage as the crowd went wild. Every slight adjustment of her legs and suggestive bite of the pizza had the front row make it rain with dollar bills. When it became obvious that she was going to eat the whole slice, they started beating on the front of the stage.

"Now this is worth the price of admission," Paloma said, leaning into Ellis. "I wouldn't want to have missed this."

He nodded cautiously and they both looked at Neely, who was transfixed, watching Lea Tune. They wondered if he might soon be in the front row.

The back door from the alley opened and four guys dressed in black walked in. Ellis elbowed Paloma and nodded to them. The band. Two guys matched Willem's and Gary's description of a "Mexican," one carrying a drumstick bag, but they looked more Middle Eastern. Two other white guys, a little chunky, both wearing black, had tats all over their arms. Evan couldn't be one of them unless he very recently inked up and gained thirty pounds. Huddled at the back door by the wall of clown paintings, they shook their heads at Lea Tune, then went back out into the alley.

Ellis pushed off from the table, breaking Neely's trance as they followed out the backdoor. In the alley, three of the band guys, standing in front of a six-foot-tall plexiglass martini glass, stood in a tight circle passing a pre-roll.

Ellis called out, "Hey, Evan."

The band guys looked around, as though also looking for Evan.

"On his way. We'll be in when she's done eating the fucking pizza," one guy said flatly, turning back to the circle.

"Camel Smile, right?"

The band members rolled their eyes.

"We need to talk about a guitar. An Epiphone," Paloma said.

"Don't know what you're talking about. Who the fuck are

you?" one of the white guys said, all twenty-something attitude.

The other members of the band turned to look at them, not disguising their concern. Paloma quickly snapped their photos.

"Hey, what the fuck?"

"Epiphone Casino? Dung Beetle sticker on the back? Benji? Ring a bell?" Ellis said, stepping up, Neely and Paloma moving to either flank.

The members of the band looked quizzical, wide eyed. Paloma thought they should never play poker.

Suddenly the back door of the club swung open and two big, muscular guys came bounding out. Like linebackers, big and fast. One went to grab the dark-skinned guy. Neely instinctively wheeled on him and landed a punch, slowing him down. Ellis and Paloma didn't react fast enough and were taken down by the other guy, arms spread, hit midsection, and sent flying back hard to the ground.

Without missing a beat, the thugs grabbed the darker skinned guy and dragged him down the alley as a black SUV roared up, the rear hatch opening, and they tossed the guy in. The other two band members were frozen in place.

"Where's the skinny one?" the driver shouted.

"Didn't see him," the guy whom Neely punched said, now holding something in his hand. Neely advanced on him, but this time he blocked Neely's punch and hit him with a lead and leather sap on the side of the head, which jerked back sharply and he went down hard. Backing up to the waiting SUV, the guy dared anyone else who wanted a taste. He got in and the SUV sped away, towards Hollywood Boulevard.

Paloma rolled and got up as the other band guys ran down the alley and split. She went to Neely, putting her sweatshirt under his head. He was out and didn't look good, pale and his hair full of blood.

"Shit, couldn't see the SUV plate," Paloma said as Ellis got up.

From behind a dumpster, the drummer came out, having heard the commotion, a quizzical look on his face. He had chosen a good time to take a leak.

"What happened? Where's everybody? They go in?" the drummer said, looking around.

"What's your name?" Ellis demanded.

"Husani. Where's my brother? The band?"

"Some guys just threw your brother in a SUV," Paloma said, looking up from Neely.

"Who were they?" Ellis said. "You guys owe drug dealers?"

"Oh shit." Husani took a beat. "I mean no. I've never been here before. We've been waiting for our guitar player to show up so we can do our set."

"Waiting for Evan?" Ellis said tersely.

"Uh, yeah. You know him?" Husani sounded surprised.

"We need to talk to him. About a guitar."

"A guitar?" he said.

"Yeah, the guitar switch?"

"My brother doesn't know anything. Got nothing to do with it," Husani blurted out in his panic.

There was a moment of silence. He looked like he was going to cry.

"Owwwwwwww," Neely said as he opened his eyes, which roamed all over as his head rocked back and forth.

"His color sucks. We need to get him to an emergency room," Paloma said. "Keys." She held up her hand and Ellis threw them to her in a well-rehearsed move.

"Nothing to do with what?" Ellis said, taking her place with Neely.

"What's gonna happen to my brother?" Husani wailed.

"Well, if it's about drugs and he has the money, he'll probably be able to dance and eat apples in the future. If it's something else, like the whereabouts of a certain guitar, who knows."

"That old ratty guitar? I told Evan it was a bad idea."

"No, it's about the other guitar. Keep talking," Ellis said, holding the sweatshirt to help Neely.

"I didn't know anything. He asked me to drive him to some repair shop. He said some guy offered him five hundred for his guitar and a fist full of money if he would do a switch. Said the guy came from out of nowhere. I thought maybe he was playing some kind of joke on his friend, you know? Evan said it was easy. If we got caught, just act stupid and say sorry. No one in the shop even blinked."

"Stupid is what it is," Ellis replied.

The BMW came tearing into the alley in reverse. Paloma jumped out of the car and went to help pick Neely up.

"Where's the other guitar you switched for? The Country Gentleman?" Ellis demanded.

"The what? I don't know! I dropped Evan off at a supermarket parking lot and he told me to come back in an hour. When I did, he had a big roll of money and a party-sized bottle of Oxy. Pills aren't my thing, but he gave me a hundy for driving."

"Gimme your driver's license," Ellis commanded.

"What?"

Ellis pushed him against the giant martini glass, spun him around and took his wallet as Paloma helped Neely into the car.

"This your address?" Ellis said, waving the license. Husani nodded. "I'm going to return this to you early in the morning,"

Ellis said. "Think of anything else you can tell me. I hope your brother is okay."

"Hospital. Now!" Paloma said.

"Wait. How will I get home? My brother has my keys," Husani said.

"Try Uber," Ellis said, climbing into the car.

"Aw, c'mon. This is Hollywood," he said as though he was in Kazakhstan. Pacific Palisades and Brentwood were his bubble, where he felt safe. "Wait, wait. You can track them. There is this Airtag thingy on my keys. My mom got it for me last Eid because I'm always losing them."

"Pull it up on your phone."

"Um, I don't know that part; just got the app and connected it."

"You just got a ride," Ellis said, pushing Husani into the front seat while he slid in back next to Neely, conscious but looking like shit, holding Paloma's sweatshirt against the wound on his head. Ellis forcefully told Husani to give him the passcode for the phone and called Neighbor Dave for help with setting up the Airtag software to track them.

"No hospital; go after those guys," Neely croaked as Paloma drove to the head of the alley, waiting for directions.

"They won't really hurt him, right?" Husani said.

There was a moment of silence in the car. Husani's shoulders sank.

"We'll figure it out once we find them," Paloma said.

"I want a piece of that guy who sapped me," Neely bleated to Ellis. "You still have bats in the trunk?" Neely didn't like to give up.

"Ok, Dave, stay on with us," Ellis said. "Here goes."

He fired up the app and a map appeared on the phone. The

tracker worked by using every Apple device using Bluetooth anywhere near it. For thirty dollars it was incredible. After about twenty seconds, Ellis shouted, "Yesssss." There was a blip on the map. The SUV was heading north from Jumbo's on Western Blvd.

"Going north on Western," he said to Paloma.

She slid the car onto Winona, the parallel side street, and raced north.

"Shit, it doesn't go through," she said when she got to Franklin Blvd., looking across at a long cinder block retaining wall and a string of beat-up RVs.

Husani sat quietly, still in shock about his brother and awestruck by the coordination inside the car.

"They're headed to the park," Ellis said. "The signal is flashing."

She tried to gain ground in the Saturday night gawker traffic.

Neighbor Dave was listening in. "The park is not good. No Bluetooth signals for the tag to latch on to."

"They must have their phones turned off, or the park had shitty cell coverage. Probably both. You think these guys are pros?"

Paloma said, "I can floor it on the park road, catch up to them."

"What are you guys, like detectives?" Husani said enthusiastically.

Paloma accelerated into the turn onto Western, clear of the traffic clog. The chase was on and she wanted to catch up, but they were losing the signal in the park.

"There's only a couple of roads in the park; I can catch them."

Neely was quiet and Ellis looked over. He was trying to focus and looked pretty bad.

"Change of plan. Let's get Neely to a hospital. Now!" Ellis declared.

Paloma didn't want to give up, but trusted Ellis' read.

"St. John's in Santa Monica," he croaked.

"Too far away," Ellis said.

"St. John's, please. Doctor Mike works there. Don't worry. I'll make it."

Paloma looked in the rearview and met Ellis' eyes. He had been on the road with Neely for years and trusted his judgment. Paloma slid into a U-turn and gunned it. Franklin was parallel to Hollywood Boulevard, and usually was a faster "taxi road" heading west from Hollywood.

Husani sat shotgun with eyes like saucers and one hand gripping onto the dash. He had never seen someone work a stick shift and drive like Paloma. The power and the handling of her 528 BMW was awsome.

"What about my brother?" Husani shouted.

"You could get out and track him if you want. We gotta get this guy to the hospital. Call one of the other band guys."

"Are you guys PIs? Like detectives?" Husani asked. "Maybe my mom should hire you."

"So those guys were about the guitar, not drugs, right?" Ellis hissed.

"I don't do drugs," he replied.

"The guitar for sure," Paloma said. "They must have been following us. They fit right in at Jumbo's. Saw the band, followed us out. Figured they would grab and go. Didn't know Evan was late, just like a junkie."

"You guys are on a case? To find the guitar Evan took? Wow! I could work with you, you know, help out. I've watched *Law & Order* since I was like seven."

Paloma looked in the rearview again and saw Ellis shaking his head in bemused amazement. The drummer was half a cop groupie.

"You helped steal it. You want to help? Where is it?"

"Uh, I don't know," Husani pleaded. "Evan must know who he sold it to."

"Kidnapping your brother. That's fucked up. You guys are rich kids, right?" Paloma said to Husani. "That means the five of you probably have, what, twelve or fifteen parents between you? One of them has to be a lawyer."

"Uh, more than that, I think," Husani replied meekly.

Paloma sliced through La Brea traffic to the highway, heading to St. John's emergency room.

"If these are Ralston's guys, fuck it. Not what I signed up for," Paloma declared, gunning the car onto the Santa Monica freeway. "If not, who are they?"

"Wait. Ralston? RimShot Tommy Ralston? You guys work for him?" Husani half shouted, very excited.

"You helped steal his guitar. How's that sound? He's not happy about it," Paloma said. "Probably why those guys drove off with your brother. They took the wrong guy, huh? Should have been you."

"Oh shit. What are they going to do? I didn't know till it was happening. I just drove. Evan was the guy. He is like a junkie with that Oxy. I knew we shouldn't have let him in the band."

"Neely, you with us?" Ellis asked.

"I don't feel so great."

Husani looked around with wonder at what was going on around him.

"Be there in ten minutes. Husani, call an Uber to pick you up at St. John's emergency. Keep watching that tracker. If he shows up, call us," Paloma said as she downshifted and slid the BMW. "Hang on."

Husani grabbed for the roof, his eyes wide with fear.

"Do you guys carry guns?"

The emergency room doctor admitted Neely. His color was a weird shade of blue. Because of protocols, Ellis and Paloma had to hang around outside the hospital, getting wobbly text updates from him until he told them to go home but to come back in the morning with two bacon, egg and cheese bagel sandwiches and real coffee. Always planning ahead, he would live.

With Ellis now driving home, Paloma texted Benny and said they needed to meet in the morning with him and Soloff. Benny questioned why Soloff should be there and she just texted back, "*See you at 10:30 at the RimShot office.*"

"*Make it ten at the Culver stage. We're rehearsing for the benefit. Tommy really wants to play that guitar.*"

Back at the Electric Avenue house, they took off their blood-stained clothes and climbed into the shower, examining their bruises. Arms and knees took the brunt of the fall, with Paloma, the surfer, having a bit more agility in covering up on the way down. Ellis' ear had scraped on the alley and was now scabbed up and purple.

"Those fucking guys hit hard. Not like eating it on a surf-board, that's for sure."

Lying in bed close, coming off the adrenaline rush and a hot shower, Paloma said something about the girl eating a slice of pizza as they quickly drifted off to sleep.

9

Chapter 9

July 3

At 2:00 am, Husani texted. His brother was back on the grid in Hollywood. Ellis replied they would be there at eight. Husani had to lead them to Evan and what he did with the guitar. The whole thing could be over soon.

The guys who jumped them at Jumbo's knew too much about Husani and Evan, as described by Gary and Willem. Someone else was trying to get the guitar back, piggybacking on their investigation. Not good.

Husani and his brother lived in a nice condo overlooking the business district of Pacific Palisades, an upscale neighborhood of West Los Angeles. Back in the BMW, Paloma circled and scoped the area to check if they were followed before parking a few blocks away. They rang the buzzer and Husani let them in.

His brother Karim came out, hair askew, eyes scared wide. His arms and face were scratched and bruised. Husani handed him a cup of tea and he sat down at the kitchen counter.

"These guys are real private eyes I told you about," Husani said, excitedly. "They are working for Tommy Ralston, the guitar player in RimShot."

"Really? What's it got to do with you?"

"We're trying to find the guitar your brother and Evan walked out of a shop," Ellis replied.

"No. Evan took a guitar. Turns out it was Ralston's," Husani said.

"That's what last night was all about! And you know about it? How?"

"I didn't know at the time. I just drove to some guitar fixer place and Evan walked out with a different guitar. Then he said he had to meet some other guy and I should drop him off and pick him up in an hour. Then he didn't have the guitar anymore."

"Well, you're an idiot. Those guys could have killed me in the park. You didn't think to tell me what was going on?" Karim was obviously the older brother.

"Those thugs were looking for two guys. A skinny, pale white guy and a pasty 'Mexican.' As your brother was taking a leak behind the dumpster, they took the only brown guy they saw. Evan nodded out somewhere?" Ellis asked.

"Mexican? Fuck, you got brown skin around here and everyone thinks you're a Mexican. We're Egyptian," Karim said, shaking his head. "Camel Smile is our band. Evan is a loser, but his stepdad bought us new amps."

"We tracked you with that key thing. These guys are like real detectives. They called a guy to set up my phone. We lost you in the park, though," Husani added.

Karim shook his head at his brother, then told them of the wild ride last night, not knowing what it was about but thinking he would be murdered when they put a hood on his head, not understanding the thugs' questions.

They took him to some deserted parking lot in the park and made him kneel. He swore that he didn't know anything about a guitar or where Evan was since he was waiting for him to show. While they smacked him a few times with a book, the thugs got into a shouting match with each other, one saying they went too soon and should go back to Jumbo's, the other cursing, saying the mosquitos were killing him. Karim said they were idiots. They knocked him around a few more times, then showed him which road led out of the park, took his phone and his shoes and told him to count to one hundred, something they probably saw in a movie. He imagined they were going back to the Clown Room.

"Shit, my license. They know where we live. We have to get out of here."

"Which address is on there? When did you get the license?" Husani asked urgently.

"When I turned twenty-one and got the horizontal one, I was still at USC. So it could be that shitty apartment I had along the highway with the fancy name. No one will know me there."

"Not Mom's house in Brentwood? She would kill you."

"Me? You're the moron, getting involved in all this," Karim said, scolding his brother.

Ellis stepped in.

"Ok, here's the deal, Husani. We need to find Evan before those guys do. They will surely fuck him up to find the guitar, and you too. You want to help us, right?"

"Well, yeah. Uh, what's going to happen to me? I mean if they find me?"

"Start thinking where Evan might be and we'll be back soon.

Stay off the street, both of you."

"Shouldn't I come with you now?"

"No. Have your food delivered."

"Uh, we already do that."

After picking up the bagel sandwiches at Izzy's Deli, they swung by the hospital before going to see Benny. No answer on Neely's cell, so they called up the nurses' station. The nurse said he was sleeping and might be sent home later in the day. The front desk said they would send the food up.

Driving across town to the Culver Studios, Ellis called Duffy, explaining about what had gone on last night.

"You think other PIs working for the band guy?" he asked.

"If so, we're going to have a heart-to-heart. This isn't a competition."

"No honor. It doesn't work that way."

"Well, now we have one of the guitar thieves helping us find the other guy and get it back."

"Great. How's your pal Neely?"

"They're watching him at Saint John's. Might get home today."

"He got that Obama insurance?"

"Luckily. Earl's Court's manager paid this year's premium with some PPP money."

"That's good. Let me know if there are any uncovered medical expenses. I look out for the people who work for us, even contractors. I'm glad we got signed agreements with your west coast leftovers."

"Irregulars, and thanks," Paloma replied.

The rest of the way to Culver City, their conversation was about the best way to say "fuck you." Professionalism was important and Ellis was concerned that Paloma might go off on Ralston. She took a deep breath, agreed with him. Again, they had no proof of any intervention by Ralston, Benny, or Soloff, yet not many people outside of their organizations knew the descriptions of the two thieves. Ellis had known of Benny for a while and didn't think he was someone who needed to prove his loyalty.

They picked up their drive-on pass and drove through the movie lot to the soundstage. This time the scene was different. No dancers, cranes, cameras, video trucks. They walked into the cavernous soundstage, past the concert stage setup. More lights hung above. A different backdrop with the RimShot logo framed the stage. Amps were stacked high on either side of the clear plexiglass drum riser, where the drum tech was thudding a snare drum every few seconds for the house mixer to EQ. Many, many times. Ellis thought about his late friend Eddie, who believed that a cheap Shure microphone was best for getting a great snare drum sound. Now it was all about triggers and samples.

"Don't miss it," Ellis said without breaking a step. They walked over to the trailer village, where Ralston was sitting on a couch, wearing his "The Most" softball jersey, talking with Maggie and Benny. The rest of the band hadn't arrived yet. Gary was busy setting up coffee at a table by one of the trailers. He was not pleased to see them.

"You've found the guitar?" Benny started. Hello would be way too formal for this crew.

"Nope, we're close but some dipshits are getting in the way," Paloma said. "You said after a week or so you would bring in the police. Probably a good idea, if you want to collect any insurance money."

As she said that, Soloff walked in, dressed in all black with shades high on his curly hair. He appeared to dress like the musicians he liked. Lindsey Buckingham in the '80s was his model. Paloma didn't acknowledge him.

"Last night three goons followed us and grabbed up a guy who fit the description of the ashy-Mexican."

"Grabbed up?"

"Kidnapped. KGB style. You agreed that we were working this alone, remember?" Paloma looked around at them. Silence.

"Not part of our deal," Ellis added.

Ralston, Benny and Maggie looked to Soloff, who shrugged and sank down into a couch. He looked around, trying to read the room, being careful what he said.

"Kidnapping? C'mon. Don't be ridiculous. We're not involved in that sort of thing."

"The guy we want never showed up at Jumbo's. Ever think this band from Brentwood might have parents with weight downtown? Who else knows we're looking for the guitar?"

"These are serious allegations you are making," Soloff said stiffly. "My reputation is my business. You say this in public, I'll sue your asses all the way to Cleveland."

"They kidnapped the guy. How's that gonna play with the cops?" Ellis asked. "We don't need to be assaulted by 'friendlies.' Neely's in the damn hospital."

Benny looked to Ralston who looked to Soloff.

"Sorry about your friend. But for the second time this week, you've got the wrong guy. If they were my professionals, they would help you, not attack you. They are good at working with people," Soloff said, playing to Ralston.

Trying to cool down the conversation, Benny stepped in.

"Okay, look. You know Tommy wants to play that guitar tomorrow at the benefit concert for all the nurses and doctors working ridiculous hours during the pandemic. Johnny Christo's in on it too. You said you're close. Find it. You've got a day left. It'll be huge."

"Yeah, stay with it and think about letting Marc get some guys in to help," Ralston added, defending his financial manager. "You've been at it almost a week."

Ellis started to explain but Paloma cut him off.

"We've been straight about our ground rules, including telling you to go to the police. We don't need to be looking over our shoulders to do this," she said, getting up from the sofa.

"You mean you can't find it," Soloff said pointedly. "Or you scraped your knees and don't like it when the big boys play rough. Are you guys cut out for this line of work?"

Ellis knew Paloma was seconds away from going off on him. He was almost there himself.

Maggie leaned over to Ralston and spoke softly in his ear. She had learned never to tell him to do something when others could hear. He was a sensitive ego maniac who had watched *The Godfather* too many times.

"Ellis, wait," Ralston said, finally standing up from the sofa, trying to cool things down. "I know you guys are on it. If not by tomorrow, just find it."

Ralston seemed sincere.

"Look, we're probably going on the road soon. A big tour, pent-up demand after Covid. Fans are gonna be great. Of course, only people who are vaccinated, all that safety stuff," he explained.

Ralston was selling, big time.

"Be our tour manager. Put it together for us. Charley Eliot moved to Montana and said he's out. You can bring some of your guys with you," Ralston said, leaning forward on the couch as Maggie nodded and smiled along with his words.

Ellis glanced over to Gary. His face was flush. Of course, he wanted the job.

"Sorry. I'm with the FAQ detective agency. Not going out on tours."

Paloma glanced over. He was charming.

"Aw, everyone is saying that," Soloff added, backing off his harsh tone, becoming the business manager. "We'll give you a great deal, a top salary, per diem plus pay for your room service, everything. We fly on a nice party plane. Even hire Paloma for something."

Paloma tilted her head slightly. *Oh boy, not good*, Ellis thought.

"C'mon, the Hoovers and The Most can coexist," Ralston said, smiling, popping his jersey, and making a hands-out gesture. "We could be a super team, like the Dodgers."

"Thanks very much, but I gotta pass," Ellis replied, looking at Ralston, then Soloff. "We're working hard on getting your Country Gentleman back. We think we're close, but you should go to the cops soon because if they weren't your guy's last night, then someone else knows all about it and who took it. I'm not sold that they are trying to get it back, for you. Any ideas?"

A look around the couch came up empty.

They walked out of the soundstage to the crack of the snare drum being hit every three seconds. Crack. Crack. Crack.

"Don't miss it at all," Ellis said.

"I guess we sorta forgot to tell them about Husani," Paloma

said.

"Yeah, but we still gotta find Evan," Ellis said casually. "First."

"Who are those people?" Paloma said, driving back to the Palisades. "A bunch of fuckups who got lucky with some three chord songs?"

"Ralston seems tight with Soloff. We walk a fine line trying to get between them."

"And what was that about offering you the tour manager job and finding 'something' for me to do," Paloma said.

"Thought you were gonna launch for that. You see Gary boiling in the corner?"

"You know we probably stirred a hornet's nest. What's the next move if they are not their guys? Everyone wants to score bonus points with Ralston. Must be that drug called rock n' roll."

"What the fuck's up with them?" Soloff asked, getting up off the couch and grabbing a Fiji water. "They really got a hair up their ass for me. What did I do?"

"You're just too cool," Ralston said, distracted by his phone.

"I guess since you offered to help, they think they're your guys," Benny added.

"So who would have roughed them up? Any ideas?" Ralston asked.

"Gary, the guys who stole the guitar looked like junkies, right?"

Gary nodded from the coffee table.

"That buys you a bunch of reasons to get roughed up, like unhappy dealers," Soloff added.

Now Ralston took command.

"Benny, get Mountain Moran up to speed on this. The manager at Jumbo's must have a contact for that band. See if we can pick them up from there."

Mountain Moran ran stage and hotel security for RimShot. His size earned him the nickname long ago.

"If you want, I can have someone follow them? They said they thought they were close. She doesn't seem to be someone who gives up too easily," Soloff said.

"I want that fuckin' guitar back and I want the low-life shit-head junkies who stole it."

Ellis kept an eye on the side view as they picked up Husani, who volunteered a few ideas where he thought that Evan might be crashing.

"He's a messed-up guy. Can't believe he talked me into driving to get that guitar. I had no idea what was going to happen," Husani said again.

Driving east on Sunset, past Bel-Air and the 405, they dropped down through UCLA to a student-filled courtyard-type apartment building where Husani said Evan lived. Ellis knocked, waking up one of the roommates, who answered the door, a bloated face, smelling of stale beer and sweat. This guy hadn't not missed a meal in a while. Mentioning that they were detectives woke him up. They chose to leave out the FAQ part until the end of the conversation. He didn't know if Evan was around.

"Hey, Evan, some people here to see you, man," he shouted over his shoulder. There was no answer.

"He's in my band; let me go wake him up," Husani said.

The roommate grunted and Husani went down the hallway; Ellis and Paloma followed. Husani entered the darkened room. Ellis pulled open the curtains in the sour-smelling room, revealing the unmade bed and a pile of laundry, most of it black, spilling out of the closet. There was no one there. A Gibson acoustic guitar with a broken string was on a stand, but no other guitar or case anywhere in the room. On the dresser and night table there were a few candles, some loose change and a broken plastic oral retainer.

"I guess he went out," his roommate said, picking at something in his ear.

Ellis thanked him, handing him an FAQ card. Almost as an afterthought, the roommate said they could check out his sometimes girlfriend Sandy, who lived in an apartment in one of the high rises further down Wilshire. He showed them where the address was written in pencil, on the wall in the kitchen, near the former landline.

"Oh man, Sandy Wilshire. I met her at a gig once. She is smokin' hot. One of those influencers with her own YouTube channel and everything," Husani said excitedly from the back seat, fumbling with his phone to find the YouTube app.

Sandy Wilshire? Paloma rolled her eyes. She was part of the same generation, but her surfer / rock n' roll thing was a world apart from her phone-hugging, YouTube-watching, Instagram-posting, TikTok-making peers.

They drove along the mile of high rises along Wilshire boulevard in Westwood that once was referred to as "Gucci Gulch," named for the shoes preferred by the rich international owners of the original apartments there. Before it was fashionable, wealthy foreign business types would park money in LA real estate, maybe spending a few weeks a year there. It was not uncommon for more than half the windows of a high rise to be dark on any given evening.

Ellis found the address among the glittering glass towers and parked on one of the side streets that didn't require a permit. In the lobby the doorman called up to the apartment and pointed them to the elevator.

"Let us do the talking, okay, Husani?" Ellis said as the high-speed elevator rocketed them up to the fifteenth floor.

"Yeah, sure," he replied eagerly, eyes opened wide, jazzed about being in on the hunt for Evan.

Paloma went to ring the bell when the door was opened by a tall woman with short dark hair, glasses and wearing a business suit. She looked like Rachel Maddow.

"That's not her," Husani blurted out, earning a head shake from Ellis and another eye roll from Paloma.

"Hello, I'm Justine, Sandy's associate. Is there something I can help you with?"

"We work with the FAQ detective agency," she said, handing over a business card. "My name is Paloma, and this is Ellis. We'd like to talk with her about her friend Evan. It's important." She didn't introduce Husani, yet.

"Evan? Uh, she is just finishing up a fitting. You can wait in here," she said, stepping back and pointing to a large room that favored Southwestern lodge type furniture and floor-to-ceiling glass windows. The southern view would be breathtaking on a clear winter day, mostly smogged up on this early July morning.

"This place is amazing," Husani blurted out. "Look at this YouTube. Must have been shot here."

Sandy was tall and lean, with long dark hair and plenty of makeup around her eyes, extolling the virtues of a green drink she said made her feel "light and airy" that was sold in dispensaries in five of the western states where pot was legal. A scroll across the bottom of the screen was a description of the cowl-necked cashmere sweater, watch, earrings, makeup, and yoga pants she was wearing, including a QR code for more information and ordering. She didn't miss a beat.

"Breakfast of champions," Sandy said, standing in the doorway. "I actually drink that stuff." She was dressed in a variation of the video.

She sauntered into the room with the confidence of a twenty-two-year-old woman who grossed north of a million dollars, with as many followers. As "Sandy Wilshire," her brand was a mix of uptown elegance with ripped jeans, Boho sweaters, large handbags, and larger sunglasses. Behind her a stylist pushed a rack of clothing through the entrance hall.

Paloma stood and introduced everyone. She was the same height as Sandy, though less curvy, especially as her breasts were natural compared to what seemed to be Sandy's '40s "sweater girl" look.

"So, Justine says you are looking for Evan," Sandy said, sitting down on the couch, tucking her bare feet under her. "He comes and goes like an outdoor cat. So cute. Why are you looking for him?"

"We're looking for a guitar and he might be able to help us find it," Paloma said.

"He loves to play guitar," she said, as though she would say more.

"Have you seen him recently?" Ellis asked.

"Maybe a few or five days ago? He was supposed to come by

late last night or this morning. I try to work in some 'fun time' because I've been super busy meeting new product people. I'm branching out. My manager is on top of keeping our numbers up."

They nodded.

"You see, there's this girl from New Roads School, who calls herself Penny Paradisio, trying to copy me. She's so low rent. Probably shops downtown. I'm going to crush her."

Paloma took a few seconds for that to sink in. A war between influencers. Totally first-world. She looked at Sandy.

"How was he the last time you were with him?"

"Oh, you mean was he fucked up? I'd say half. I've known him since high school," she said casually. "Always was a druggie because he played guitar in bands. He could get pretty messed up. Such a bad boy. He needs me to take care of him sometime," she said with self-pride.

Paloma bristled and looked at Ellis. She did not want to stick to the script.

"Did Evan leave a guitar here?" Ellis jumped in.

"No, but sometimes he sings to me. I'm going to put him on my channel, and I tell you he will blow up. So cute, he'll make a fortune," she said, making a mushroom cloud type motion with her arms.

"So, any idea where we might find him now? Maybe he has a new phone number?" Ellis asked.

"I'm in his band," Husani almost shouted. "We have been calling and emailing, trying to find him. He blew off our gig at Jumbo's last night. We really need to find him."

Sandy looked at them. Husani's tone added a level of urgency she had not heard from Ellis and Paloma.

"Wait. Is he in trouble?"

"We're trying to find a guitar and his name came up."

"Probably fell asleep somewhere. I haven't called because I've been so busy. He turns up, usually late. He's so cute that way."

There was silence in the room. Did she realize she was a booty call? Evan "falling asleep" was kinder than "nodded out." His Oxy use was the elephant in the room.

"Is there another cell phone number?" Ellis asked again.

"Nope," she said, looking at her jewel-encrusted large-format phone. Paloma thought it was big enough to be an iPad. Her patience was streaming away, so she moved over to the couch and sat next to Sandy.

"Okay, here's the deal. Evan is in danger because he stole a guitar for someone. He got money and a party bottle of Oxy for the guitar. This guy helped. We're the good guys who need to find him first. There are other guys looking for him, bad guys, who put our friend in the hospital and beat up this guy's brother. We want to find the guitar, but protecting Evan is our most important mission."

Paloma threw that in as a kicker, figuring that Sandy watched bad cable movies that might trigger her imagination as to what could happen to Evan.

Sandy sat silently. She avoided looking at anyone else in the room, rocking slowly back and forth on the couch.

"You say you're the good guys. Who's paying you to find him?"

Ellis gave a "shut the fuck up" look to Husani. It was nobody's business.

"We're paid to find the guitar by the owner. Now there is some rogue faction that took matters into their own hands. After this guy's brother was kidnapped, we could see that Evan was in danger."

Sandy looked to Paloma, who nodded her head slightly in agreement with what Ellis had said. Husani was transfixed with what was going on.

"Then I'll pay you to find him."

Paloma and Ellis shared a look.

"I've known him since high school. I know that if he got that much Oxy, and cash money, he'll be out of it, unaware of the danger you say he is in, or much else. I'm hiring you to find Evan, and if he has it, the guitar too," she said proudly. "You accept the Black card? Justine will give you my information and I'll E-sign whatever." She was all business.

The Sandy Wilshire facade came down. "Please find him."

"Give us a minute," Paloma replied, leading Ellis to the corner of the windows. Husani started to follow, but a quick look from Ellis stopped him.

"Do we want to work for her?" Ellis whispered. "She's a little self-absorbed."

"After working for Ralston, are you kidding? We're looking for him already, why not get paid again?"

"We knew Ralston was an ass."

"C'mon. We're close. I can feel it," she said.

Ellis looked at her. "Feel it?"

"Shut up, we're doing it," she said, smiling and giving him a soft pat on his chest.

"Okay, you can hire us to find Evan," Paloma said, holding out her hand. "This will do until we get the signed paperwork, which our office will email over. Please have Justine text your info to the number on our card."

"Thank you very much," Sandy said, now kind of Disney "doe eyed." "Find him and I'll keep him safe."

"Gonna try. Anywhere else you think we should look for him?"

She gave them the address of Evan's stepfather, on the 11th Helena Dr. in Brentwood, near where Marilyn Monroe had lived.

The house was a massive New England–style cottage on a large lot. You could live in one part of the house and never see someone living in the other part. According to the housekeeper, Evan's stepdad had been out of town for two weeks and when they asked about a wife, she said "ashram, and hadn't seen Evan's car lately. This was not the kind of place they could just walk in and check his room.

"Husani, you have to earn your keep. Anywhere else we can look for this guy?"

"Earn my keep? Are you guys paying me?" he said, very excited.

"No," Ellis replied. "We're letting you hang out with us and we'll buy you lunch. Where else?"

"Let me text the other guys in the band, see if they have any ideas."

"Now that's thinking like a detective," Paloma told him.

After wolfing down the two bagel sandwiches, Neely dressed slowly and looked at his phone to see if Alena had arrived. There was a bandage on the lump on his head, but seeing in the mirror that his color was edging closer to that of a human, he decided to check himself out. He wanted no part of being in the hospital, even though Covid patients were in a separate wing.

"A hospital is a great place to get sick," his Uncle Joey had told him. He agreed.

The nurse, working her fourth twelve-hour shift of the week, was more than happy to roll him out to the driveway where Alena was waiting. She came over, gave him a long hug and helped him into the car.

On the drive home he explained the "case" he was working on for FAQ and apologized for the days he had missed at the ghost kitchen.

"Neely, do you see a pattern here? You work with them and pretty soon there is a brawl with you involved," she said.

"Hey, did not see it coming. We were watching a girl eat a piece of pizza at Jumbo's Clown Room and then we were in the alley getting attacked," he said.

"Yeah, just like that night at the Moose Lodge."

"C'mon, you know I need to move around. It's hard being in the kitchen all day, even if they are famous rock stars' dishes."

"I thought you wanted to help," she said, driving to Mar Vista.

"I do, I did. I do. Look, let's figure out a way to split my time. This case is important to rock n' roll, to the entertainment world! We're looking for George Harrison's guitar, the one he played on *Ed Sullivan*."

"No shit? I know what that means to you, but to me, you're not dependable. I'm running a business, trying to keep my nose above water during this fucking pandemic. You disappearing for days sucks."

"Until this 'rock' on my head goes down, I'm low and slow. Ellis needs my help on this. You're the best at looking out for me," he said, reaching for a kiss.

She pulled back and looked at him.

"I think we should take a break. Covid has made me edgy,

and I need some *me* time."

"I know I let you down at the kitchen. Covid has made everyone edgy." He looked at her. "I kinda figured this was coming."

"Sorry to drop this on you with a lump on your head and your bizarre bluish color. Of course, if you need help, let me know, but no more sleepovers."

Alena kissed Neely goodbye on the cheek. They had been moving apart in little ways. Without the road, he had been kind of drifting from one thing to the next. Ellis and Paloma had thrown themselves into FAQ, but he had no passion or drive for anything but going on the road with rock n' roll bands.

He texted Ellis that other than a large lump on his head and a disturbing bluish-purple color, he checked himself out of St. John's and was home. He thanked them for the bagel sandwiches and ended the text with "I'm there if you need me."

While Husani had feelers out to other guys who knew Evan, they went to lunch, believing Evan, and maybe Husani, knew who had approached him about stealing the guitar. It was smart to keep him close.

Finding a meter in Westwood, no small feat, they tried Gyu-Kaku, a Korean barbeque. Too crowded, so they wandered over to the Corner Bakery, more of a soup and sandwich place on Westwood Blvd. After ordering at the counter, Husani excused himself and went off to wash his hands.

"Good idea. Here, use this hand sanitizer," Paloma said, reaching into her backpack's outer pocket. "Remember washing our hands twenty times a day? Your hands got all cracked after the first week. Amazing how some things you never thought about became omni present during the pandemic."

Ellis said he was in awe of the houses he had been in. Ralston's place was elegant and sprawling, with a huge backyard and a pool. Evan's stepfather's place was massive, like a New England cottage house on steroids. Even without going inside, he was impressed by the sheer presence of it, shingled and shuttered. His little two-bedroom bungalow on Electric Avenue was fine, yet he wondered if there would be another step up, when he had a family. So much in the national media made him apprehensive of the future. From relentless Covid to climate decline, he wondered if he should be thinking about not having a family. That thought evaporated when he looked at Paloma. She was the one, the only person he ever thought about starting a family with. Of course, he would retire from touring. FAQ was just the first step.

Their food arrived, so Ellis got up to let Husani know. Opening the bathroom door, he saw Husani held up against the wall by a guy with an arm across his throat. Before he could react, a large fist slammed into his head. He hit the tile floor hard and tried to stay clear, grabbing helplessly at the three sets of shoes he saw leaving the room. Focus was difficult as the blue-tile room seemed to be off axis. Probably his brain was.

Ellis got as far as his knees before pausing as the room spun. He might throw up. On all fours, he tried to make sense of what just happened. They were followed again? And some guys were grabbing Husani. How did he miss the tail?

Holding on to the sink counter, Ellis stood and tried to get his eyes to focus. He turned to go to the door to get help and had to stop. Bending over, putting hands on knees, he took a few deep breaths and noticed a phone on the floor in the corner, by one of the stall supports. Reaching for it, still bent over, he saw a smiling camel cartoon and realized that it was Husani's.

He palmed the phone when Paloma burst in. Behind her were a few of the waiters who saw the guys run out dragging Husani.

"They grabbed him up."

"Call the paramedics," one of the waiters said. "He doesn't look great."

"No, I'm fine," Ellis said, showing Paloma the phone cupped in his hand.

"Husani's? Did he drop it for us?" Paloma asked quietly.

"Maybe. Or when they jumped him. Blindsided me, for sure."

She led Ellis out of the bathroom, threw some cash down on the table and led him outside.

"You're alright?"

"Just got my bell rung. The moons and stars are gone."

"You know, if he has his keys, we can track him," she said.

"Sure. He told me the password last night when we called Neighbor Dave. Shit, what was it?"

"Jeez, that was last night?"

"It was a name, remember? Sounded Middle Eastern."

"Oh yeah. I made a joke in my head, a mnemonic."

"Go for it. We only get a few chances."

"Thinking isn't coming easy right now?"

"You can do it."

"Something like 'Yes Sir.'"

"You mean like the Cockney rhyming slang?"

"Kinda. Yassir?"

"Like Arrafat?"

"Naw, not that. Did he say if it was a woman's name? Maybe his mom?"

Paloma was on her phone, looking for a name that sounded right and had six letters. What was it that caused passwords to be six numbers?

"Anippe, Bahini, Chione, Edrice," she kept scanning down.

"Essrra! That sounds like 'Yes Sir,' right?"

"Yeah, let's try it. Where did you find it?"

"Top one hundred Egyptian women's names website. Who knew?"

They tried the code and it worked. Paloma smiled as she tapped the tracking app they had used the other night after Jumbo's.

Ellis looked at her with wonder.

"Really? Of course, I remembered her name," she said.

A hand to his head, Ellis said, "Let's hope he has his keys."

"I listened in as Dave walked you through it."

Then the phone chirped with a text.

"*I'm there.*"

It was from Evan.

They raced to the car, watching the Airtag signal go west on Wilshire Blvd. towards the 405.

"That lying SOB. We should let them have Husani. Save us the trouble," Paloma said.

"Good act, his 'gee, you guys are real detectives? I watch *Law & Order.*'"

"If you needed to go to the hospital, you would tell me, right?" Paloma said.

"Oh yeah. Hang with Neely? I'm okay. Just got my bell rung."

The text log showed that Husani had been texting Evan, telling him where *not* to be as they looked for him. Evan first texted early in the morning, before they picked Husani up, saying he had totally nodded out last night and missed the gig. Husani replied with a condensed version of the story of what happened at Jumbo's and that there were detectives and thugs looking for him and the guitar.

"Stay away from your apt and Sandy's," he had texted.

"These fucking guys. They've been playing with us."

Paloma picked her way through Westwood traffic to reach the 405 freeway. They heard a chirp from the back seat. Then another. Ellis turned his head around too fast and saw stars.

Paloma pulled over and listened, trying to zero in on the chirping sound. It sounded muffled, so she jumped out of the car to look in the trunk. Then another chirp and she saw it. An Airtag that had been stuck into the rubber rear window seal.

"Oh great. No wonder we didn't see anyone following us. They were on us. Probably since when?" she said, holding up the tracker and slamming the car into gear.

"They are tracking us like we're tracking them?" Ellis said, taking it from her. He opened the window and tossed the Airtag into the back of a pickup that drove past. "Track that, you fuckers."

Powering through the Sepulveda pass, Ellis could see on the phone that they had ground to make up.

"We have been *so* played. Husani should get an Oscar because everything he has told us since Jumbo's is pure bullshit."

"Keep reading the texts," she said, sliding around cars that were slower.

"Looks like a lot of jumble; Evan must be fucked up. Husani told him to go to his mother's and she would let him crash in the guest house," he said, looking through the contacts for the address. They raced across the valley floor, trying to make up some ground.

"Is Husani or Evan the guy? We get him back and have a conversation about 'life.' Maybe get the older brother involved.

He didn't seem too pleased with the whole guitar thing."

"About almost getting murdered in the park?"

"That would be a great motivator."

"If they take the 118 Exit, I got a bad feeling where we're headed."

"No way. Paul's? Wait, we looked at him for stealing the guitar. Why would he be trying to find out where it is by grabbing Husani?"

"Maybe it makes him a hero with Ralston and gets Benny off his case. Or, and bear with me, he stole the guitar and is now pretending to get it back."

"But we're not sure we are headed to Paul's."

Paloma's reaction was to hit the gas. Part of her Grant DNA.

They took the turnoff onto the 118, then the DeSoto exit. It was like they were following directions to Paul's house.

"Getting warmer," she said, jerking the wheel.

Then Paloma made a phone call.

The tracker on Husani's keys had led them right to Paul's. The black Escalade was parked, in front of the house this time.

Paloma slid the BMW to the curb and compared the plate to the photo she had given Duffy. "Same SUV as last time. Could be the one from Jumbo's," Ellis said.

They sat in the car, the air conditioner on "stun," looking around the quiet cul-de-sac.

"Got to be an idiot to bring him back here."

"Remember, Paul is the cousin of the wife of a famous rock star," she said, sarcastically.

"We passed an alley that might run behind the house. Maybe I can see over the fence into the large windows in that room we were in."

"Dude, with that bruise, you should wait here, in case they try to leave. Not a good idea for you to be running around."

"No, I'm good."

"Flip you for it," Paloma said, digging around in the ashtray for a coin.

"Flip me? Really?"

"Yup." She pulled a penny from the cup holder. "Call it."

Darting down the alley behind the house, Paloma found garbage bins that made a perfect platform for her to crouch on and look over the wooden fence, two mature orange trees giving her cover. She remembered there were no curtains on the back sliders. It didn't matter, they were sitting outside. She ducked down to call Ellis.

"Looks like the guys who jumped us at Jumbo's," she said. "Probably the same guys who tried to follow us."

They were more brawny than big, developed upper bodies for sure. One had a bushy head and chest of hair and a gold chain around his neck. The other was taller with deep-set eyes.

"Must have been a sale on Adidas tracksuits," she murmured. "Looks like "Goodfellas.""

"What?"

"Never mind. You're not going to believe what I'm looking at," she whispered to Ellis as she peeked over the fence.

"Husani? Is he tied up somewhere?" Ellis asked urgently.

"These morons are hanging out, drinking beers."

"But can you see him—Husani?"

"Yeah. He's sitting with them, drinking a beer. What the F is this all about?"

"Wait, he's hanging with them?

"Yup. Looking pretty chummy. Sounds like one of their

names is Rick. He for sure is one of the guys from Jumbo's."

"What about Paul?"

"I haven't seen him yet. Let's wait to see if he comes out."

"You think Ralston knows they are searching for the guitar or are they freelancing?"

"Paul struck me as a guy who needs to score points. Gotta go," she whispered.

Ellis touched his head to feel the small welt that had grown from hitting the bathroom floor. How do they grow so fast? What was Husani doing? *"Do you carry guns?"* he had said, while feeding Evan bad information the whole time. Now was he rolling over for these guys or playing them too?

Paloma carefully crawled to another garbage can to better hear what they were saying. Then Paul came out.

"Do you remember your friend's phone number yet?"

"Speed dial, you know. I think there are a lot of threes."

Paul just looked at him.

"Look, for the five thousand I'll take you to Evan and he will lead you right to the guitar. I get the signed RimShot stuff too, right?" He was playing them.

Damn, he is good, Paloma thought.

Waiting in the car, Ellis unlocked Husani's phone to read the messages again. In the backyard the Airtag on Husani's keys started chirping. Rick jumped up and grabbed him.

"What the fuck, man?" he shouted.

"That's my key thingy. It's beeping."

"No shit," Rick said. "I thought you lost your phone at the restaurant."

"I did," Husani bleated. Paul asked where Ellis and Paloma were.

Rick checked his phone.

"On the one-ten in Pasadena."

Paul stood silently for a moment, trying to put the pieces together.

"Fuck, check outside," Paul said, shaking his head as they headed into the house.

Paloma lay down on the garbage cans and called Ellis.

"The friggin' Airtag went off. Guys headed your way," she whispered.

Ellis realized he triggered the Airtag by turning on the phone. So much for the element of surprise. He got out of the car and popped the trunk, rummaging through the duffle of softball bats he kept there. He was still woozy but might as well be prepared.

Paul went into the house after them and Paloma saw her chance. She grabbed a limb of the orange tree and swung into the backyard. Husani froze with beer in hand.

"Come with me right now if you want to live," she said, taking his arm, with the straightest face she could muster. A classic line but wanted to freak him out. It worked.

"What?" He could barely talk.

"These are really bad guys," she said, opening the back gate. "Whatever they promised you is bullshit. They'll dump you in a gully behind the big rocks."

She pulled him out the back gate.

Paul and Rick came walking down the driveway, Rick pimp rolling with arms flapping. The other guy standing in the driveway.

"Hey fucko's," Ellis said. "Bring the kid out."

"Give us the phone, get in your car and shove off," Paul said as he came to a stop, posturing with his chest puffed and shoulders back, like a superhero poster he had seen.

"Oh wait. Jumbo's?" Ellis said to Rick. "You're the guy who threw me down."

Ellis lifted the bat and smashed the side-view mirror with the bat.

Rick started to step to Ellis, so he smashed the driver's-side window. Paul stared in disbelief.

"You're bringing a world of trouble on yourself," Paul said. He had heard it in a movie once. "Tommy leases this car."

"Good. Call Tommy then bring Husani out," Ellis said, motioning with the bat to keep them at bay. "Paul, this your kind of party? You trying to be the hero for Tommy?"

Sharing a look, Rick took a few steps away from Paul for a better angle on Ellis.

"Or are you freelancing today? Trying to show Ralston or Benny you can get the right guy this time? Bring him out. Now"

He used half swings of the bat to keep them away, maybe buying Paloma some time to get Husani. Paul reached for the bat and cursed as a full swing caught a few of his fingers. Rick came at Ellis before he could recover from the swing and slammed him into the SUV door. The bat dropped and rolled under the car.

Rick held Ellis against the SUV as Paul stepped up.

"You leave blondie behind? That welt on your head looks painful. You want more? You're going to get the fuck out of here, now. We're taking over. We'll have that guitar for Tommy by tonight," he said and slammed his fist into Ellis' midsection, doubling him over.

A black Dodge Avenger slid to a stop in the street. Rosato and Jim-O, Eddy's pals and rock and roll truck drivers, got out. Although not wearing colors, they reeked of "biker" in heavy boots, jeans, and long-sleeve tees. Rosato, bearded, broad shoulders and black hair slicked back, yanked Paul away from Ellis. Jim-O stepped to Rick, who froze where he was.

Rosato looked around for Paloma, who had called him on the drive up. Ellis pushed off the car, eyes on Paul.

"These the fuckups jumped you and my god-daughtah at Jumbo's?" he asked, studying Paul, his Quincy, Massachusetts, accent leaving no doubt of his origins.

"And they like to grab people and take them for rides?" Ellis nodded.

"Oh yeah? You fellas feel like going for a ride?" Rosato continued in his thick Quincy accent, pointing to the Avenger.

Rick and Paul were still processing what was happening. Paul slowly tried to step back. He tended to shy away from "conflict."

"Who the fuck are you?" Rick finally said, puffing out his chest.

"I already told you. I'm the fuckin' Godfathah'. You deaf?" They still stood frozen.

"Nice tracksuits. You part of some club? Secret handshake kinda shit?" Rosato said, mocking them as he stepped to them. There was the clank of something heavy and metal. Jim-O was at the trunk of the Avenger.

"So, we come to decision time," Rosato said. "The inside guy comes with us, and you boys can play badminton, or we settle this a different way."

"The guy wants to hang out. We have business," Paul said defiantly, taking two steps back.

Paloma came out through the empty lot with a very frightened Husani. His eyes were wide as saucers as she held onto the back of his belt and quick-walked him down the street. Rick looked at Paul, his leader. He gave him a WTF look since they had left Husani unguarded. He then took a step towards Paloma to stop her but Paul, having a much better sense of the situation they were in, grabbed his arm and shook his head.

Rosato waited for Paloma and Husani, then walked with them to the BMW. Jim-O still stood by the open trunk as Ellis backed up.

"Thanks for coming, Rosato," she said.

"You bet. FYI, don't look now but there's a surveillance van parked down the street. Must be some kinda cops."

"As my uncle Leon used to say, 'The jig is up,' Husani," Paloma said, as they drove back to Venice.

"You found my phone, right? I knew you guys would figure out the key thingy to find me. Those guys were huge. Really scary. I was so scared and didn't know what I was going to do. You saved me. You guys are great detectives."

"We remembered your password from the other night."

Paloma waited a beat for that to sink in. It didn't.

"We read the texts. With Evan."

Husani was quick.

"Wait, I was just keeping him safe till I was sure those other guys were out of the picture."

Paloma slid the BMW onto the 118 ramp.

"One chance to tell us everything or I swear *I'll* leave you tied to a tree in Griffith Park at midnight," Ellis said.

Husani played dumb.

"I saw you in the backyard, drinking a beer. Five grand plus the swag?" she said, looking at him. "You must be an idiot if you thought those guys would give you anything."

"Okay, let's pick up Evan. He'll tell you now," Husani said.

"You're a pretty good bullshitter, you know that?" Paloma

said.

"I am?" he said, looking at them both with a smile.

"Not a compliment. We haven't decided if we are turning you over to the cops or Ralston's guys."

"Weren't those Ralston's guys?" Husani said, bewildered.

"No, those were amateurs. Ralston has real guys," Paloma said. "Break you like a twig." She grabbed a look at Ellis.

"Is he at your mom's? Is that what he meant by *'I'm here'*?"

"Anita, off of San Vicente," he said, resigned to the fact that his act was over.

On the drive they got today's version of the story. Evan was approached at a bar after a gig by some guy in a black hoodie who made the offer for his Epiphone guitar. Maybe the guy saw Evan was strung out. Then they talked about making the switch. He said if they were caught just say, "oops, my mistake." The hook was set with the promise of a party-sized bottle of Oxy, a few samples in hand. He knew a junkie would show up and deliver, for money and drugs. It helped if he didn't know the true value of the guitar he would be taking.

Someone knew Gary would be there at two o'clock.

On the day, Husani said, they parked down the street and waited in the car. A guy walked up but wasn't carrying a case. Another guy pulled up into the driveway and pulled a guitar out of the back. Agreeing this must be the guy, they went in and made the switch, Husani amazed that Evan was so cool about it. Walking a block down the street from the shop, he put the guitar in the trunk and turned around for the drive to Mitsuwa market parking lot to collect his reward.

Husani said Evan asked him to swing around the store and come back into the parking lot to be a lookout while he waited by the soda machine. In the time it took him to do that, Evan said a different guy from the one who originally approached him showed up to take the guitar, a manilla envelope with cash and the Oxy in hand. He was also wearing a black baseball cap and a hoodie. Then he walked away.

"Did he look at the guitar?

"I guess; I couldn't see from where I was."

"Black baseball cap and hoodie? What kind of car did he get into?" Ellis asked.

"I dunno. I couldn't get around the store fast enough. There was a delivery truck blocking the way. Evan was anxious, walking to the car carrying the package and said to get out of there, so we drove to his place. Bouncing up and down, shaking it with excitement, he chewed two pills in the car."

"How did the guy who first approached Evan know what time Gary was getting there?" Paloma said, looking back to Husani, then Ellis.

"Who's Gary?" asked Husani.

"The guy with the guitar you stole," she replied.

Paloma took the 405 ramp and up to San Vicente, racing to get to Husani's mom's house. They needed to get Evan's story. Fast. Who would trust Husani? He lied as easily as the former President. Turning onto Anita Road, Husani directed them. The fire engine and ambulance parked out front made it easy to find.

Jumping out of the car, they approached the front door as the paramedics were wheeling Evan out, slight under a blanket, more gray than white, an oxygen mask strapped to his face. Husani's mother was wringing her hands, eye makeup dripping, looking to Husani for some explanation.

"Mom, what happened?"

"I thought he was dead. He almost was. Oh no, in my house! They said he had the OD and gave him some medicines."

Paloma ran to the gurney to see if Evan was with it at all, but he was out and looked bad.

"Hey, Evan, wake up. It's important," she shouted at him. The lead paramedic gave her some side eye and continued to the ambulance. She knew once he got into the hospital they would be shut out.

"Let me ride with you guys," she said to the paramedic as they loaded him in. "I'm a private detective."

"Not today. See him at the hospital," he said.

"Where are you taking him?"

"Westwood."

She knew that, like at St. Johns, under Covid protocols, they probably would not be allowed in. The paramedic knew that too.

Husani's brother, Karim, pulled up in his car and was shouting at his brother in Arabic as he approached. The tone was obviously in the "you fuckin' idiot" mode. Husani appeared to shrink under his brother's tirade, the family retreating into the house with Ellis and Paloma left standing in the driveway as the ambulance pulled out.

"What the hell just happened?" Ellis said.

"Home," Paloma replied, shaking her head.

As they drove down Anita Drive, Husani jumped out of some bushes into the middle of the street, furiously waving them down.

"My mom's freaked and my brother's a dick. Please, please get me out of here," he said, grabbing for the back door.

Ellis looked at Paloma, who gave a slight nod then unlocked the doors.

"Go, go, go," Husani said as he lay down prone across the back seat, covering his head with his hands.

"You realize nobody's shooting at us?" Paloma said. "It's friggin' Brentwood."

"You really need me to do this? Neely said, standing on the porch of his house. "Uh, I kinda got a new friend coming over for dinner tonight,"

"New friend?"

"Alena dumped me. I missed too many shifts at the kitchen. She didn't want an undependable boyfriend. We were probably one of the Covid romances."

Ellis shot Paloma a look and she laughed.

"What?" Neely said.

"We wondered the same thing about us."

"You guys? No way," Neely said, looking at them for a reply. Nothing.

Neely looked at Husani sitting in the car.

"Okay, I'll babysit. My head is feeling better with a few peach gummies in me. Okay if I lock him in the guest room?"

"Yeah, your color is more human, less 'Avatar,'" Ellis said.

"Maybe Dina from the Grandview will think of it as an adventure," Neely said with a question leaking into his voice. They brought him up to speed on the day's events.

"Give him something to eat and put him in the other room. We'll come get him in the morning. His friend should be 'with it' by then and we'll get another story. This guy is a class A bullshitter."

"I hope he likes Ralph's vegetarian chili. I'm trying to use up the stuff I bought at the start of the pandemic."

Paloma looked at Ellis. They had some too.

10

Chapter 10

July 3 Evening

A phone call confirmed that Evan was admitted to Westwood Hospital, so at least he was alive. With Neely babysitting Husani, they went to the Murtosa Cafe to regroup. The welt on the side of Ellis' head was way down.

Joaquim was happy to see them, expressing concern for Ellis and immediately wiping down one of the outdoor tables. A snack plate of cheese and meat appeared on the table with a basket of bread. As always, Joaquim encouraged them to visit Portugal, where his many cousins still lived, from Porto to Murtosa to the Algarve.

Duffy waddled in, gave Joaquim a stiff hug and slid into the outdoor booth with them.

"You come here too? Love this place," he said, settling in. "Almost bought the building years ago when Alice the owner was moving to Costa Rica. Boy, she was a pip! Total mom to the Venice skate kids and surfers. I hear there are good breaks down there."

Joaquim took their orders.

"Duffy, you surf?" Paloma said.

"Used to in the bad old days. You know, the big boards." he said, holding his hand up in the air. "You do, right?"

"Yeah, my whole life. I'm out most mornings early. Good group: we could spot you an extra board. A bit shorter than they used to be."

"Nope, the knees. They don't have the bend they used to."

Ellis just stared in amazement. Duffy must have been a trip in his twenties.

Over soup, they brought him up to speed about Jumbo's and the day's activities, then asked Duffy if he had a connection at the Westwood Hospital who might get them in. With his necktie thrown over his shoulder, he slurped his soup and shook his head no.

"Yeah, there is a violent side of the job. Had a husband go at me in the parking lot of the Tattle Tale lounge once. I had snooped the guy at the old Culver City drive-in with a woman other than his wife. Tried to slam my head into a car door. Some people get pissed off at our kind of work."

"I'm going to anticipate more. I should remember the guys who tried to take Ellis down in Seattle. But we still have to find that guitar," Paloma said.

Ellis nodded.

"Oh yeah, the guitar. A woman called, about a card in her door you guys left, a video doorbell on the guitar guy street. Martha Kowalski. Said she was visiting her daughter and grandkids in Kettleman City. You know that place on the 5? Just got back."

"Great. We'll go over. Maybe it shows the other side of the street."

"Taken care of—just came from there," Duffy said with a

smile and a little rock back and forth.

Ellis and Paloma shared a look.

"Okay, you watched it. Anything? Get a copy of the video?"

"Well, first, Martha couldn't figure out how to get it off the cloud thing. Me neither, so I came up with plan B."

"Do tell," Ellis said, looking over to Paloma, anticipating the story to come.

"Back in the day, there wasn't video tape, so they filmed the TV screen to preserve live shows. Called a kinescope. So that's what I did with my phone camera on her phone screen showing the video. Cool, huh?" he said, gesturing with his phone, then jabbing it with his short, fat fingers. "Couldn't quite remember the time I was looking for, but I remembered you talking about a guy going for a nooner, so I figured after lunchtime. Had a few of those over the years. Took a little while to find the fast-forward."

They huddled around his phone and Ellis propped it up against a water glass. The video showed the missing view of the street to the right of Willem's shop. The image was shaky as Duffy's hand was during the time he held it, for most of an hour. In the background they could hear Duffy and Ms. Kowalski talking.

". . . *zinger tea?*" they heard her say. "*How about another lemon cookie?*"

"*Don't mind if I do on both,*" Duffy replied, happily.

They could hear the rattle of china teacups and plates. Duffy's hand jiggled the video.

They fast-forwarded. Empty street.

". . . *a few nice collections here,*" Duffy said. "*. . . the glass animals.*"

Fast-forward.

". . . are those spoons from?"

"Oh those? My late husband Oscar and I would buy a spoon whenever we . . ."

Fast-forward.

". . .is Carlsbad Caverns, Branson Missouri and of course the Excalibur one. Oscar loved the jousting and knights."

"Medieval Times! I used to go in Pomona."

While this went on, Paloma and Ellis saw some of the cars they recognized from the first tape. They were getting close.

Fast-forward.

". . . is Mitten and the other is Socks. Pure alley cats." She laughed.

Then they saw them, Evan and Husani for sure, enter the frame, walking towards Willem's shop. Heads down, not talking, Evan carried the guitar and his gait seemed steady. Junkies focus on things that are important to them. This guy knew what he was about to do. Switch the guitar, get money and drugs. It was a straight line. If he pulled this off, he would be really high an hour from now. If not, no harm, no foul. Picked up the wrong case. Sorry. Already got five hundred for his trouble, although he had probably blown most of it.

". . . that baking show too. The British one. Prue and that darling Paul Hollywood."

Based on what Willem had said, the guys weren't in his shop more than a few minutes before leaving. Ellis went to fast-forward again, but Paloma touched his hand to let it play. Street activity at this point would be important if there were other people involved.

"They make it look so easy. I'm afraid my efforts are not very successful," Duffy said.

"I got a few tricks," Ms. Kowalski replied.

"I bet you do," Duffy said.

Paloma and Ellis looked up at Duffy, who was busy eating.

The guys leaving Willem's broke the frame of the video. They walked quicker than the approach, Evan with a slightly different guitar case. Of course, Evan was closer to a party bottle of Oxy and cash in his pocket. Husani was following his friend on a grand adventure. Did they know the true value of the guitar they stole? Evan would have tried to renegotiate or sell it. A junkie always wants more, scheming how to get over.

"I could show you how to make rum cake."

They walked out of frame, where they came from originally. Must have driven off, never crossing either camera. Ellis was about to stop it, but Paloma touched his hand.

"Let it play," she said.

About two minutes later, Gary entered the frame, walking quickly, urgently, looking in a blue car, another car, a driveway. Then right near the edge of the wide video frame, Gary stopped. He just stood there, looking down the street.

"What's he doing?" Ellis asked. Gary was small in the frame.

"Not a lot. What is he looking at?"

"Can't see his face; he's so small in the frame."

From what they remembered, there were six or seven more houses before the corner. Cars in driveways and on the street.

Gary rocked on his feet, for about fifteen seconds. Then he returned around.

"Now he's looking in the same cars and he's watching something the other way. Probably Willem running from car to car. Less urgency. We have to sync these two tapes up, see both sides."

Duffy tried to follow their narration.

"You think the guy's wrong? Inside job. Usually is," Duffy

said, using his napkin.

"Starting to look that way," Ellis asked.

"Duffy, gotta thank Miss Kowalski for this."

"Thank her? We're baking a Bundt cake next week," he said.

Returning to the office, Paloma loaded the video she had sent from Duffy's phone while Ellis called to check in with Neely. His next call was to Leon to see if he was available after work, maybe have him hang at the hospital.

Putting the two laptops next to each other, she synced up the time codes on both Ring videos.

Gary had stopped and reacted to something he saw, out of frame. A video further down the street would be nice.

"Recanvass the block for more video?"

"There weren't any more cameras, Ring or otherwise. It's in my notes."

"He's less animated on the walk back. He saw something that literally stopped him in his tracks. We need to talk to him, alone. Let's leave Benny out of it this time."

Paloma pulled up a new tab and set to finding Gary's address. She didn't want to ask Benny. How many people named Gary Edison could there be in Los Angeles?

"Got 'em. Two Gary Edisons and one is eighty-nine, the other forty-two and lives in West LA," she said.

"The fuck you want?" Gary said as he opened the door to his small bungalow. "Aren't you out looking for the guitar? Or you think I took it."

"Gary, help us. Five minutes."

"I just got in from the office. The concert is tomorrow. Tommy really thought you guys would have found the guitar by now." A shot across the bow.

Gary kept his foot braced behind the door, as though they might try to push in. He looked them up and down, his eyes a little bleary; he gave off post–happy hour vibes.

"We even brought visual aids," Paloma said, pointing to her laptop. "You can be the first kid on your block to watch it."

"Or Ralston, I mean Tommy, can be first." Ellis said, playing the card he knew would get his attention. They had pegged Gary right. His past, present and future were all Ralston all the time. His identity was built on his relationship with a rock star. That's how his friends, relatives and lovers knew him. Gary was a rock star's right-hand man. For years, whether it was tickets or swag, or hospitality passes, Gary was a good guy to know. However, he always came up short of joining the management team, repping his own bands, being "the man."

"Okay, amuse me," he said, letting them into his house. The walls of the living room were covered with RimShot concert posters, silver records and photos of Gary with Ralston and Maggie in some tropical locale. Kinda like a shrine, or a room to impress civilians.

Paloma went to one side of the room that transitioned into the kitchen. She set up the laptop on the counter and opened the cued-up video, with the sound off. Gary, with a fuck-you look on his face, watched the video. Then he became animated.

"Yeah, that's them! You got names? You can see the case is different," Gary pointed emphatically. Paloma let it play until Gary appeared, working his way along the street, looking in cars and driveways.

Then he stopped. He looked at something for about fifteen seconds, took a slow step back and looked over his shoulder, probably to see what Willem was doing, and turned around, relooking at the cars he just passed. Slower, with less urgency.

Gary shrugged. "A video of me searching for those fuckin' assholes that took the guitar," he said, pointing at the screen. "You have one of Willem too? Why are you wasting my time?"

The good offense theory.

Paloma ran the video back.

"What did you see, Gary?" Ellis said, pointing to him, frozen on the screen. Looking. He tried not to sound confrontational.

"Nothing."

"It's okay if you forgot something. Does this help you remember?" Paloma asked, also trying to be gentle.

"Yeah, I remember that Willem let two scumbags walk out of his shop with the fuckin' Harrison guitar. What you're seeing here is me realizing that A, I don't see the guys and B, I'm so fucked with Tommy. Big time fucked," he said, shaking his head and pacing away across the living room.

Paloma and Ellis shared a look.

"C'mon, Gary, we want to find the guitar. George Harrison's Country Gentleman is an important piece of rock n' roll history," he said, pointing to the living room shrine to RimShot.

"Oh great. Thanks for reminding me."

"We are not trying to make trouble. We're just following up anything we come across, like this video. You sure you can't help us?"

Gary mellowed a bit but stayed defensive.

"Look, if you find those guys who took the guitar, let me put them in the hospital, and you guys can have dinner somewhere."

They didn't mention Evan and Husani.

"Are you sure you don't remember who else knew you would be getting to Willem's at two o'clock?" Paloma asked. "How did you make the appointment? Email, phone, text?"

Gary looked at her. "I called Willem from the office after Tommy asked me to bring the guitar in. Added it to my list of calls. I was in the lounge, by the kitchen. Nice leather chairs. I like to hang out there where people can find me if they need me."

Which meant after many years Gary didn't have an office or even a cubicle.

They had walked past the lounge area when they spoke to Gary in Ralston's office. Off the main hallway, anyone could have walked past or been in the kitchen area, which seemed well populated during their visit.

"Do you remember anyone else there when you were setting up the appointment?" Ellis continued. "Hanging out in the kitchen maybe?"

"You been there. People in and out all the time. I dunno, the usual, I guess. We were starting pre-production on the video, so it was busy. You think someone overheard me? Set me up?" he asked.

"They knew you were coming," Paloma said.

"Hey, I'm not getting hung for this."

Paloma and Ellis stood staring at him.

"How about Willem? He knew when I was coming."

"True that. However, the guy is going to lose his shop. That's his whole life."

"Well maybe he wants to trade the glue and varnish for a beach in Belize."

"The thief is a junkie. He was 'Narcaned' back from an OD today and is in the hospital. We're hoping to get to him in the morning, with Covid regulations and all."

"Where? What's his name? Let me talk to him and I'll have

the information in five minutes. What hospital?"

"In the morning." What Ellis didn't say was that they also had Husani, who was a lying piece of shit. There was silence.

"Don't know what else to say except you let me know when I can talk to him," he said, walking towards the door to usher them out.

"Thanks for taking the time," Ellis replied.

Walking back to the car, Paloma said she regretted not having the totally illegal Stingray device to use on Gary's phone. She was sure there was more he was not saying. Her premise was everybody lies, which didn't make her feel good about people. Ellis checked in with Neely, getting a quick reply that he had put Husani in a room because he never fucking stopped talking and might be injured by morning. Then he texted Leon and told him they wanted to stake out Gary to see where he went, or who came to see him.

Who or what did Gary see?

Leon said he was good for the night shift starting at eleven. They texted him the address.

"I guess Sandy Wilshire owes us for finding Evan," Ellis reminded her.

"That's right, even if he's on a stretcher," she said, opening the car door. "Text her. Be right back."

Paloma skipped across the street and dropped low along the side of Gary's bungalow. No high-tech gizmos tonight. The old-fashioned way, listen by the window. Not the smartest way to go, but a way. Peering over the window ledge, she saw Gary leaning against the kitchen counter, two fingers of Jack and his cell in front of him, tapping his keys on the granite top. Thinking of going out? She wished he would or pick up his phone and call someone. He didn't.

Ten minutes later, Ellis, shaking his head, watched her skipping back to the car.

"Nada, nothing. Drinking at the counter."

"Kinda dangerous peeping, isn't it? Next-door neighbor could be a dock worker or a fireman. Big and burly."

"I'm fast, remember?" she said with a big smile.

"Did we make a mistake telling him Evan had OD'd and was in the hospital?

"Maybe, but we didn't use his name, right?"

Leon texted that he was almost there.

Ellis was about to reply when his phone chirped. It was Longworth. Paloma answered and put it on speaker. He sounded stressed.

"They said pay or they're shutting me down. I'm dying here. Did you find anything? Anyone? My engineers are failing at a work around. Is that on purpose? I'm going to pay the ransom," Longworth said. "I can't afford to wait."

"Woah, slow down," Paloma said. "We understand your problem, but you're gonna give them a million cash?"

"I have to. I told you I'm negotiating a big funding round right now, which will lead to a 'SPAC' buying the company. Many millions will follow."

"When are you going to pay?"

"Tomorrow," he said.

Ellis and Paloma shared a look. This was not good.

"They said before I give them the money, they will give me the key code on an SD card that I can uplink to my engineers to verify right away."

"You believe that?" Ellis said.

"Yes."

Trying to stall him, Paloma said, "You can put together a million dollars in cash?"

"Yes."

"On a holiday weekend?"

"Let's just say I have emergency cash."

Paloma shook her head. Her emergency cash would fit in an envelope. She looked at Ellis.

"Then let us make the drop. Maybe we can grab them up," he said.

"No, they said I have to come alone."

"You spoke with them?"

"Yes. The voice was distorted, and no number was displayed."

"Where's the drop?" Ellis asked.

"I'll know that at six o'clock in the evening. Can't come soon enough."

Longworth was stressed big time. More than finding out his wife was cheating on him with a beautiful woman.

And tomorrow was July fourth.

11

Chapter 11

July 4 –Way to Early

Paloma woke up with a start. She heard something. Reaching over to wake Ellis, she found the bed empty, and the clock said 2:52. Opening the bedroom door, she heard a crash of glass and looked around for a weapon. She grabbed a baseball off the dresser that sat in a ceramic mitt she made as a kid. Creeping down the dark hallway, she peeked into the kitchen, then the living room.

Someone was bent over the back of the couch. It was Ellis who looked up as she entered the room.

"Careful, I just broke a juice glass."

"What's going on?" she asked softly, turning on a lamp.

"Couldn't sleep. Didn't want to wake you."

"Well, glad you're up. We have to go talk to Evan. Now. We can't lose him.

"Now? They said he wouldn't be discharged until noon, and besides they won't let us in."

"Now. Middle of the night is the best time. We show our FAQ credentials, say his dad sent us. Or maybe, I'm his older sister, just flew in from Portland. We cannot lose this guy."

"Lose him from the hospital?"

"We made a mistake telling Gary the guy was in the hospital," Paloma said. "Or if Husani gave up a name to Paul's guys for the promised cash. We gotta go. Now."

Ellis nodded and followed her down the hall to get dressed.

"What would have happened if Rosato hadn't shown up?" he said

"It might have been ugly."

"Cause I lost the bat?"

Ellis reached for his pants. "Is that a baseball in your hand?"

"Yeah, I thought someone broke in. I was going to throw it at their head," she said.

"Your dad's 1957 New York Giants autographed baseball?"

"Yup."

"The last Giants team to play at the Polo Grounds?"

"Uh huh."

"Signed by Bobby Thompson *and* Willie Mays!?"

She flipped the ball in her hand and looked at him with a big smile. "Would have made Willie proud."

The drive to Westwood was fast at 3:10 am on a holiday. The "side shows" of souped-up cars burning rubber and spinning around intersections had ended. Everyone who was leaving town had left.

They settled on a plan for Paloma to enter through the emergency entrance, carrying the duffle bag from the trunk, claiming to be Evan's distraught sister who just flew in from Portland. Injuries from backyard fireworks usually meant the emergency room would be a circus. It was.

The overworked night shift desk orderly melted with her

urgent smile and settled for a mask and her vaccination card, even with a different last name, and sent her on her way to Evan's room. At the elevator, she nodded to Ellis, who took a seat in the bustling waiting room.

The fourth-floor hallway was hospital half dark, silent and eerie, like a scary movie. A nurse was entering a room with a blinking call light down the hall. The nurses' station was empty, lit by a few monitors. A muffled cough, a moan. Not where Paloma wanted to be, Covid or no Covid. Finding his room, she looked in through the vertical window.

A machine was beeping as she entered, vital signs displayed on a screen. As thin and gray as Evan looked on the stretcher, he looked worse in the dim nightlight. His breathing was labored with oxygen tubes feeding into his nose. He didn't look like a guy who was getting discharged in the morning. How long he had OD'd before getting the Narcan would determine the course of his recovery.

She had just noticed a chair pulled up to the side of the bed when the door opened behind her. A fit, handsome, tired-looking silver-haired man in a very expensive suit entered, carrying a sandwich wrapped in plastic. His look went from her to Evan and back.

"Who are you?" he demanded, half whispered, taking long strides into the room, getting between her and the bed. "What are you doing in my son's room?"

Obviously, she wasn't Evan's sister.

"I'm Paloma Grant, a private detective hired by your son's girlfriend, Sandy Wilshire, to find him," she whispered, handing him an FAQ business card. "I spoke to your housekeeper trying to locate Evan. Back from your trip, Mister Garvin?"

"I'm Alvin Crosset. Evan is my stepson," he said, totally

off balance. Paloma gathered that he was an executive type, used to being in control of situations. This was not one of them. "I've just flown in from Dallas. You say a 'Sandy Wilshire' hired you?"

"Yes. She knew him at Crossroads School. Lives in a tower on Wilshire. She does a lot of internet stuff."

"Porn?" he asked responsively.

"Uh, no. She's an influencer. Reps a bunch of products on her YouTube channel. Has a few million followers. Maybe you knew her as Sandy Baer."

"From Crossroads. Why the hell did she hire you to find Evan? Was he missing?"

"His band's drummer was concerned for his welfare when he didn't show up for a show, so we looked at Evan's apartment, your home in Brentwood and Sandy's. She hadn't seen him in days, couldn't reach him and was concerned. I need to ask him a few questions. About a case I am working on."

"In the middle of the night? My son has had drug problems, and with what the nurses told me, a serious relapse. Two times in top Malibu rehabs. But you were looking for him already? I wish you had found him sooner."

Paloma had to decide how much to tell and how to tell it.

"Evan picked up the wrong guitar at a repair shop. We are trying to find that guitar and return it to its owner."

"The wrong guitar. You mean he stole it."

"A few questions with him would help us determine that."

"He's a junkie. He stole it." He said directly.

Paloma studied Alvin. The guy had real money, and this was at least his second family. A stepfather who knew Evan was a junkie, mostly out of town and probably paying for the apartment and other things that Evan couldn't sell for cash.

She hesitated to ask after Evan's mom at the ashram.

"If he was awake and lucid, we could probably figure it all out pretty quickly," she said gently.

"He's been out since I arrived. They say he took Oxy. A lot. He might have had a small seizure on the way here."

Paloma decided to pass on telling him the rest of what she knew, and about seeing him wheeled to the ambulance.

Her phone chirped with a "?" from Ellis. She replied with a quick "*all good, hang out.*"

"Who are you texting? Let me see that," he shouted, reaching for the phone. Paloma spun away to the other side of the room. "What's your game with Evan? Are you his dealer? Seeing if he is still alive? Or this Sandy Wilshire? These business cards are cheap to make," he continued, agitated, and stepping towards her.

"Woah, cool your jets, dude. It's my partner downstairs. There have been some tough guys looking for him, for the guitar. They already roughed up members of his band. Kidnapped one of them and almost left him tied to a tree in Griffith Park. We're watching out for him." She hoped this would get his attention.

"I can protect him. I know people."

"Well, so far our clients haven't gone to the cops."

"Cops don't care about a stolen guitar. Take them a week just to call you back," he said scornfully.

"They do when the guitar is worth north of 800k, maybe more."

Those kinds of numbers got his attention.

"You've heard of the Beatles? *Ed Sullivan Show?*"

He stood ramrod straight. He was of the right age.

"You're serious?"

"SO very," she said.

Alvin looked at Evan, so pale in the bed and shook his head. He had married Evan's mother because she looked good on his arm and made him feel twenty years younger in bed. Evan was part of the package, Alvin figuring he would soon be off to college. A string of wrecked cars and thefts at friends' houses proved his thinking wrong. Her being away at yoga retreats in India left him to deal with this mess.

"Wake him up and let me talk to him. Three or four questions," she said.

It was a moot point as Evan opened his eyes and seeing Alvin, groaned. He looked at Paloma.

"Is there water? My mouth is full of sand," he said in a hoarse, forced voice, then turned half eyed to his stepfather. "Alvin? You're here? The Gulfstream run out of gas?" he said sarcastically. What a prick.

Alvin took the hit with no reply. Paloma filled a cup and put a bent straw in.

"Are you my plainclothes nurse?" Evan croaked, looking her up and down, taking labored deep breaths. "You work for him?"

"Nope. Sandy Wilshire hired me. You know, during Husani's wild goose chase."

It took a few seconds to register in Evan's addled brain.

"Had you going there, didn't we? I just needed to crash for a while," he said, trying to take a breath. "Sandy paid you to find me? What a girl!" he said with a slight smile. "She's loaded, you know."

"Evan, she says you stole a very famous, expensive guitar. Tell her now. Where is it?" Alvin demanded, stepping to the bed.

"Me? An expensive guitar? Did you ever give me an expensive guitar, Alvin?"

"No police are involved yet, so where is it?"

Paloma immediately realized she messed up telling Alvin the pedigree of the guitar. She hadn't found out yet if Evan had known.

Evan looked around to see what he was hooked up to, if there were any buttons to push for pain meds. A junkie always hoped.

"Who approached you to make the switch? Who paid you for it in the parking lot?" she asked.

"I don't feel so good. You think we could get out of here?"

"Husani's mom flushed your Oxy if you're thinking of going there," she lied. "The rest of the party bottle stashed at your apartment?"

"Wow, aggressive," he said.

"Evan!" Alvin shouted.

"Get him the fuck out of here," Evan croaked, pointing at Alvin.

"No, he should hear this too," Paloma said quietly. "The guy who owns the guitar is of course pissed, well connected and ready to go to the police." She lied. "He has two people who can identify you."

Evan was silent. He didn't look too good.

The door opened and Paloma wheeled around to see if it was a nurse who would throw her out. Dressed up in a tight, short dress after a night of clubbing, Sandy Wilshire strode into the room, her jeweled phone in one hand, ending a call with two kissing sounds. A well placed $50 bill got her upstairs. She was surprised to see Paloma and Alvin, but the sight of Evan lying in the bed caused her to cover her mouth with her free hand.

She started to move to the bed as Alvin stepped in front of

her.

"Who are you?" he asked somewhat bewildered, as she was dressed in heels and filmy club wear.

"I'm his girlfriend. Who are you?" she said with the attitude of a woman with a couple of million followers and millions in the bank.

Alvin looked to Paloma, as though he knew her after ten minutes.

"Alvin, meet Sandy Wilshire, the woman I was speaking about. Sandy, this is Alvin, Evan's stepdad."

She nodded to Paloma. "Thanks for finding him."

Alvin held out his hand as Sandy blew past him and went to hold Evan's hand as he feebly waved to her to come close, then pulled her head to his.

"There's a bindle behind the handle of Tito's in your living room," he whispered. "You want to get it for me? These folks are driving me crazy."

Not a greeting or a kiss. Normally Evan was so affectionate. When he was stoned. Sandy stood up and turned. The look on Paloma's face made her wonder if Evan's whisper had made it halfway across the room.

"I love you too," Sandy said, turning back to Evan, trying to cover. "I was so worried about you when they called."

Paloma hesitated to point out she had been out clubbing, building her brand until three in the morning, before deciding or remembering he was here.

Paloma's phone chirped.

"Two of Ralston's security guys downstairs! Trying to get room #. Not Paul's guys. Get him lost."

Paloma looked at Alvin. "Some guys you don't want to meet are headed up here. We have to move. Now."

Richie Cortina and Mountain Moran worked tour and hotel security for RimShot and other bands. They traveled with the band, supervised security at concerts and made the halls safe at hotels, always carrying themselves like they were important and belonged. The LA security "uniform," a gray sports coat over a black T-shirt, stood out in the rock world where jeans and tees were the usual. Between the two, it was obvious which one was Mountain.

With their generic "security" ID's, they easily convinced the overwhelmed desk orderly that they were sent by the family and to give them Evan's room number, even though Richie, with a raw bruised face, looked like he needed the ER.

In the dim fourth-floor hallway, Mountain sniffed a few times and made a face. Disinfectant, chemicals, sweat and who knows what else assaulted his nose. And this was a nice hospital. He pointed to the discolored, swollen area on the side of Richie's face.

"Shoulda checked you in here," Moran joked.

Two middle fingers were Richie's reply.

There was no name on the room number they had been given. Sharing a look, they walked down the hall to check a few other name plates, then went back to the first one. The IV lines were hanging down, monitors and computers off and the mattress had been folded over. This could mean the patient had died. Recently.

Richie inspected the IV bags that were half full. Moran looked in the bathroom and closet, empty of any personal items. He unfolded the mattress and saw a small blood stain. He touched it. It was wet. He put his palm down on the sheets and they were warm. Fuck. They bolted out of the room and looked down the hallways, where a man was pushing a patient in a wheelchair.

Ellis had watched the two guys enter the ER and get in line to speak to the orderly behind the desk. He recognized them from Ralston's softball team and security at the Forum. Richie something and "Mountain" Moran. Using the cover of a guy walking into the ER, wailing with hand injuries from a fireworks explosion, he ducked past the front desk into a stairway, hoping to get upstairs before they did. He raced up to the fourth floor, peeking through the door window to see if the two guys had made it up. He texted Paloma that he was there.

With Alvin's help and Sandy asking endless questions, Paloma had disconnected his monitors, oxygen and IV, then helped Alvin get Evan from the bed. She told Sandy to grab Evan's clothes. With a mighty heave, Paloma turned the mattress in half like she had seen in some movie, hoping they would think that Evan had died. On the way out she ripped the name tag off the door, then made their way down the hall towards the stairs, ducking into a room when they heard the elevator ding. She looked around in the semi darkness; an elderly patient in the room was snoring vigorously. They had to move fast.

Ellis peeked through the stairway door as the guys came off the elevator and walked down the hall, checking rooms, when they went into one, he ducked in the room Paloma had texted. She held her finger to her lips, nodded towards Sandy, who was trying to dress Evan, and held out a hospital robe for him while hiking up his jeans and removing his trainers. Alvin held up Evan, who seemed to be less with it and nodded.

"I've met these guys before. Ralston's tour security. One of them looks like he was just in a brawl," he whispered.

"Ralston is back-dooring us?"

"Or Benny, who knows?"

She peeked out the doorway. The hall was empty.

"I'm taking Evan. This is Alvin, his stepdad. He'll explain. Text me when you're out; meet at the car," Paloma said, heading to the stairway.

"I'm coming with you," Sandy hissed, not wanting to miss this grand adventure.

Alvin told Ellis to sit on his shoes in the old man's wheelchair while explaining how it all might work as he wheeled him out into the hall, hoping to give Paloma enough time to get Evan down the stairs.

A nurse came out of the med room and asked what they were doing. Richie showed her his bogus security pass and told her to stand by, since they might need her help. Moran headed down the hall, fast for such a huge guy, and stepped up to Alvin, reaching for the wheelchair.

"What are you doing?" Alvin hissed in his best CEO voice.

"Shut the fuck up!" Moran said offhandedly.

Richie caught up as Moran spun the wheelchair around.

"I will not shut the fuck up. Leave my son alone," he said, standing his ground.

Ellis, head bobbing slightly, looked up at them, eyes unfocused and mouth slightly ajar. Not the junkie they were expecting. The robe covered his Hawaiian shirt and his rolled-up pants. They didn't recognize Ellis from the Hoovers softball games. He sure recognized them.

"Shit, where is he?" Moran threatened.

"I don't know or care what you are talking about," he said as Ellis lowered his head, trying to get into a better position to jump out at them if it came to that.

"Where's Evan? What's your name?"

"Alvin Crosset. What's yours?"

They chose not to answer.

"My son is recovering from a stroke. I spend most nights with him," Alvin said, getting up in Moran's grill. "I don't know this Evan you are looking for, so fuck off. I do a lot of business in this town and know plenty of cops and judges," he said, looking at the "security pass" that had his name on it.

"Mister Moran. You could lose your license tomorrow." Ellis stifled a smile. Alvin gave a commendable performance.

Going down the stairs with Evan was like carrying a smelly bag of potatoes. At least he wasn't a heavy bag. Holding him upright, she could feel bones through his clothes. He seemed out of it, but Paloma had no trust that he wasn't faking and would take off, so she made sure of her grip on his belt as they went down to the main floor. Sandy cursed broadly as she took her heels off to navigate the stairs.

Were there more of Ralston's guys waiting outside the entrance? Paloma parked Evan and Sandy in the stairway as she looked out into the ER. She texted Ellis.

"We will meet you at the In-n-Out burger parking lot. Not sure if there are more guys outside so I am going to another building to exit," she texted.

"Okay, we are headed to the south stairs. Alvin has a friggin' driver."

The ride back to the FAQ office was silent, everyone trying to digest what had just happened. Following in the BMW, Ellis tried to put together the events of the last two days. The fight at Jumbo's, Husani being snatched by Paul's guys, Evan's OD and then the security guys at the hospital. Now Ralston knew Evan's name.

Did Paul get Evan's name from Husani and offer that up to show Ralston and Benny what a trusted, loyal, dependable guy he was? Did he engineer the whole guitar theft just to be the hero in the end?

With these security guys in the hunt, not knowing if they were allied with Paul's crew, the next hour or so with Evan was going to be critical. They would need to get him talking, since they couldn't legally hold him, and Alvin could walk him out at any moment. If he was a good liar like Husani, it could be a dead end. They would have to give Ralston the information about the two, hoping he would use the police and not Mountain and Richie to get better answers.

A day in the city jail would show the rich boys from Brentwood another side of Los Angeles. Then the truth would probably come out pretty fast, with their parents' expensive lawyers cutting a deal for the guitar's return. Would Ralston go to the police when he learned Evan would be protected by his stepdad?

Willem could press charges, but he was in a weak position, believing it would destroy his business. They weren't sure if Gary could press charges, his resistance from an ongoing sense of loyalty to do whatever Ralston wanted. Part of what kept OFOW's around. They did what they were told.

Abbot Kinney was quiet and still at 5:00 am on July Fourth as they arrived at the FAQ office. Parking was no problem. Alvin, Sandy and his driver, helped Evan up the stairs as Paloma went ahead to unlock the door.

The door was open, wood splintered around the strike plate.

By the early light spilling in through the windows, she could see the office had been tossed and trashed. She motioned to Alvin to stop, and for Ellis to hurry up.

There was paper everywhere on the floor, wooden file cabinets and bookcases pushed over. Paloma slowly walked around the office, then heard a groan. Behind a desk she found Duffy, face bloodied, on the floor trying to roll over.

"Ellis, it's Duffy," she said, running over to him. "Don't move, man, stay down."

Duffy looked at her, trying to focus, shook his head slowly and tried to get a hold on the desk.

Paloma and Ellis helped him into his chair, the white hair on the back of his head tinted brown from dried blood. They directed Sandy to the bathroom to get a hand towel for Duffy's head.

"Out late. Saw a light on, found two fucking mastodons trashing the place. Big fellas. Knew how to handle themselves. I know I clocked one with my desk phone before it went black," he said. Duffy's desk phone was from the '80s and weighed about four pounds.

"White guys, black T's under gray sports coats? One of them really big?" Ellis said.

"Yeah, really big, that's right. You know them?"

"Kinda. We just danced with them at the hospital. Security on RimShot tours. Ralston's guys. Damn, maybe they got the hospital from the legal pad on my desk," Paloma said.

"They asked about that. Held fast," Duffy said, sitting up a little straighter. "I thought Ralston was the guy we're working for?"

"He is. Strange business."

"You landed a good shot. That guy's face was messed up.

You sure you're okay?"

"Yeah, sure. Hit him with the phone. Would have broken my hand."

Ellis introduced Duffy to Alvin and Sandy. Whatever disagreements had gone on in the past between Alvin and his stepson now seemed on hold. He had been a stand-up guy at the hospital, Paloma noticing his shift from resentment to caring. Alvin tried to never give Evan cash or anything that could easily be converted into drugs. The money he received to steal the guitar would be "copping" money. The promise of a party-sized bottle of Oxy would have been impossible for a junkie to resist.

He covered an "out of it" Evan on the couch with an LA Rams fleece, then Alvin handed his driver a hundred to go get breakfast sandwiches and coffee for everyone.

"Am I seeing right?" Duffy said.

Paloma looked at him.

"'Amen Anderson,' best running back in the Pac-12 a while back."

The driver stopped and nodded slightly, acknowledging the compliment.

"Saw you in the Rose Bowl, ran for 139 yards," Duffy exclaimed with a slight rock back and forth. "Glad to meet you."

'Amen' held out his large hand and flashed a quick grin. A blown knee his second year in the pros cost him the fame or money he might have earned. Now he was a personal driver.

As Paloma and Ellis righted a file cabinet and picked up papers strewn about, Duffy explained how he walked in on the two guys, one of them saying some nonsense about the door being open and where was the guitar guy. His "get the fuck out" was met with a punch that put him against the desk, where he managed to grab the phone and strike one of them before getting struck from behind.

Ellis reviewed the events, ending with now there were two groups willing to use violence in the hunt for the guitar: Paul and his pals and now the security guys who worked for Ralston.

They wondered if Richie and Moran might be bold enough to return to FAQ in daylight, with no lock on the door. Alvin made a call. He told them in an hour a few off-duty sheriffs would be parked in front of his home so they could move Evan there. He really was connected downtown.

Ellis texted Neely and asked him to bring Husani over when he woke up. Neely called immediately, saying he couldn't get there soon enough. Anything to get rid of Husani.

Then they heard footsteps coming up the stairs and moved to defensive positions, Alvin moving between Evan and the doorway, Paloma and Ellis in front of him.

It was Leon. Finished with his Gary watch, he saw the lights on as he headed home. He looked around at all the people in the office.

"Damn, you guys start early, even on a holiday," he said to Ellis, who nodded his head. "Whoever trashed this place it wasn't Gary. He spent the night passed out in his clothes, drooling on the couch."

Neely then stomped in with a bleary-eyed, reluctant Husani in tow, eager to be done with him. After seeing all the platinum records and posters around Neely's living room, Husani had pestered him, full of gee whiz, about bands and drummers he had worked for. Neely knew about Husani's relationship with bullshit, finally telling him after half an hour to get in the bedroom. Luckily for Neely, Dina had looked on in amused wonder. They had a wonderful first night.

Paloma squeezed Ellis' hand. "If any more people come in here, it's gonna feel like that Marx Brothers movie on the boat."

They huddled with Duffy, relaying all the versions of the story Husani had told them in the last two days. Duffy said that the ring video was enough, with Willem or Ralston pressing charges, to turn the two "kids" over to the cops, but FAQ couldn't be the ones to press charges. He added not to mention that part.

Amen Anderson returned with breakfast. Paloma told Alvin it was time to wake Evan up and get some coffee into him while Ellis and Duffy took Husani back to the glassed-in office that no one used.

"Okay, Husani, it's showtime," Ellis said. "The real story. If you and Evan 'Oxy' over there are on the same page and we believe you, you don't get turned over to the police."

Husani hadn't met Horace "Amen" Anderson, whom they had quietly enlisted to be Duffy's "big guy" in the room. He entered the office and removed his jacket and tie, sitting down just behind Husani, the wooden chair creaking under his weight. Husani looked over at Amen, who was slowly removing his watch and rolling up his sleeves, then turned back to Ellis and Duffy, a sharply different look on his face than the gee whiz real detectives he had been playing. Ellis marveled at Horace's unrehearsed performance. He doubted if Husani had ever taken a beating.

Neely sat by the window and watched Alvin get coffee into Evan. He had spent the last few days hunting for this guy. A skinny, pale junkie, as described, why didn't he feel sympathy for him? Neely had lost friends to drugs, all of whom didn't have the privilege Evan had. Or maybe because he fucking stole the Harrison guitar, part of rock n' roll history that he revered. Or both. Now was the make it or break it. Paloma pulled Leon aside and asked him if he would play the silent heavy with Evan.

"Damn, this is getting interesting at six in the morning. Yeah, sure, what do you need?"

"I don't know. You got any East LA?"

Next, she asked Alvin to stay out of the "discussion" for now, since Evan had shown nothing but defiance of his stepfather. With the hospital drugs wearing off, he would be feeling bad pretty soon.

From her experience with her mom, Paloma knew that a junkie was most vulnerable when they were hoping for their next fix. Tell you anything you want to hear to get out that door. Paloma set her chair between Evan and the front door, the goal line he needed to cross to race to his stash. Sandy sat next to him looking at her phone, unfazed and seemingly uninterested in what was going on. Leon came over and silently took a seat to his right while Paloma sat in front of him. Alvin walked away to a desk by the window to watch.

"Remember the hospital you were just in? You know why you're not there all busted up right now? We saved your ass from two guys who were paid to convince you the hard way to tell them where the guitar is. The one you stole. Then they were going to dump you in the woods like Husani's brother. He's lucky he isn't eating his meals through a straw for the next two months."

Evan sat slumped with lidded eyes and a smirk on his face.

"So, who hired you?"

"Can't help you, plainclothes nurse" was his opening.

"The guy who approached you for the guitar. What did he look like?"

Evan just looked at her. Paloma gave a slight nod to Leon, who got up to remind Evan he was there. He put his hand on his shoulder.

Paloma tilted her head slightly. Evan was a rich boy Brentwood brat.

"Gosh, Ese. It would be terrible if you tripped and fell down the stairs on your way to jail," Leon said, trying not to laugh, leaning in, getting close to Evan. A bit extreme, but that might get his attention.

Evan stiffened in the chair.

"Walk me through it," Paloma said, starting the Ring video, Duffy's soundtrack turned off. "Here you are carrying the Epiphone guitar, walking to the shop, and three minutes later you are walking away with a different case."

He squinted at the screen. "Does that look like me? Husani, for sure. But you have it all wrong. I was trying to get the frets on my Epiphone worked on. Didn't realize I left with the wrong guitar."

"Wrong guitar, huh?"

"Yeah. Then we went over to the market to get some sushi lunch and this guy saw me with the case and said he needed a guitar for a gig in Palm Springs, pronto. Would I sell it on the spot? Would you believe it? I told him about needing a fret job, but he offered a fistful of cash. I said yes," he shrugged.

"So you walked to the market carrying the guitar?" He must have been working on this version of the story while he was nodding. Junkies can think up some wild shit.

"Hey, I didn't want to leave it in the car. When Husani parked it might get stolen," he mugged to Sandy, still working her phone with her thumbs.

"What about the party bottle of Oxy?"

"What? Who, that guy? I wish."

The bullshit was making Paloma a bit crazy.

"So, what did the guy who bought your guitar look like?"

"You know, some dude, maybe thirty, hoodie, white guy," he said in his helpful voice.

"You do realize that Husani is in the back room giving you up?" she said, pointing to the back office.

"Man, he's got it all wrong. He was parking the car," Evan said with a smirk. "You know about drummers, right?" He thought it was a good joke and laughed at it himself.

"What's he got wrong? You don't know what he told us."

Evan gave a shrug, which was like a "fuck you." Was he always such a prick, or did he feel like with Alvin there he wouldn't fall down the stairs?

"Okay. Here's the choice. Tell where the guitar really went and who paid you or wind up in the city jail downtown. You don't feel too well? How about two or three days from now? Puking into a stainless-steel bowl in a jail cell. This is grand theft, well over the thousand-dollar limit for a hand slap. Alvin's lawyers will take a while to get you out on bail. You could get three years in state prison. I'll let you fill in the blanks about that life. To get drugs there, people do things they never imagined doing on the outside."

Evan looked over at Alvin by the window.

"You get me arrested and my *real* dad will have me out in an hour." He bragged. Alvin slumped slightly, defeated. There was nothing he could say or threaten him with, although a few days in jail was appealing.

Paloma, frustrated, walked over to Neely. He had heard the conversation. They searched for these two guys for days. After finally finding and rescuing each of them, they were no closer to the guitar. They couldn't get Evan arrested. Ralston or Willem had to be the ones, but so far Ralston wouldn't bring in the police. They had to report to Ralston that they found Evan and show the video, Husani too. Maybe then he would get the police involved. Or let Moran and Richie go at it.

Willem was a long shot. Would he change his mind and defy Ralston? The guitar was stolen out of his shop, after all. Getting him to file the police and required insurance report was worth another try.

Ellis and Duffy came out of the office and joined the huddle. Husani repeated the same story he had told them in the car. Except, in this version he had seen the guy and the guitar entering the CVS next door to Mitsuwa. Where there were cameras. Maybe they could get a look.

Paloma walked back towards Evan.

"Okay, this is enough," Alvin said, standing up. "Off-duty sheriffs will be at my house when we get there. I'm taking him home."

"Good idea. Change his clothes before he's arrested, he's kinda ripe," Paloma said, pissed that she couldn't get anywhere with him, couldn't resist the snark.

Putting Husani in an Uber, they told him to expect to be arrested, not to leave town and they would try to keep his mother out of it. Duffy sat on the couch and held a frozen bottle of vodka against his head wound, half joking that in another hour it could be time for a drink.

Reviewing the stories, it was obvious that having finally spoken with both guys involved gave them one thin hope. The CVS video. Duffy said it wasn't easy to get videos from large corporations, but he would go when the store opened. The fourth of July holiday would preclude the corporate office being open, but maybe the manager would be helpful.

If Husani's latest story was true, then the guitar thief had picked Evan perfectly. A junkie from a rich family with confidence in himself. Paloma wondered aloud if the guy knew him.

Ellis was stuck on who was the inside source who knew when the guitar was getting to Willem's. He recounted the video and the visit to Gary last night. Anyone in that office could have heard Gary making the appointment. Or Gary himself.

Duffy took the bottle down from his head.

"You've talked to Gary twice, right?" he asked.

"Yup," Ellis answered.

"Back in the seventies, there was this Son of Sam guy's shooting rampage in New York," Duffy said. "The police squad canvas turned up a dog walker who told them about a parking ticket written near one of the murder streets. When they asked the beat cop, he said he didn't write any tickets that night. They went back to the dog walker, who was positive there was a ticket. They went back to the cop two more times before he finally told them he had written the ticket but hadn't turned that and others in."

"You're saying we should talk to Gary yet again."

"Yes," Duffy replied. "You see, when they finally got the info on the car with the parking ticket, they called the police department in the town where the car was registered, hoping the owner might have seen someone, and when they repeated Berkowitz's name to the police operator, she said something like 'That guy's crazy. He shot my father's dog.' Like that, the good guys win." Duffy raised his fist. "He sees something on that tape. Maybe his accomplice, maybe he recognizes a car."

Leon spoke up. "I know nothing about this, but I agree.

Something he sees stops him. Maybe he's scared to tell you and not scared enough not to tell you."

They all looked at Leon. His Westside facade was the smooth, hip guy at the valet stand. Obviously, his background was closer to the street.

"On that note I'm going home to sleep. Call me if you need me. Restaurants closed for the holiday," he said, getting up from the chair.

Ellis asked him to wait while he wrote out a check for last night. Leon stood and looked at the whiteboard Paloma had laid out of the two cases they were working on, the brogrammers party photos, Ralston in full thrash, "The Most" team photo and the rest.

"White Tesla, killer green Maserati and a black AMG," Leon said, looking at two of the photos on the wall. "Dinner a couple of times."

"Wait. You recognize people and you know their cars? Really?" Paloma asked.

"I told you; I never forget a face. Never. Ever. I'm what they call a 'super-recognizer.' Some kind of syndrome. If I see somebody once, I remember their face."

"For a long time?" Paloma asked.

"Oh yeah," Leon replied.

Ellis bolted over from his desk. "Which people do you recognize?"

First Leon pointed to Longworth and then Ralston and Soloff.

"Don't know if any of them were together or not."

"Well, that deserves one of Duffy's little lines," Paloma said, reaching for the sharpie.

Duffy nodded to Leon. "I've heard about people like you. In London they have a squad that watches CCTV all day for bad guys. Caught a bunch."

"Really? Doesn't sound like much fun," Leon noted.

"It's pretty important."

Leon looked over at Neely. "I've seen you walking on Abbot Kinney a bunch of times with a shorter woman, sometimes wearing a flowered peasant shirt and a great smile."

"Yikes, that's Alena. Man, you are good," Neely replied.

"Then of course there's the redhead with the rented X6."

"I bet you remember her," Duffy said, trying not to smile.

"Yeah, put a line to her," he said, pointing to one of the brogrammers party photos where a clutch of revelers was dancing together with a shirtless Marik. They all tried to huddle around the photo. There was no redhead.

"Don't see her. Where?" Paloma asked.

Leon pointed to a woman with long blonde hair whose hand was on Rusty's bare chest, her mouth open with the "yah" look.

"Wearing a wig or dyed it, but it's her."

Paloma pulled the photo of Michael at Mona's off the board and held it next to the party one. The high cheekbones and the smile were very similar. She opened her laptop and showed Leon other brogrammer party photos. He picked her out in three others in no time.

Michael now became more than just Mona's lover from the gym. She also hung out with the brogrammers. Based on what Neighbor Dave had mapped out, if she had slept with one of them, she could have gained access to a router and the code. But they had checked, Marik's and Riina's. But what about the router at Longworth's?

Who looks at the back of a router? It's usually stashed in some corner of a room or a closet. Two possible points of entry had to be inspected.

Now.

Ellis was pissed that they had gotten so involved with finding the guitar that they never followed up with Rusty at his home. The rookie mistakes kept mounting up. Didn't happen in his rock n' roll jobs. He had to let it go, for now. There was much to do.

12

Chapter 12

Michael

Red hair, killer body, the Westside of Los Angeles was the perfect place for Michael to land after the situation got hot in Scottsdale. She had been bartending in a logo bikini top at the poolside swim up bar of a resort hotel. A horny bellman had found a key-making machine and how to turn off the key logger. The plan was to rip off newly arrived guests while they were at the pool.

An unpacked bag meant a theft could be blamed on airline personnel in the dark bowels of luggage claim. An expensive watch or jewelry went missing that way all the time. She knew a fence in New Mexico. After a few weeks they moved to another hotel. With her looks, it was easy to get hired. Seeing the hustle had a limited shelf life, she took her money and split to Los Angeles. Her partner didn't and was busted a week later.

Growing up in the Midwest, her parents moved around. A lot. Often with little notice, pulling her out of school one day, waking her in the middle of the night, even while she hung out at Starbucks.

Her boxes of belongings were already packed in the van. She learned to embrace the adventure.

Her dad was a "confidence man', who would find a moderate-sized city and get a readily available sales job. He would approach small business owners and convince them he could get the products they sold very cheaply, usually with a wink, that it might be a little shady. He would supply a small amount super cheap, taking a loss at first, then build up to the larger order that of course would never come. Sometimes with his wife, for a little cash and fun, they ran the "lost ring" scam, hoping that the mark had not seen the movie Zombieland.

When the Iraq and Afghanistan conflicts came along, he found gold in towns near military bases. First, he would print up fake Veterans Administration business cards, then find the local bars where off-duty sergeants hung out. There were always a few who enjoyed someone buying them drinks.

On the base, these sergeants ruled the lives of their men, trusting eighteen- and nineteen-year-olds away from home for the first time, about to be shipped to overseas combat zones. The sergeants would introduce him to his men, and they would line up to purchase non-existent life insurance policies backed by the "VA."

If a casino was nearby, her mom Chandra hit the tables and usually turned a few hundred into "getting out of town money" or a bail fund. She had a knack with blackjack, and started calling a casino "my ATM."

Their daughter, Michael, grew into a real beauty, her developing body and flaming red hair driving boys crazy. To give her a break from the family business, they sent her to Arizona State for four years, where she studied for real but kept up the skills she had picked from her parents. College guys were easy marks.

The Westside of Los Angeles and the beach appealed to her after

Phoenix. A red bikini made it easy to meet people. Lots of people. Either hanging around near the tony beach clubs or going for a drink at a trendy bar, she could be choosy about men. She liked rich ones and bedded a few, learning about the local scene. Her informal poll led her to a fancy, expensive gym. She could put down roots and do what she did best. Hustle.

Figuring out the scene, she found the best gym which was pleased to have her as a coach since she was not a licensed trainer, to encourage people during their workouts. Form-fitting gym attire suited her very well and she was quickly in demand. Like Scottsdale, she was determined that some of the wealth around her should come her way.

When Covid shut the gym down, she was caught with no real work, so it was time to freestyle for a while.

13

Chapter 13

July 4 - Morning

Venice on a hot fourth of July. The daily newspaper scoreboards showed fewer people were dying of Covid. The beaches were crowded again, though with distance between the umbrellas, Abbot Kinney was jumping, and the night's fireworks were back on in the Marina.

Paloma listed on the whiteboard all the things they could do before tonight, hoping to short-circuit the payment Longworth wanted to make. Michael had become a "person of interest," but it could be as much about sex as tech. In a last-ditch effort, they needed to sweep Longworth's and Rusty's for a compromised router or something, anything that might lead them to the hackers. Ellis texted Neighbor Dave, hoping he hadn't left town.

As for finding the guitar, they had struck out with Evan and Husani with Ralston refusing police intervention. It was over a week ago and probably a long shot, but Paloma would go to CVS when they opened and speak with the manager about the security recording. Duffy, sporting a Rams watch cap to hide a gauze pad on his head wound, was leading the move. Even though it was early, she texted Willem the photos for ID, hoping he could be convinced to press charges.

She would have to prepare the summary for Ralston, including the names and addresses of Evan and Husani, and the two Ring "street videos." They agreed not to edit Gary's erratic behavior out of the second video, still not sure what he knew.

A lot to get done on a crowded holiday. With no working lock on the door of FAQ, they asked the Thorazine Kid to have his breakfast while watching the office.

Duffy, a little blurry from his injury, tossed Paloma the keys to his car, a '69 four on the floor Cutlass 442, to drive over to the CVS store on Centinela.

"Quite a car," she said, sliding it into gear, heading down Abbot Kinney Venice Boulevard. "Where's the Caddy?"

"I keep this in my garage. A classic. Got it as payment for finding a guy's daughter in some Topanga commune many years ago. He was big in the movies." Duffy didn't kiss and tell.

At the CVS parking lot, Paloma looked around to reconcile what they had been told about the geography by Husani. An anonymous place to make the switch.

Asking the sleepy-eyed CVS cashier for the manager, they were sent to the end cap of aisle seven. A young woman was shelving tubes of sunscreen for the holiday rush. Duffy, ears sticking out of the watch cap, handed her an FAQ card and Paloma asked about the security video.

"I'm just filling in for the holiday. You would have to ask the manager, who would have to ask the regional office," Anita said.

Expecting this from a large corporation, Paloma tried to play the importance of the guitar.

"I know I can trust you with this information," she said leaning in. "We are looking for a stolen guitar. It belonged to George Harrison," she confided.

There was a blank look on the managers face.

"He was one of the Beatles," Duffy added enthusiastically.

"Oh? My grandparents have a few of those CDs. But you'll have to come back tomorrow. I'm just holding down the fort."

Prewash was already in the yard and greeted Ellis and Neely. Neighbor Dave came out on the porch, holding a cup of coffee as they approached.

"Eight am. You guys look like you're on a mission. Been up a while?"

"We have a winner, ladies and germs," Neely shouted.

Sitting on the porch, they brought Dave up to speed, telling him about the redhead in the "brogrammer" photos and needing to check Rusty's home and Longworth's, ASAP. Ellis' call to Rusty went to voicemail—the same with Longworth. Neely left to sit on Rusty's place, and they would go to Longworth's. Dave said he was hoping to go to a party on the canal later but otherwise was ready to go.

Duffy refused to see a doctor, so Paloma dropped him at his house and jogged the mile back to FAQ to start working on the recap for Ralston. She punched up the narrative, again urging them to file charges with the police. instead of having Cortina and Mountain Moran try to beat it out of them. It being the day of the benefit concert, she hoped they would be busy with security meetings at the arena. She left out the off-duty sheriff's protecting Evan. No hurry. It could be sent tomorrow.

A call to Willem went to voicemail, then he picked up, screening his calls. He reluctantly identified the photos of Evan and Husani, adding that he would love to press charges, but still wouldn't because of Ralston. Paloma tried convincing him that he would wind up getting screwed by Ralston either way. Like the former President, Ralston could always find someone else to blame. Willem's life was his craftsmanship and his reputation. He believed that if the theft of the guitar from his shop was made public, which a police report would surely do, his reputation would be ruined in the music community. The Thorazine Kid picked up a phone extension to give support to do the right thing. Willem listened but was unmoved.

Ironically, if they found the guitar, the story of its theft and recovery would get out, first in the music world, then who knows. Ellis was reluctant to point that out.

Was now the time to tell Gary to be careful and maybe get him to give it up? Once they sent the file and Ralston saw the Ring video, he could be in trouble. Loyal to a fault, was Gary part of stealing the guitar? For money or did he plan on being the hero and getting it back? Which is the same thing she wondered about Paul. A guy like Paul "on the outside" getting the guitar back would earn big props from Ralston and RimShot.

Everyone wanted to please Ralston, the rock star, the blazing sun that they orbited around, basking in the light of his stardom. The entourage, the fans, all worshiped him everywhere he went, which eventually limited the places he could go without a disguise. Celebrity did have some downsides.

Gary's phone went to voicemail.

Getting nowhere with Evan, Husani and CVS put them at a

dead end. They would get paid for finding the guys, but they had failed to return the guitar. Maybe Ralston's guys would beat the answer out of them. Was that the way to get it done? A junkie with rich parents but no money of his own had been a good target. Who had the information to target him? Lots of questions. Too few answers.

Ellis called Paloma to discuss this as he and Dave drove over to Longworth's. She had spoken to Duffy and relayed the conversation he had with "Amen" Anderson after Evan was dropped off at his stepfather's. Amen believed in confidentiality in the car he drove, but in this case, because he believed Evan had stolen the guitar, he told her that all the way home Evan only spoke to Sandy, whining to get her to pick something up at her apartment and bring it to him. Had to be drugs.

They had never met Mona Longworth but imagined she would not be pleased to see them. Paloma would meet them there.

"He's not here," Mona said, through the doorbell speaker. "He's out on his bike with that bunch of ya-hoo's he rides with. Dressed up like it's the Tour de France with those stupid hats."

"We're the detectives Banshee hired for the ransomware attack. We really need to check your internet hookup," Paloma said, holding an FAQ card to the camera, while Ellis and Neighbor Dave waited.

"I know who you are. You're the ones who ratted me out. Spied on me. Go fuck yourself," she said, slightly opening the door.

Paloma tilted her head slightly and studied her.

"Hey, you like the house, the cars, the fuck-you money? If the apps shut everything down, Banshee's SPAC goes away and your husband is gonna lose a ton of money."

"We already have a ton of money," she said defiantly. Looking Paloma up and down, then Ellis and Dave, she nodded her head towards the garage. "He said you were coming. It's in there. I'll open up. Make it quick."

They walked around to the alley, sharing a look, something like "what a bitch." The garage door opened, and she pointed them to a cabinet containing their alarm system and the router. The wires were all mounted in perfect lines. Neighbor Dave opened his kit and started checking connections.

"Any chance Michael came out to the garage?" Ellis asked.

Mona was surprised at their use of her name.

"No, we were having too much fun," she said, all bratty.

"Ok, if I plug into your router to run a few tests?" Dave asked.

"Well, you're here. Make it quick; I have to be somewhere."

A very rich woman who had been caught with a lover by detectives her husband had hired. And they were still together because her husband didn't want to split his second fortune with her. Or maybe it just got him off since he had kept the photo file.

Dave ran tests on the IP address to see if there was DNS spoofing or a "man-in -the-middle" attack going on and traced the wires to see if a device had been inserted in the line. Nothing. It was apparent that Mona was not going to let them in the house without Glenn home.

"I see you have several Wi-Fi networks. Any chance someone has your passwords?" Dave asked.

Mona looked at him, then Ellis. She had a problem with Paloma.

"My assistant and the housekeepers use the guest password."

"Did Michael ask you for the password?" Paloma said.

"You keep bringing her up. Didn't you fuck things up enough?"

"Mona, we're trying to save Banshee from going down in flames. Did you give her the password?"

"Possibly. I can't remember. She may have said she needed to send her gym schedule in. I was pretty stoned that night. I can't believe those videos you took are legal. I should sue you."

"Videos are illegal. We took photos. Your husband hired us; it's his property too so it's legal. Talk to him."

"I will. Now get out of my fuckin' garage."

They handed an envelope to Mona. "Please give this to him. Instructions for tonight. It's important."

Back out in the alley, Ellis noticed a modern barrel-roofed guest house right next to the garage.

He turned to her standing in the garage, watching them leave.

"Is that little guest house yours?"

"It's his office; guests are in a separate wing," she said. "And no, I don't have the key."

After waiting for an hour outside Rusty's, Neely got impatient. Banging on the door and ringing the bell, he didn't care if he woke Rusty up. He got some side eye from a dog walker, then Riina's voice came through the Ring doorbell, saying Rusty was out of town. When he told her he was with FAQ, she told him she had a key to feed the cat and would text Rusty for permission to let them in. She figured Rusty was watching on his phone, wherever he was.

Everyone arrived at Rusty's, Riina saying Rusty wasn't thrilled and wanted to watch them on FaceTime. Paloma shrugged.

"No problem with that," she said.

Neighbor Dave set to work in the living room, testing the router and cables with Paloma's help.

Ellis called the gym where Michael worked. It was closed for the holiday, so he drove back to the office with Neely to relieve the Thorazine Kid. They needed to plan for Longworth's ill-advised money drop.

"Geez, guess how much a million dollars weighs?" Neely said, stabbing at his phone.

"In what denomination?" Ellis replied.

"Hundies." Neely liked the way Husani had said it. Ellis shook his head.

"Let's see. Ten thousand is about this," he said, holding his fingers apart less than an inch. Ellis as a tour manager had experience with large amounts of cash. "Thirty pounds maybe?"

"Close, but no cigar. About twenty-two pounds. Says you could fit it in an attaché case. Damn," he said, miming holding up a case, bouncing his hand.

"Longworth could carry that. We have to be able to follow him and track the case. A small duffle would be better. I put an Airtag for him to use in the envelope.

"See, Rusty, they're just doing a router check, just like at my place," Riina said on the phone.

"Glenn already had my lines checked. We've got encryption up the wazoo. I don't want them poking around," he implored.

"Afraid we'll find your sex toys? Black mask and Viagra in the night table?" she teased. "If we had cracked the ransomware code, they wouldn't be here now. You know some of us are still 'pulling the oars,' dude. Where the hell are you?"

Rusty protested that he was burned out, went to a friends cabin and was still working on it. Riina rolled her eyes and made a face to Paloma, showing her lack of sympathy. All the brogrammers had been jamming the past few days, trying to figure out a work-around before the Banshee apps stopped working. Much of their future wealth was tied up in the possible SPAC purchase, which would be torpedoed when the apps slowed down enough to make news.

Neighbor Dave splayed his hands out to tell Paloma he found nothing.

"There has to be something here," Paloma said. "Rusty, did this woman ever come to your house? Sleepover?" She showed a photo of Michael in the blonde wig.

"None of your fucking business." He was pissed.

Paloma let the insult go.

"Look at the photo. You partied with her at some raves. She's all over you."

He was defensive. "I can't believe we are having this conversation. You're really something."

Riina gave a look to Paloma, who nodded yes. "Hey, Rusty, I haven't coded my ass off for the last eighteen months to have my stock options turn to dog shit. I danced with her too. She's the one who works at a gym. Great body. This might be the only chance we have left."

"Okay, okay. She came over. By the way, that's a wig in the picture. She's really a redhead and a freakin' all-star."

"So, a sleepover over?"

"No, I guess she took an Uber home. We took some 'love drug,' rocked the bed and when I woke up, she was gone. Man, redheads are something else."

Paloma shrugged it off. "Who had the love drug? What was

it?"

"She had it. Put it on her tongue and kissed me down to my kidneys."

Riina rolled her eyes. Rusty might be a great coder, but to her he was an idiot.

"You let her drug you, moron," Riina said.

"No, man, I drank a lot that night. And I'm not a moron."

Paloma held up her hands like a referee.

"Dave, anything else we can try?"

He had traced down all the internet cables outside the house, looking for any interruption in the lines for a key logger or such.

"Ok, we try a different approach," Dave said. "Let's turn off the Wi-Fi and all phones, anything that is transmitting a signal."

Rusty protested as Riina said bye and shut off the phone. Dave unplugged the router and put on headphones, using a radiofrequency scanner to look for a signal. He moved from the living room through the kitchen then, to the "coding cave" bedroom. Similar to Marik's, it was a random collection of hard drives and other devices, multicolored wires reaching down to the floor to form a messy nest.

Riina started to say something snarky about the condition of the room when Dave held up his hand for her to be quiet. Kneeling to look on the floor, there were two power strips for the computer gear, wires clumped everywhere. He came up and put his finger to his lips, waving Paloma over with the other hand and pointing to the power strip. He shined his light on what looked like a USB thumb drive plugged into a regulation white cube charger. Riina leaned in to see as well.

Dave wiggled his fingers as he moved his hands away from

the drive, signaling it was a transmitter. He also pointed to his mouth then shrugged, suggesting a microphone was nearby. Paloma crawled under the desk next to him and looked up. In the far corner of the desk was a clump of sticky clay that held a 9-volt battery with wires leading to the side of the desk. Sliding over a bit, she saw a tiny microphone. She pantomimed to Dave and then Riina to follow her out of the room, then out of the condo.

"His place is bugged? A friggin' microphone and a transmitter? How does that help? Does he recite code out loud?" Paloma said. Riina shook her head.

Neighbor Dave was busy looking up something on his phone, then called a Navy pal. After a short conversation, Dave explained, softly.

"Now this is some sci-fi shit. It's called 'acoustic cryptanalysis.' Each key on the keyboard makes a slightly different sound, a distinct signature, when pressed down. With Rusty passed out, she would have set up the microphone and transmitter, then typed a prepared page or two on his computer that used all the keys a few times to get a baseline sound for each. You take that recording and write a program to determine what each key sounds like. Whenever Rusty was coding, the program read out what was being typed. And it all happens pre-encryption.

"He must have written enough of the code for them to see the honey pots and find a way in. The thumb drive might be the main or a backup transmitter. Probably a car or a van parked on the street recorded the keystrokes automatically. Brilliant. Whomever we are dealing with is pretty advanced. She isn't doing this alone."

They powered everything back up, and in the living room Riina Face Timed Rusty again so Dave could explain what they had found.

"My house is bugged? Are you sure it's her?" He was freaking out.

"Nope," Paloma said, "but she's all we got. Any cars or vans been parked around your place regularly?"

"You think I would notice? We've been jamming code."

"If she, they, whoever worked with the code you wrote, that would cut down on what we have to look for," Riina said.

"Rusty, how many times were you with her?" Paloma asked.

"Jeez, once. Or maybe twice. Those raves kinda blend together."

Dave's theory about how she inserted the bad code would wait. No need for the brogrammers to know about Longworth, Mona, and Michael. They got Ellis on the phone as they drove to the office.

"So here's the timeline. We watched Mona and Michael eight days ago. Then Longworth hired you to investigate the ransomware, right?"

"Yeah. A few days later. We were surprised to hear from him," Ellis said. "From the time stamp on the rave photos, she was with Rusty a few months ago."

"Let's say she goes fishing at these raves, finds targets and bugs them, this time Rusty, gets the code and writes the ransomware program, but has to get it into the server. She's found Mona at the gym, maybe overhears her talking to a friend, sees a familiar logo on her gym bag and jackpot. She figures Longworth's computer has ultimo access, so she seduces Mona and inserts the malware code while she is crashed out from the weed and wine and whatever 'love drug' she used on Rusty. Probably groomed her for a while before the big night."

"That's some devious shit," Ellis said.

"Wouldn't they see it came from his computer?"

"Maybe no one looked there. Whoever is writing this stuff is really good. Maybe she has help. Disgruntled former employee?"

"Yeah, we brought it up at the first meeting. Nada."

"The Kid fixed the office door. Meet me at the house. We gotta figure out what's next."

14

Chapter 14

Michael and Henry

Exercise gyms were seen as virus petri dishes during the first year of Covid and closed. Uber Eats, Door Dash were the only growth industries. To help with the rent, Michael posted for a roommate on Craigslist. No one responded for a week until Henry came to the door. With his mask on, she could only see his neck beard sticking out and his thin eyes with a brow that didn't seem to move. A master-blaster T-shirt hung on his tall, slim frame; his hair could be described as an "FBI cut.". Not the type she had hoped for but he explained that he was an Army vet with a disability pension, ensuring he could pay the rent. "I work in tech," he said, as though trying to impress her. He paid two months up front and moved into the small second bedroom.

At first, she ignored him, but as the limited quarantine went on, they ate dinner together. Fruit Loops for him, Michael favored Trader Joe's pre-made meals. Henry started talking about his time in Iraq, where he repaired electronics on one of the large Army bases. Like most men, he was smitten with her.

A loner, Henry had a workbench in a repair trailer. He was not a member of the warrior class that went out on patrol every day, at first referred to as a "geek" by the nineteen-year-old country boys who hung out together on the base. The fact that electronics and sand were a bad combination and his choice to play heavy metal music meant he eventually was shown respect

At the mess, he heard that the daily patrols were being given copious amounts of Klonopin and Zoloft to keep them inspired to go out and get shot at or blown up by IEDs. Henry easily hacked into the base computer and put him onto the list. Nobody questioned this or his dosage. After that, he was blitzed most of the time.

A heightened sense of well-being from the drugs and the boredom of military life led him to more hacks, like base electrical grid, causing mysterious rounds of blackouts or the lights coming on at 3 am in the officers' quarters. School hijinks.

With rotation of personnel from the states, he was promoted and put in charge of the electronic infrastructure on the entire base, including internet services. He lowered the cost of internet for each soldier in his dorm to one dollar, earning him a following among those who ventured off base every day.

He trained the troops to use the "Wasp", a drone that could be carried in a backpack and launched like a balsa wood kids toy, allowing patrols to get a glimpse of what was behind village walls. In the evening, he loved showing off crazy things he could do with it.

After two tours, he had saved money and mustered out as an E-5 sergeant with a disability pension, claiming one ear had been damaged during an IED incident that he had not been anywhere nearby. As a vet, he was eagerly recruited by several tech companies. Cranky from a reduced Klonopin and Zoloft ration, and people saying, "thank you for your service," Henry found working for others challenging.

He had been toying with small computer hacks since Iraq, and after hearing Michael describe the scams her parents ran, believed he had found the perfect partner. They brainstormed how to work together although she found most of his ideas far-fetched. He jokingly called these sessions crime school.

Michael was no fool. She thought of him as a useful idiot and made sure he "accidentally" saw her topless occasionally to keep him "in the pocket."

The Scottsdale scam was a nonstarter at the gym with cameras everywhere, so Michael proposed something simple. Fleecing rich techies, she met there. Henry wanted something big. He had heard about a ransomware attack in Atlanta, holding various parts of the city government hostage. Michael doubted he was up to the task.

In the meantime, they ran a few break-ins. Michael in a bikini near the beach clubs, finding a rich techie took about ten minutes. After accepting a date, she would drop an AirTag tracking device in his beach bag, Henry, using an RF matching device, would open the date's garage while they were out, override the alarm and was careful to steal only a few expensive things. A fence she knew in Phoenix paid them a decent amount.

When the Covid raves started in the Hollywood Hills, Michael tapped a "Molly" connection from college and opened shop for eager party goers. She wore the blonde wig, so hopefully no one might recognize her, and made good money. Henry came along sometimes, hoping to get lucky. His chin beard all but nixed that. The raves were wild. Drinking and drugging, dancing to loud music, sometimes the cops were called. Lots of young nearly rich people from Silicon Beach attended.

So far, Michael's scams didn't have her sleeping with anyone to make a score; rather she had teased and tempted, dancing in the crowd, rubbing up just enough to have some techie begging. For a large payday, she figured if she found the right mark, she could handle it, since she wasn't regularly sleeping with anyone.

When the gyms finally opened, she looked for tech company logos on gym bags and fleeces. Like rock tours, tech companies were big on swag. Then she found Mona and started monitoring her workouts. She lived on the canals, was married to the often-absent founder of an app company called Banshee and complained about him often. When she met the "brogrammers" in their logo gear at a rave, her plan fell into place. She proposed that they target Banshee.

"I want to come to the gym," Henry said one night.

"You've never exercised in your life. Your muscles are mush."

"You could train me next to her."

"You just want to look at her ass."

"No, no, research. See what I can pick up from a technical end."

"Forget it. We can make this work if your computer skills are as advertised."

"I've got mad skills," he said.

"Shut up, Henry. Get to work."

Henry stayed up for two days and studied the apps that Banshee offered. He checked on "dark web" sites, finding little of value from the Romanian or Russian hackers who might have worked on the code. A long exchange with a friend who lived in the high desert town of Landers gave Henry insight into various ways he could steal their code and insert it into the server. The guy also talked up Bitcoin, declaring it would be the real currency after the militias took over the government, turning Henry into a believer.

"Bitcoin is the future. Untraceable. You can't even see it except for a string of words," Henry said, parroting what his friend had

told him.

"I heard the FBI learned how to get it back," she replied.

"That's one case. Much bigger deal. They're not going to have anything to do with this. Believe me. And the price is going up. That million could be two in a few months. Besides, a million in cash, what can you do with it?"

"Get the fuck out of here is what I can do with it," she replied.

The hack was coming together. The tech blogs reported that Banshee was out for a new funding round, and probably a SPAC, this year's trendy buyout vehicle. To insert the ransomware, Michael gave up her long-standing resistance to sleeping with brogrammers and with Mona. For half a million in cash, no problem.

Henry went to the Banshee office at lunch to see who the caterers were and promptly applied for a delivery job so he could get some inside read of the company and who they might target.

Rusty was first, and he crashed hard from the "love drug". She had no problem installing the bug. It worked great, and Henry followed along with the code Rusty was writing, then did his own with the ransomware hack included. It would look just like Rusty's code. Working days and jamming all night, he was no joy for Michael to live with, as his eating and bathing habits fell by the wayside. His constant consultation on the project with Facebook friends built up to a moment where Michael declared he could share his half with whomever he wanted, but do not think about sharing hers.

Her night with Mona got her the Wi-Fi password and as Mona slept, she inserted the malware into the server. They baited the hook by starting to slow down only one app. Longworth, under extreme pressure, bit on the ransom demand hard. It was almost too easy to get him to offer the million in cash. Henry wanted to wait a few more days for the ransom after hearing how stressed Longworth sounded. Delivering lunch each day to Banshee, he sensed the tension, and liked it. Why not string him along? Henry got off on that. Let him squirm, maybe have him add some bitcoin to the ransom.

His survivalist army buddy had continued to tout digital currency being the next big thing. CNBC and CNN tracked its dramatic price swings; FinTech companies like Robinhood and Square set up trading platforms for the average investor, who during the darkest days of quarantine had flocked to them. Many people were working from home, and tales of overnight bitcoin millionaires burned up the Slack channels of young professionals. People were using it to buy Tesla's. Gas stations were selling it through ATM-type machines.

Michael, showing she had paid some attention at ASU, disagreed, calling Crypto "tulips," a reference to the Dutch investment craze in the 1600s. If she couldn't touch it, forget it. She was old fashioned that way.

"We're not waiting. July 4th is the perfect time," she said.

Henry whined at first, but saw she wasn't going to give in. He wondered if she would let him screw her laying on all the money, like in the movies.

The return of the Marina fireworks would bring huge crowds of people. The whole district would be a chaotic mess for the evening, fireworks painting the sky. With everyone looking up to the west, it would be perfect for them to make the exchange and get out.

Studying a Marina map, she liked the Ballona marsh nearby, with a trail through bushes and tall reeds, and easy access to the main north south drag of Lincoln Blvd.

Henry liked the marsh too.

15

Chapter 15

Venice holiday crowds returned to the beach, getting ready for the fireworks later in the evening, pretending that the dark hand of Covid was passing. Paloma and Neighbor Dave dodged traffic and pulled up in the driveway, much to the delight of Prewash, who had been lounging on the porch.

Ellis was pacing in the yard, bummed about not finding the guitar after rescuing both guys who stole it. Ralston wouldn't and Willem felt he couldn't press charges, so their threats were toothless, and they had to let Evan and Husani walk away. Not great for his morale. Ralston was a dick, but they knew that going in. Bringing in Mountain Moran still had to be dealt with. He had to put all that aside today and deal with Banshee and the money drop.

Paloma was bummed too, but hoped pizzas from Abbot's would cheer Ellis up. Dave grabbed some beers. They would go at Gary again tomorrow, inspired by Duffy's Son of Sam story.

Today he would be attached at the hip to Ralston at the Forum concert.

Waiting for the where and when of the money drop, they needed at least a generic plan to cover the exchange on the 4th of July. Everyone was surprised that he had that amount of cash when banks were closed.

"In my letter I told him the drop has to be an exchange, money for a provable code he can check on a cellular SD reader," Ellis said. "And to use the Airtag."

"Make the switch outside, if possible," Neely added.

Dave nodded. "Yes, better to follow with the drone cam."

"The bag he's going to carry is going to weigh north of twenty-two pounds, so it might slow down whoever takes the drop."

"Is that all a million dollars weighs?" Paloma asked.

"That's a lot of hundies!" Neely added.

"We break up into teams, one watching the exchange using the drone while the others can bracket the drop point," Paloma continued.

"Drone has about two miles or less of transmission, so we have to be right on them. Then the Airtag will take over."

"Traffic will be a bear tonight. Fireworks from nine to nine-thirty; the Marina and beach will be so packed. Let's hope the swap is inland."

"Longworth gets the SD card with the release code; we follow with the drone and get the money back?" Neely wondered.

"In a righteous world, yeah, fuck 'em. And we bring some detective stuff with us in case we catch them," Paloma said.

"Detective stuff?" Dave asked.

"Yup."

While waiting for Longworth's call, Paloma still wondered how to convince Willem or Ralston to press charges and scare the truth out of the Brentwood brats. The LA City jail could do that.

"Ellis, you and Dave spot him with the drone. Neely should ride with the Kid, and I'll be with Leon. That gives us flexibility if it all goes to shit," Paloma said. "Friggin' Fourth of July. They're smart. It'll be crazy everywhere."

"All goes to shit?" Ellis asked.

"I read a Michener book where he described a native American attack on soldiers on their land. They would stay up all night planning, then two minutes into the battle, it was every man for himself. Gotta be flexible."

Longworth had returned from his bike ride to an irate Mona, complaining about his "fuckin' spies" coming around the house to question her about who she gave the wireless password to and check the router. He shrugged and said he was trying to save the company. She handed him the envelope as he went off to shower. Mona wasn't sure if she should text Michael and tell her these detectives were asking questions about her.

Everyone was waiting on the porch, now chowing down Neighbor Dave's fabulous pulled pork sandwiches. When the call from Longworth finally came, it was late, around 7:55. The drop would be on the westside, at the Ballona Marsh at 8:55 pm. There Longworth would be given a coded SD card to transmit and verify, Riina and Marik standing by at the office to check, then if it was real, administer the code to relieve the attack. The Airtag they had given Longworth would help track the money.

They pulled the marsh up on Google Maps.

"Jeez, that place sucks," Neely offered. "It's dark with lots of bushes to get lost in."

"Near enough to the Marina tonight to really suck, right as the fireworks start. They are looking to use the total chaos down there. Good call because the streets are going to be jammed," Ellis added. "Let's go. We don't have much time to get there."

Leon spoke up. "Keep the alleys in mind if you have to dodge traffic." He was a true man of the streets.

16

Chapter 16

July 4 Evening

Ellis and Neighbor Dave drove to the wetlands in heavy traffic and Parked along Jefferson Blvd. where there was a permanent camp of dozens of battered RVs. They squeezed into a spot across the street. While Dave unloaded the drone, Ellis went down the line of RVs until he found a guy, who for a hundred dollars and a pre-roll would let them set up inside his RV. His name was Walter. Dave put the drone base in the space between the two RVs, and Walter offered to move his folding chair to hide it from anyone walking by.

"What is that smell? Something die in here?" Ellis said, squinting and making a face as they set up on the small Formica table.

"Kimchi, I think," Dave replied, firing up the screen.

Paloma and Leon sat at one of the benches near the path entrance, looking like a couple hanging out, eating sandwiches. If Michael was involved and walked by in disguise, Leon would recognize her. If the drone showed someone on the path, they could enter the marsh from either entrances. Neely and the

Kid would be parked at one of the Marina streets near Lincoln Blvd. with good access to follow in any direction.

Dave reminded Ellis of the drone limitations in this part of town. Any direction but west, where the tall Marina condo towers interfered with his signal should be okay. With backyard fireworks going off everywhere, the wetlands were one of the lone dark, clear places. Following the money would be another story. Everyone in pursuit would have to move quickly before the drone was out of range and the Airtag took over. Then they would be relying on Bluetooth signals.

Paloma watched Longworth squeeze his Tesla between two RVs and park on the hard gravel. He walked to the entrance, carrying a gold-colored metal briefcase, not the duffle they implored him to use. Walking into the wetlands at night carrying a gold briefcase—might as well put a neon sign in his hand. His arm was fully extended under the twenty-plus pounds of the money. He tried unsuccessfully not to look at them on the bench while he reached for his phone.

Ellis had instructed Longworth to keep his phone turned on in his pocket so they could hear what was going on. Everyone wore earbuds and were grouped on the call. Neighbor Dave finished putting tape over the red lights on the drone, shrugged a "one more felony" look to Ellis and prepared to launch. With the souped-up battery pack, he figured he had at most thirty to forty minutes of flight time before he would need to land.

"I'm going in," Longworth told them.

Ellis nodded and Dave launched the drone while Ellis controlled the camera, tilting it down to look for Longworth on the path. His plan once he found him was to switch to the heat sensor to see if there was anyone lurking in the reeds, staying wide at first so Dave could get his bearings.

"Okay, I see him. Let's do a quick infrared sweep then zoom in." The gold-colored briefcase stood out in the darkened marsh.

"She's got 'tats' where?" the Thorazine Kid exclaimed.

"Oh man, you wouldn't believe it. It's like Fantasia coming to life up the side of her body," Neely said, slapping on the dashboard. "I guess you get a discount working at a parlor. Get this, she wants to open a chocolate store. Bean to bar. Do the whole thing."

They were parked near the Marina marketplace, muted but listening to the group call.

The Kid considered him. "What's with you and cooks?"

"Dunno, I guess the way to my heart."

"Stop, don't say it. Probably because you're stoned all the time and like to eat, though you seem to burn it up."

"Oh man, we were burnin' it up last night after I finally got that Husani guy to shut up and go to sleep. I don't like babysitting."

"Ready to tour? I am. It's too quiet working on guitars, even with Hendrix booming from my studio speakers."

"Staying up early on a tour bus? I'm getting there, although I heard about the new 'improved' Delta offspring of Covid that sounds pretty rough. Things could shut down again. I guess I could quarantine with Dina," he said, all smiles and delighted at the prospect. "Make and eat chocolate all day."

They heard Ellis talking with Longworth.

"Guy's fuckin' crazy, you know that right?" Neely said.

"My kinda crazy. A hot wife, a house on the canals and a pool full of money. Sign me up, coach," the Kid replied.

"Wild night. Glad not to be working the valet stand for this one," Leon said, looking at the crowds passing by. Leon had learned to filter faces because at times it got overwhelming. He could recognize someone he saw once on a bus five years ago, someone he sat next to eating breakfast when he was seventeen. He never forgot a face.

"Pent-up celebrations. Where do people get all the fireworks?" she asked.

"Everywhere. My dad used to tell this story about a fourth of July when he and his pal Roger were on Grant Street in San Fran. He said you had to go from doorway to doorway, there was so much firepower on the streets. Three blocks took an hour."

"Bad craziness."

Paloma and Leon listened to the group phone call. Everyone was muted but would hear. Leon studied a map of the area to locate what was around them as two joggers passed by, neither one he recognized.

Neighbor Dave took the drone high as Ellis widened out and switched to infrared, looking for the heat of anyone on the path or in the weeds. Satisfied, they zoomed back to Longworth, now heading to the bend where the path turned away from Lincoln Blvd., entering the remotest part of the wetlands. Longworth used a second phone to call his office to triple-check that his engineers were standing by for him to transmit the code he would be given. They had taken precautions that whatever code they were given was isolated from the main server in case it was a trick.

"Don't go any farther down the path," Ellis said into Longworth's earbud. "It gets kinda hairy the further in you go. Let them come to you."

"Look, they said walk down the path and that's what I have been doing. I can go in a bit more."

Ellis shook his head. The further in he got, the harder it would be for someone to help him on the path if he needed it.

There was a blur across the screen. "What was that? Fireworks?" Dave asked. "Widen out."

Ellis zoomed out, working the joystick.

"What the hell is that?"

On the screen a drone came into view. A big drone, with six powerful rotors and two "arms" dangling down with claws at the end. Dave's drone was dwarfed by it.

"Shit, it's a heavy-lift drone. A huge one. With fucking arms," Dave said for all to hear.

"Is that you?" Longworth said. Ellis wasn't sure if he was talking to them or the drone.

"No. It's them. Don't talk to us," Ellis said.

Dave kept his drone up above them with Ellis zooming in as far as he could. The other drone had not seen them.

"Paloma, go, go. They're using a drone, at the bend near Lincoln."

"It has two arms with claws on the end!" Longworth whispered.

"Get out of there, man, this is no good," Ellis implored.

A male voice from the drone said, "Take the envelope the claw just dropped. The SD card is in there. When you are satisfied with the code, we will take the briefcase," a male voice said. "Do it now."

Longworth was shaken by the appearance of the drone, big and loud hovering above him. He grabbed the envelope and ripped it open, pulling out the SD card. He put the briefcase down to get his card reader/transmitter out of its case to send the code.

The drone lunged towards him, six large blades slicing, claws extended, pushing him away from the briefcase.

"Whoever is flying that drone is a pro," Dave said. They watched the claw paw at the handle and finally grab it and lift the briefcase up, then lunge at Longworth, catching his knees.

"Shit, they're grabbing the money!"

While he was doubled over, the drone swung again at his forehead, knocking him down.

"Take over the camera?" Ellis said, putting the joystick by Dave as he raced to the RV door.

"Yeah, go help him," Dave replied. "I'll narrate what I see."

With Longworth dazed on the ground, the drone strained to lift the weight of the briefcase. Ellis ran to the path while Paloma and Leon ran up from the west. Dave brought the drone down a little lower for a better angle on what was happening.

"He's bleeding, guys," Dave said, "and the drone is still there. Try to grab it."

From his angle, he couldn't tell if it was having trouble lifting. Longworth lay on the path, dazed with the drone hovering over him. He struggled to get the SD card into the reader and hit send. His hands were covered with blood.

Paloma raced down the path while Leon split off to come in the back way. Ellis came running up as the large drone rose, turning as though to look at him. The two claw arms holding the briefcase gave the drone the look of some giant insect.

"It's really big, Dave," Ellis shouted as he ran to Longworth, whose face was covered with blood while the code was sent. He looked up dazed as Ellis held the arm of his sweatshirt to the head wound.

Paloma arrived in time to hear Longworth shouting that the code was a bust. The drone was higher and starting to lean away.

"The drone is heading towards Lincoln. I don't think they have seen me. I'll stay above and track them," Dave said.

Ellis looked up at Paloma. "I got this. You guys follow the Airtag."

"There is no Airtag. I left it off," Longworth groaned.

Ellis looked at Paloma, and with the slightest shake of her head, she was off down the path, unmuting her phone, telling Leon to meet her at the car.

"It's headed towards Lincoln," Dave called out. "Damn, there's a lot of fireworks smoke." He could hear the big booms from the Marina reverberating off the towers.

Joining Leon on the dirt path, Paloma looked toward Lincoln and at all the red taillights. Traffic was barely crawling. Police flares had changed traffic lanes to accommodate the crush around the Marina. Paloma shouted, "Forget the car," running down to the line of RVs where many bicycles in various stages of repair were strewn about. Leon shouted, "Who's Walter?"

Walter raised his hand and stood up, like in grade school.

"Any of these work?" Paloma asked, pointing to a mess of bikes. Walter nodded his head and pointed to a few leaning against a bench. They grabbed two and threw a couple of twenties down as they raced off to the boulevard.

Ellis helped Longworth to his feet. Back at the office, the engineers, led by Riina, told them. It was a fake. He was livid.

"A fucking drone? What the hell?" he shouted. "You guys prepared for that?"

Ellis held him steady, putting Longworth's hand on the

sweatshirt against the gushing cut. "Our drone is tracking him now, so yes, we were prepared."

"The Airtag. I thought . . .," Longworth said.

"It's okay. Let's get you some help."

Dave watched as the drone turned onto Lincoln.

"Everybody, seems like they might use Lincoln as a drone path, crossing the creek still heading north." From the map on his screen, Dave figured, *if they knew we were following, they would have cut us off at the creek.* It was a large drone and normally would outfly him, except for the weight of the briefcase. Dave's calculations from his sparse knowledge of heavy-lift drones, he figured it was close to its weight limit.

Quick walking out of the marsh, Ellis wanted to take Longworth to an Urgent Care nearby, but Longworth insisted they go back to his house on the canals.

"Dave, can you keep doing both? I'm gonna take Mister Longworth home," he said on the group phone call.

"Uh, yeah. Still going north on Lincoln." Dave was keenly aware that every minute of flight, his range was decreasing. Had he anticipated a drone, Dave knew of a few "under the desk" devices he would have loved to use. Now he needed to upset the path of the drone to see if it was now on autopilot returning to its base.

"Paloma stood as she pedaled, Leon with her. "We're coming out of the marsh near Fiji way. Where is it, Dave?"

"Ahead of you, towards McDonald's."

Paloma grabbed looks into the sky, ahead of her for the drone lights, or a reflection off the briefcase. The air was smokey from fireworks that seemed to be going off in every backyard. She raced between the stalled cars, Leon to her right. The marine layer of fog coming in off the Pacific didn't help visibility.

"How can I not see a friggin' flying gold briefcase?" she said for the phone audience.

Dave dropped his drone down and turned the camera for a closer look at the large drones' structure, hoping for a weak point. It was big. With no match for the big drone, surprise could be on his side.

"Neely, you guys over by Marina Towers? I'm going to see if I can force him to the marketplace side."

"Might take a bit to cross Lincoln, but moving now," the Kid said. He looked at Neely, who nodded.

Walter, the RV owner, popped his head in.

"Everything okay?" he said.

"Come here and guide this camera for me."

"What?" Walter was baked.

"You ever used a joystick? Old computer games maybe?" Dave asked.

Walter stared at him. "Like Atari?"

"Just like that. Get over here, man."

Walter came over and Dave gave him a ten-second course in moving the camera. He had him widen out to keep the drone on the screen. Keep it simple.

"Everybody, I'm going to try to slow him down, see if it's on autopilot or being flown manually. Then with any luck I can push it East to the Marketplace."

Dave's drone was faster since it wasn't carrying twenty-three pounds or so. Now speed versus battery life came into play. Dave shrugged and said "fuck it" under his breath. He was about to dive down to engage when the image on the screen shook. Walter yelled. Suddenly Dave needed to wrestle with the controller to stabilize the drone. Jeez, the backyard fireworks were relentless, with rockets exploding along the boulevard.

Driving Longworth back to the house on the canals, Ellis hoped they could get to Admiralty Way, where traffic would be better. Already there were knots of people leaving the Marina, crossing the boulevard. Really large crowds would follow, since the main fireworks' "blow off" had reverberated through the Marina a few minutes earlier.

Maneuvering his drone down to about five yards to one side of the larger one, Dave got his first good look. Six blades and two claw arms clutching the metal briefcase. Dave needed to expose his drone to see if the other was locked in on a GPS heading or being manually controlled. It didn't take long. Dave pulled out into the path of the big drone; it made a quick jerk to the right. Someone was controlling it for sure.

And that someone was struggling.

The large payload hanging below the drone was acting like a pendulum weight and the pilot fought to stop the swaying as it tried to evade Dave. Sudden moves would make the big drone unstable. Dave hoped he could use that to bring it down. He followed the drone as exploding fireworks blinded the camera.

"Are people shooting at you?" Walter asked.

"Fireworks. You're doing great. Keep the camera on him."

Passing McDonald's and nearing the Marina Marketplace, Paloma spotted the drone, high above Lincoln Blvd. The gold-colored metal case did a great job reflecting light. She wondered how many other people saw it as fireworks painted the sky.

"We see it!" she exclaimed to everyone on the phone. "Rocking back and forth."

"Yeah, giving him a hard time right now." Dave did his best Chuck Yeager impression. Walter was doing his best to hold the camera on the drone.

"Uh, passing the Ralphs, turning towards Maxella. I don't see you though."

The explosions in the air got heavier as the big drone headed northeast over the Marketplace. Dave wondered how long the batteries on both drones would last. Whoever was guiding the other drone had to be nearby.

"Guys, they're probably chewing up batteries with that weight," he said as a rocket swooshed by the camera. "Is there a park nearby where they might land?"

Ellis was stuck in traffic, trying to get Longworth home. "Could they put it down in a backyard?" he asked.

"Tricky with trees and wires. It's a big-ass machine."

"Paloma, can you guys still see it?" Ellis asked.

"Lost it behind a hotel. We are taking a detour to cut through to Maxella," she said as they leapt a curb and went down a grassy area between the hotel and apartment building, the bikes rattling on uneven ground, threatening to come apart.

Holding a burning emergency flare in your hand is not the safest idea, yet it was perfect for the Thorazine Kid to stop traffic, so Neely could get his car across Lincoln. Acting like a concerned citizen, he leapt out into the first lane of creeping traffic, waving the flare with one hand while pumping his arm furiously, like a traffic cop, signaling Neely to pull out. As he moved to the next lane, a Tesla driver rolled down his window to shout something at the Kid until their eyes met, for a few seconds. That's all it took for the "maniacal danger" that is the Thorazine Kid to be transmitted. The Tesla driver rolled up his window and looked at his shoes.

With the flare spewing flame and fumes, the Kid's eyes burning, he managed to get Neely across six lanes of Lincoln Blvd. traffic. After tossing the flare down a sewer drain, he heard Paloma say she saw the drone. Looking in that direction he caught a glimpse of the briefcase, hanging from the big drone, reflecting light before going behind a large apartment building. Backyard fireworks lit up the sky.

Dave had a decision to make. His drone was nearing the far end of its range. When that happened, it would automatically turn around and return to the base station outside the RV. He needed to interfere with the big drone enough so that everyone on the ground could catch up and follow. Naked eye visuals were getting harder as the big drone entered an area near Glencoe Blvd., which was flanked by six-story apartment buildings.

"Fuck it, I'm going in," Dave said to everyone on the phone call. "Walter, you got the hang of it? Think you can keep the camera on the drone if I start moving around it?"

"This shit's real, right?" he said, not taking his eyes off the screen.

"You bet."

"Okay, I got it," Walter said, glancing over at Dave, as though he were from a distant planet.

More fireworks exploded, the camera flaring each time and causing Walter to jump back in his seat. Dave pushed his drone in front again, and the big drone took evasive action, setting it to rocking, the pilot struggling to keep control.

Then the big drone surged towards him, trying to get the

briefcase into the blades of Dave's drone.

"Dude, look out!" Walter cried out, seeing the floating briefcase head towards them.

Dave managed to drop down and to the side, losing speed in the maneuver. He figured he had one more try. He needed to destabilize the drone enough that the weight would bring it down. He needed to attack the props. Drone "kamikaze" might be the only way once Paloma and Leon were close.

Where the big drone had legs and the claw arms that acted like legs, Dave's drone had two skids that hung down on either side of the camera to land on. If he could get the skid into one of the big drone blades, that might break it off and unbalance the big drone. It was a precision move that Dave had never imagined before. If he missed, those blades would chew up his drone, sending it to earth in pieces.

"Dave, are you on it? We are in a canyon of apartment buildings and see nothing but friggin' fireworks," Paloma said, pedaling the rickety bike furiously.

"We saw it for a second then lost it," Neely added. "Maybe over at Glencoe."

Another explosion in the sky. Walter dropped the joystick, shook his head then picked it up.

"Walter, where is he? Where did he go?"

"Uh, not sure. Let me twist this around."

There was a flash on the screen, different from the fireworks. The big drone had maneuvered in front of him and was now swinging the briefcase. Right at the camera.

"This is crazy; I'm walking," Longworth said as the Tesla sat in the stalled Admiralty Way traffic, full of cars and people leaving the Marina. The bleeding had stopped but Ellis wondered if

Longworth could make the walk.

He crept the Tesla into the lot at the Ritz and Longworth gave the guy a fifty to park the car. He would have someone get it later. Removing the sweatshirt from his forehead, Longworth looked in the side mirror to see that the large purple bump was forming, and blood smeared all over his face.

They set out to walk the rest of the way on the now jammed sidewalks, fireworks going off everywhere, even from the back of a pickup truck.

In an instant, Dave gave the drone maximum lift to avoid the briefcase.

On the way up, one of the rotors hit his camera, cracking the lens. Walter jumped. Dave told Walter to tilt the camera so he could see the big drones next move, but it was frozen from the hit. He rotated his drone to see two of the six rotors damaged on the big drone that now was swinging radically back and forth.

"We see it," Paloma shouted. "Heading down Glencoe. We're about a block away."

"Costco at the end of the street, right?" Ellis said, walking with Longworth. "Big empty parking lot. Gotta be the base. Neely, can you get there? We had to ditch the car. We're walking to his house."

This was it. The last gasps of power and range for Dave's drone. With the big drone swinging back and forth and two rotors out, it was time to bring it down any way he could. Kamikaze. Just drop down from above and take out a rotor or two while it is swinging, surely destroying his drone.

A bright flash blinded the camera, then another. Walter kept the camera wide.

"People are shooting at the drone from on top of the apartment buildings. It's lower now, the perfect target. Damn, there's serious firepower," Paloma said as she and Leon pedaled furiously to catch up. Dave pushed his drone higher. He could tell the big drone pilot was struggling with the swing that was compounded by a missing rotor. The fireworks were bouncing off the big gold briefcase hanging down, and a few hit the drone. Leon and Paloma hoped the drone didn't go down on an apartment roof.

"It's coming down. Costco is a block away. We're under it," she said.

"We're coming up Beach Street," Neely said as he gunned the engine.

In front of the Marina Marriott, Longworth started to sway. Ellis grabbed his arm and lowered him onto the short wall by the parking lot.

"I just need a minute. We're almost there," he said to Ellis.

"They're closing in on the drone. It's going down near Costco."

"Does it still have the money? Let's go there," he said, wobbly, trying to rise off the wall.

"Don't think so. You're not running a marathon today. Anyway, people are shooting fireworks at it. Crazy."

"That's my money!"

"And Paloma and our guys are on it. You sure you don't want urgent care?"

"Just one more minute," he said, staying seated on the wall.

Paloma and Leon followed the descending, wobbling drone

into the Costco parking lot, headed for the side of the building where the shopping carts were stored. A lone car was parked nearby in the lot.

"Neely, Kid. The far side of the building, where the carts are," she said.

Racing across the lot, the drone came down fast, listing badly to one side. They could see the silhouette of someone standing near the car, working the controls. On landing, the briefcase slid, causing the drone, and everything, to slide sideways. The rotors smashed into the pavement, sending splintered plastic in all directions. The man running the controller hit the deck to avoid the shrapnel.

Dave landed his drone nearby in the parking lot, having performed above and beyond what it was designed for. Walter looked over, his eyes wide. Dave nodded to him. "Great job," as Walter, his shirt soaked through, slumped back in the chair.

Michael was crawling and reaching out to pry the briefcase from the drone, so Paloma aimed her bike and ran over her outstretched arm. She howled but grabbed at the case while Paloma slid the dismount.

The car lurched forward at Leon, and Paloma yelled to him. He let the bike roll out from under him, smashing into the car, jumping out of the way. The driver then backed the car up and threw open the passenger door for Michael to jump in with the case. Instead, it was Leon jumping in through the door, his forearm smashing into the driver, who had tried to open his door and escape.

Michael freed the case and was holding it with her good arm when Paloma ran at her. She swung it at Paloma to keep her back as she moved towards the car.

"Where's the SD card with the real code?"

"Fuck off," she said, swinging the case again. "We gave it to him."

Paloma timed the grab when the swing was ending, going for the handle while trying to trip Michael up. Michael, who worked in a gym, was in good shape, strong arms and good balance. Paloma, the surfer, was too. They struggled with the case. She ducked a wild punch and tried to take Michael down. Heaving the case back and forth, trying to rip it out of each other's hands, Michael gave a big heave and Paloma lost her grip.

So did Michael and the case flew into the "corral" of shopping carts.

Henry fell out the door and slammed to the ground with Leon on top of him. He struggled and got free. Leon's foot was tangled in the seat belt. While Leon was trying to free himself, Henry went to the trunk and came out with a tire iron crowbar. He went to smash down when Leon got his foot free and rolled to the side, the iron bar banging on the asphalt. When he raised it again, Leon shot out his leg and caught Henry's knee, pushing the leg into a position it was not meant to be in. Henry howled as he half swung the tire iron, then dropped to the ground. Leon grabbed him up, and half threw him into the open trunk.

Like a cat, Michael leapt onto the rows of red shopping carts and on all fours sped down to where she thought the case had landed. It had slipped between two rows of carts. Paloma followed alongside, crouched down, realizing that Michael was cornered in the corral. She quietly told Neely where she was, then realized that her earbuds were gone, and she had been disconnected from the group. She saw Michael prone across the tops of the carts, reaching her arm down between two rows for the case.

No time to wait.

Vaulting up onto the carts, Paloma ran along the uneven surface. She calculated the jump onto Michael's back and leapt, only to land on Michael having rolled over holding the case in front of her, knocking the wind out of them both. Damn, she was quick. Pushing the recovering Paloma off her, Michael tried to roll off the carts, but Paloma caught her leg and held on. As Michael hung over the side of the carts, she tried to swing the case at Palomas hand. Instead, Neely grabbed the case as the Thorazine Kid pulled her to the ground.

"Good to see you," Paloma said, reaching for breath.

"You too," Neely replied, pointing to the case he was holding.

"Get the fuck off of me," Michael said as the Kid took some "detective things," zip ties, out of his pocket.

"Where's the real SD card? Do I have to search you?"

"You got it in the marsh," she exclaimed.

"Nope, that was a dummy."

"Fuck off," she said to Paloma, getting furious that Henry hadn't given them the real SD card. It was supposed to be a simple exchange, but idiot Henry insisted on using the drone that his pal had dropped off. She figured he got his thrills from being an asshole.

Leon dragged Henry around the car and dropped him on the ground. He held up a plastic baggie he had removed from Henry's pocket with an SD card in it.

"You fuckin' moron," Michael yelled at him. Henry tried to look up at her, but his mind was swimming from getting punched in the head.

Leon asked for a knife. The Thorazine Kid tossed his knife

over and Neely, handing the case to Paloma, followed. They zip tied their hands, cut the seat belts out of the back seat and used them to tie their hands over their heads. The Kid and Paloma did the same with Michael, who cursed at them and had a stream of words for Henry. Neely took their wallets before buckling them into the front seats as well. For grins, they took their belts and secured their legs to the bar that adjusted the seat for leg room.

Paloma grabbed the keys, popped the hood, and locked the car. She found the battery and wrestled the corroded battery wire until it came off. Since she had their IDs, she felt okay about leaving them tied up, locked in the car in an empty remote parking lot for a few hours. She wanted check the SD card and the money.

Neighbor Dave drove up to pick up his drone. It had survived the battle and the fireworks.

"You were something else," Leon said to Dave. "I've never seen anything like that."

"The little drone that could, I guess," Dave replied, examining the scorch marks from the firework hits. "What are you going to do with them?

"Well, we have their IDs, and they are locked in the car for a while," she said.

Leon held up the baggie with the SD card. "We need to see if this is the real code."

"How about I keep an eye on our friends until your guys figure out if it's real and what Longworth wants to do. I'm kinda beat," Dave said. "And I want to check out the drone they were using." To Dave, this was a science project.

"The traffic is clearing up," Paloma said. "Let's go to the canals."

17

Chapter 17

July 4 Night

The little caravan headed west along a relatively clear Washington Blvd. The crowds from the Marina had cleared out through the smokey air. Backyard fireworks would continue into the night. Driving over the Linnie canal bridge, they came up on Ellis and Longworth approaching the house on foot. Paloma called out and slid her bike next to Ellis, with a big smile. She saw the bloody sweatshirt against Longworth's head.

"He doing okay? What happened to the Tesla?"

"Parked for now. He didn't want urgent care."

"We have something that will make him feel a lot better."

Neely's car slowly passed them with the Kid, all crazy-man grinning, pointing to the briefcase he held up.

"No kidding." Ellis was catching up. His phone had died a while ago.

"And maybe the real SD card. Hat trick if you include Michael and Henry tied up in a locked car in the Costco parking lot. Dave's watching them."

Longworth looked at them, then punched in the door code and they entered. Mona rushed to Longworth when she saw the bloody sweatshirt and led them into the kitchen. Putting the case down on the counter, Longworth opened it to see the cash was still there. None of the FAQ people had ever seen a million in cash. It was hard not to stare.

"Try this one," Leon said, handing him the SD card.

Inserting it into the bloodied reader, Longworth called Riina, still at the office with a few brogrammers and instructed them to try the code.

"The million doesn't matter if we don't have the code. Will they get away?"

"Nope, they're tied up in the Costco parking lot. Our guy is watching them. Some ex-military guy and a woman named Michael," Paloma said, directing her eyes to Mona.

Mona looked like she had been slapped. The detectives she hated were correct and she was wrong. For a woman of recent privilege that was hard to take. Michael had thrilled her emotionally and sexually, but now she saw it for what it was, just a con.

"Here's Dave's number if you want to talk to them. You can tell us how much police involvement you want."

She led them into the expansive family room that overlooked the canal. It was a well-appointed room with a huge screen TV and bookcases on one wall that held photos and software awards.

"I'll get something to clean him up," she said, stalking off.

Longworth sat down and continued talking to Riina, nervously waiting for the code to be verified. The apps had really slowed down.

Another wall was adorned with original, framed Fillmore

and Winterland posters by Stanley Mouse and Rick Griffin. Lit up next to them were three guitars hanging on the wall, tiny spotlights raking the fretboards.

Mona came back with what looked like a camping first aid kit and opened it to clean Longworth's head gash. Her impatience with him was obvious. Paloma elbowed Ellis and with a silent head nod led him towards the back wall as Neely and the Kid watched. Hanging next to an Eddie Van Halen Fender Stratocaster and a Don Felder Les Paul was a Gretsch Country Gentleman guitar with no name plate underneath like the others. Paloma took out her phone, which was just about dead, and pulled up the auction house photos of the Harrison guitar and held it up to the small plate on the head with the serial number. The Thorazine Kid slid over and looked at the phone, then the guitar and continuing the pantomime, gave a silent freakout face refined on tour buses late at night. Neely reacted with what Paloma called a surfer wipeout face.

The serial number matched. It was the friggin' George Harrison Country Gentleman guitar, buffed and beautiful, hanging on the wall.

Paloma shook her head as Ellis looked over at Longworth. How the fuck did this guitar wind up here? Did Longworth know Evan and have the guitar stolen? Had he used a cutout as Duffy had described to do the first and or second parts?

"These are great guitars," Ellis said, his eyes imploring Neely and the Kid to be quiet.

Longworth turned, the phone still to his ear. "Yeah. Auctions. I phone in." He held up his finger, listening to the phone. His posture improved as he pumped his fist.

"You sure? Wait, let me see for myself," he said, pulling the phone down from his face and stabbing at one of his apps.

"Okay, we got it," he exclaimed. "You guys did it! The correct code and I got my ransom back. Now get to work on a patch to prevent them from getting in again. Bonus if you do it now!" Longworth was smiling as Mona tried to apply a large Band-Aid.

"Where'd you get this one?" Paloma asked innocently.

"Just got it. I tried to buy that at auction a couple of years ago. Then got it in a private sale. I'm paying a premium, in cash. In fact, that's why I had the money. It's an extremely rare guitar."

Neely was about to explode, like Roger Rabbit trying not to react to the "shave and a haircut" knocking on the door. He failed.

"It's George Harrison's fucking guitar that he played on *Ed Sullivan*! Fucking stolen a week ago," he shouted.

"What are you talking about?" Longworth shouted back, dismissively, getting up from the couch.

Ellis stepped to him. "We were hired to find this guitar which Tommy Ralston purchased at auction two years ago and was stolen from a repair shop last week."

"No, I got it from a guy. It's legit."

"A guy? What's his name?"

"That's private. But it's legit, really."

"Bill of sale?"

"Not yet. I told you I hadn't paid him since I was using the cash for the ransom. It's okay. I'll have it tomorrow."

"We were hired to find and retrieve the guitar. This guitar. It is a piece of rock n' roll history. Lucky you haven't paid for it yet," Paloma said.

"You are wrong. It's mine." Longworth stood up, a little wobbly still.

"Where's the case?" Ellis said, reaching to take it down from the wall.

"Case? You're not taking it. I'll call the police."

"That would be refreshing," Paloma said. "But right now we are taking the guitar to the legal owner. Tommy Ralston. He's playing a benefit for the very same police right now at the Forum, so you can call the cops or your brogrammers over to defend you, but it won't be pretty."

One look at the wild eyes of Neely and the Thorazine Kid gave legitimacy to her statement. Rock history and guitars were enough to turn them into stoned, deranged "superheroes." Old ways die slowly.

"You try to take that guitar and you'll have to sue me to get paid. I have lots of lawyers," he said, his eyes getting a little swimmy.

Mona looked at Paloma with softer eyes. Then the daggers came out when she looked at Longworth. She was stuck with her husband's millions. She'd survive.

"You dope. I'll get the case," Mona said, stalking out of the room shaking her head. She had an iron-clad prenup. The fact that her husband had ruined the interlude with Michael, even though it turned out to be a con, might have played large in her decision.

Ellis hoped Benny saw his text, telling him to set up a ramp pass at the Forum for them. The Covid-19 First Responders Benefit was well underway, with RimShot closing the show. Neely at the wheel, took side streets with names like Centinela and Prairie, backyard fireworks still lighting up the smoky night. Ellis pounded on the seat, sitting in the back with Paloma and Leon, the Harrison guitar case across their laps.

"We found the friggin' guitar! I can't believe it," he said.

"We're gonna circle back to Longworth. "Him saying "I can't say" won't play," Paloma added.

"Gotta be sad sack Gary! He's been hanging around for a payday for years I bet," Neely opined.

"Didn't Longworth say he bid at auctions? Could be that moron cousin Paul remembered him and set it up with his steroid buddies," Ellis proposed.

Up front, the Thorazine Kid fired up a pre-roll.

"Getting them arrested is still up to Ralston or Willem. But we have the guitar, we got the ransomware, maybe we get paid, but FAQ is on the map." Ellis needed the wins. The road was a constant "siren's call" as more and more tours were going out to make up Covid-canceled shows.

"Did Benny reply? We're getting close and this guitar shouldn't be out in a crowd," Neely said, seeing himself as a protector of rock n' roll history.

"Yeah, turn off Prairie onto Pincay Drive. He gave security our names. Drive right down."

"Like the old days," The Kid remarked, taking his last toke from the pre-roll. Who didn't like pulling up to the backstage door, being waved in by security, especially at a crowded concert. "By the way, don't worry about not getting paid." He held up five banded bundles of hundreds. Fifty thousand dollars. "Took 'em for some insurance on the ride to Longworth's."

Baraka Murphy, one of the promoter reps, met them at the back door with "crew" passes allowing full access backstage. They walked past stacks of road cases with different band names on them, then a row of remote video camera operators, joysticks in hand, faces eerily lit by their screens. She led them to the curtain for the stage right floor area, usually sprinkled with a few special band guests. For this show, the area was packed with guests and musicians from the bands on the bill.

Standing inside the curtain as security was Mountain Moran. Baraka waved them in, Moran giving Ellis a squint as he walked past. Benny came speed-walking through the crowd and huddled with Ellis and Paloma, shaking his head in disbelief, pumping their hands. Ellis nodded to Neely, who handed the guitar to Thorazine Kid to take to the tuning station under the stage. He knew Jimmy Gomes, who took care of Ralston's guitars. As the Kid handed him the case, Jimmy's eyes got wide, nodded his head vigorously and fist-bumped the Kid.

RimShot was tearing through their set. The crowd of first responders had been going nuts all night. Ralston was wearing a #34 Fernando Valenzuela Dodger uniform shirt over his usual black-on-black outfit, leading the band through one of their anthemic hits, "Soupy's Girl."

Ellis and Paloma had their arms around each other, taking it all in, nodding hello to people they recognized. Paloma saw Soloff with a young blonde about her age hanging off him, again all dressed in black like Tommy.

Maggie was dancing with a few friends and frowned when she saw them. Maybe she would cheer up when she saw the guitar. Her cousin Paul was not to be seen. Ellis doubted he would miss an event like this. Maybe Longworth had tipped him off?

Gary stood at the bottom of the stage ramp like Hachiko, the loyal Japanese dog, waiting for his master, watching the band, with a bottle of water and a towel in his hand for Ralston, should he ask for it.

"You miss it," Paloma said, looking at him watching the show. "I totally get it." He looked at her, shrugged and laughed. "Obviously not enough." She pulled him in tighter.

"Soupy's Girl" ended, and Ralston went back to switch guitars. Jimmy casually held the freshly tuned Harrison Country Gentleman out for him to play.

"What the fuck?" Ralston shouted over the roar of the crowd. A quick look at the headstock and his mouth flew open. Jimmy nodded his head to offstage right where Paloma gave him a small wave. He looked for Maggie and Soloff, making hand gestures that said "WTF. Check this out."

Running up to the microphone, Ralston excitedly spoke to the crowd.

"Okay, for all you wonderful first responders out there," the masked crowd roared. "It's been an incredibly tough year-plus, and we've tried to make tonight special for you, so now we have something *really* special tonight. This guitar," he held it up, "*this guitar*, was played by a British guy on a famous TV show in 1964. The show was *Ed Sullivan*, and the guy was George Harrison of the Beatles. A great guitar player. My idol. Wanna hear it?" The crowd roared their approval as Ralston shouted the set change to the band, faced his amp, making the low feedback sound, then quickly turned and played the opening notes of "I Feel Fine."

The crowd went nuts.

It was a moment of unexpected glory for Ralston. He was playing the Harrison guitar and sharing in the surprise with 18,000 people. The whole show had been a feel-good night, honoring the doctors, nurses, EMTs, police, firemen and teachers who had slogged through the worst days of the more-than-year-long pandemic. He looked over at Ellis and Paloma, smiled and shook his head in wonder. Soloff gave him an air victory fist bump while Maggie danced with her friends. Ellis turned to Paloma and gave her a long, tight hug.

"In the weirdest way, we friggin' did it," she said in his ear over the music.

"A real E-ticket ride. Ready to go home?" Paloma wearily nodded yes and looked to signal Neely, the Kid and Leon. They weren't around.

"Where'd the guys go?"

"Probably burning one somewhere backstage. C'mon, let's grab them. Beat the traffic out of here."

She saw Gary toss the towel and water to a crew guy and start walking quickly to the backstage curtain, following Soloff, who had ducked through ahead of him.

"You see that? Soloff left and then Gary went after him."

"What, for more towels?" Ellis snarked.

"Let's follow. C'mon."

They wove their way through the crowd of dancing guests to the curtain, Ellis making a point to look away from Mountain Moran, not wanting to give him a second look.

"Duffy said we should go back to Gary. We never did," Ellis said.

"We were caught up with Longworth."

"Hey, Paloma."

They turned to see Maggie steaming towards them, face scrunched up.

"I'm disappointed," she said. "I trusted you guys and then you guys got my cousin Paul arrested?"

"Say what?" Paloma replied.

"Yeah, he said you sent the cops to his house yesterday."

"Not us," she said, studying Maggie. "What was he busted

for? Kidnapping?"

"Huh? No, they said he had stolen goods."

"Well, if it was us, he would have been charged with kidnapping after he grabbed up one of the guys who stole the guitar. We went out there to save the guy from whatever beating they were going to lay on him." Paloma added the beating part to make it dramatic.

"Didn't he help you get the guitar back?" Maggie said eagerly.

"No. Try to be happy your man is playing that guitar right now, okay?" Ellis said as they turned to go.

"Jeez, how's that for modern American fiction? People do make up some clever stories. Knew that house didn't look right. Now where'd those two go?" she said, looking around the piles of band gear backstage.

"Dressing rooms are this way. Was Gary going after Soloff? Are they working together?" Ellis asked as he speeded up.

"Leon said he saw Soloff and Longworth at the restaurant."

"But he didn't know if they were together?"

"Starting to feel like they were?"

"Could Gary know Mona? Maybe he fooled around with her too?"

"Dude, they don't play in the same league," Paloma replied, shaking her head.

Their "crew" passes got them into the dressing room tunnel. Paloma looked into the production office to see if either one was there. Down the hall, a caterer came running out of the RimShot dressing room, almost knocking over a food cart.

"I'm not paid enough for this shit," she said, quickly walking past them.

They heard a crash and went in.

Gary and Soloff were in a clinch, falling over a small table onto the back of the couch. Gary's face was bloodied, and Soloff's face was red with rage. Gary managed to get one arm free to push back across Soloff's neck.

"I saw your face when Tommy came out with that guitar. You set me up! Fucking had the guitar stolen, didn't you?" Gary demanded. "You heard me on the phone, in the kitchen."

Soloff kicked out at Gary's knee, and he howled, releasing his arm. Then they noticed Ellis and Paloma standing in the room.

"This fucking useless guy loses the guitar and now he tries to hang it on me. Nice try, asshole," Soloff shouted, spittle projecting from his mouth. "Thanks for finding it."

Ellis moved between them, holding out his arms like a fight ref.

Soloff picked up cheese cubes from the catering tray and threw them one at a time at Gary. "Here. Free food. You're going to be out of a job tomorrow."

Paloma studied them. Gary leaving the side of the stage during a show to go after Soloff was the act of a desperate man, not a guilty man. Her dad had worked with people like Gary, and they were loyal to a fault. She stepped forward.

"Got something to say Gary?" Paloma asked.

"Yeah, this dickhead must have heard me arrange to go to Willem's. I thought I saw your car that day, but I wasn't sure."

Paloma and Ellis shared a look. That's what stopped Gary on the Ring video Duffy showed them.

"See my car? You don't even know what kind of car I have."

"Sure, I do. Black AMG. At rehearsal you throw me the keys to park it like I'm some kind of fucking valet." Gary was a storehouse of resentment.

"Isn't Tommy looking for his towel boy by now? You should get going," Soloff scoffed.

Gary charged towards Soloff and Ellis caught him. Soloff was trying to be cool, picking up his shattered sunglasses off the floor, shaking his head. Giving Ellis a slight head tilt, Paloma approached Soloff. She didn't like him from the start so figured she had nothing to lose. He was off balance, so why not throw some shit and see what sticks.

"Don't need the bad acting. The guy you sold the guitar to gave you up," she said, watching Soloff's body language.

"You're nuts."

"Longworth told us. Where do you think we got the guitar?"

"Who?"

"Russell Longworth. Banshee?"

"Fuck off. Don't know what you're talking about," he said, starting to walk out.

"You know, the guy you had dinner with, in Venice."

Soloff looked at them with thin eyes, then to the door, where Mountain Moran had been standing, listening.

"All good in here?" Moran asked, in his deep husky voice, looking at a bloodied Gary.

"Sure, these guys were just leaving," Soloff said.

Paloma looked to Ellis, both figuring how to play out her bluff with Soloff.

"He stole Tommy's guitar," Gary said to Moran. "You're fucked," Gary spat out at Soloff and started to leave.

Moran had been looking at Ellis like he recognized him. It had been less than twenty-four hours before they were at the hospital.

"Hey, you're the spaz from the hospital. All recovered, huh?" Moran said to Ellis.

Ellis smiled and shrugged, trying to gauge if Moran was sarcastic or dense.

"Nobody leaves yet," Soloff said to Moran. "Ellis, Paloma. You work for Tommy. I want you to tell me where these guys who stole the guitar for Gary live. I'll send Mountain over there and in five minutes they'll give Gary up in a heartbeat." Paloma's dad had taught her the best defense was a good offense.

Mountain Moran looked at Soloff with a quizzical look.

Paloma picked up on the look and walked right up to Moran, who towered over her.

"Mister Moran, right? I'm Paloma Grant. You may have worked with my dad Bob Grant at some point. You were busy last night." When needed, she would play the Bob Grant card. He would have loved it.

Moran looked at her.

"You were on the fourth floor of the Westwood hospital, about 4 AM, and I recognized you as the guy we have on high-definition video breaking into our FAQ office and working out on Duffy, our elderly boss. No offense, but you're kinda easy to identify. Who sent you there? Tommy, or do you work for this guy? Do you know he had Tommy's million-dollar guitar stolen and is trying to lay it off on Gary here?" she said, pointing at Soloff.

"Listen to her," Gary said.

"Shut up," Soloff said, then turned to Paloma and Ellis.

"You're finished. Your little detective agency will wither and die when my lawyers are through with you."

Paloma continued. "I bet Duffy, from his hospital bed, might be talked out of pressing charges. Breaking and entering, not horrible. But on tape assaulting an elderly man, who by the way plays cards with lots of judges and cops? That could clog up your calendar for a few years." She embellished the Duffy hospital part.

Soloff was in a rage. He took a step towards Paloma and Ellis, who stepped a few feet apart into a defensive position. He pointed at Paloma.

"Throw them out. Now!" Soloff demanded of Moran. "Grab the passes off and throw them out."

Moran was quiet.

"Did I stutter? Throw them out!"

Moran looked to Gary, whom he had known and toured with for years.

"C'mon, Gary, the show is almost over. Gotta get back to the stage," Moran ordered as he turned and walked out.

"Where are you going?" Soloff demanded from Moran.

"I gotta do my job. Tommy depends on me," he said, walking out with Gary, who threw a middle-finger salute over his shoulder.

Soloff reached for his jacket to leave. "You guys are so fucked. You're going to be out of business, and don't dream about getting paid. You crossed the line big-time. Accusing me was a bad idea," he said. "You'll never work on the road again." He pointed a finger at Ellis, tempting Ellis to punch him out.

"Second time tonight someone said they weren't going to pay us," Paloma said, shaking her head at Soloff.

Then, stumbling through the doorway, quite stoned and oblivious, were Neely, the Kid and Leon, laughing, led by Murph, a tour bus driver they had known for years.

"The dressing room is like my wine cellar. I always liberate a great bottle or two. They don't care," Murph said as they finally noticed the standoff.

"Get out, you morons," Soloff ordered.

The Thorazine Kid stood still. He wasn't a guy you called names. He stepped to Soloff.

"What did you say, you Lindsey Buckingham–looking motherfucker? Did you just call me a moron? Do I know you?" the Kid demanded, right up in his face.

No one ever knew when the Thorazine Kid might go off, or if he really ever took the antipsychotic drug he was named after. He could be scary. Not someone Soloff was used to. Leon, who had never been in a backstage dressing room, had been checking out the place, but was still listening.

"Black AMG, right? Dinner at Zanzibar, with that guy Longworth?" Leon said casually. He could stretch his powers.

"What?" Soloff said, spinning his head to Leon. "Who are you?"

"Our associate Leon. He's the invisible guy at the valet stand. Never forgets a face," Paloma said.

"Really. Some kind of syndrome," Neely added eagerly, chewing on cheese cubes and grapes from the catering trays.

"You're all fucked. I'm out of here," he said, starting to walk forward.

"Well, we have some more talking to do, don't you think?" Ellis said calmly.

Leon and the Kid stepped to Soloff and nodded, like they were agreeing with a complicated medical diagnosis.

Ralston ended the show in assault mode, screaming into the mic, "Well, shake it up, baby, Twist and Shout." Members of the other bands who had stuck around flooded the stage and crowded around vocal mics for the reply chorus. Ralston gave a head nod to Maggie, and she raced up the ramp and joined the group, some of whom were now doing a bizarre, drunken version of "the Twist." The audience was ecstatic, treated to something seriously special after the most trying year of their lives. Taking bows, the performers moved to the front of the stage, shouting thank-you to the audience, who roared with approval.

Ralston took his cue and ran up to the mic. "One more time!"

With a final flourish, Ralston leaping into the air and landing with the drummer's downbeat, the show ended. Ralston held the Harrison guitar over his head like an offering to the gods, then turned and handed it off to Jimmy Gomes, who pretended to almost drop it. He had worked for Ralston for a long time. They *knew* it was a magic moment.

The musicians came down the ramp, to the thunderous applause of the audience, and made their way to the backstage hospitality area. Benny led Ralston and Maggie, with Gary waiting for the guitar to be packed up, to the dressing room so he could dry off. Ralston sweated under the bright lights, especially wearing a flannel Dodgers jersey.

They found Ellis and Paloma on the couch, drinking some expensive wine.

"You guys found the fucking guitar! Amazing," Benny said, entering the dressing room, holding up his hand for a high-five. "I knew you were the ones to call."

Ralston came over, stripping off the jersey, reliving the moment. "I couldn't believe it! I was handing off my guitar and there is Jimmy, holding out the fuckin' Harrison! Unreal. Did you see it? The crowd went nuts. Guitar sounded great, right?" he said, nodding his head vigorously. "There's a bonus coming your way for sure."

"Thanks," Paloma replied simply.

"And I heard you found the idiots who stole it."

"Not a moment too soon," she answered.

"Yeah, they led us to some unexpected people and places," Ellis said.

Ralston looked puzzled, then stripped to his waist to towel off while Maggie got a fresh black shirt from his wardrobe case.

Maggie looked at Paloma, then turned to Ralston.

"I was wrong, babe, about that stuff with Paul. It wasn't them."

Ralston gave her a blank look, already having forgotten what she had told him.

"We should explain about the guitar," Ellis started, then turned to Paloma to continue. He remembered how Ralston and Benny tended to talk past her.

"First, we wondered about your cousin Paul, but as you said, he was arrested yesterday for something else. We found the guitar in the home of a rich tech guy. Randall Longworth. Seems he had dinner with someone who works for you. According to his unhappy wife, Mona, that person was your accountant, Mister Soloff. Maybe he wanted to replace the income you and his other music clients weren't producing during Covid. We figure managing Longworth's tech millions would more than make that up. Oh yeah, the telephone bidder at the auction when Paul bought the guitar. That was Longworth."

"This is crazy," Ralston said, looking at Maggie.

"Yup. Soloff offered the guitar as a sweetener to help get the guy's business. Millions to manage. He probably used a "cutout" from his office to set up the theft, and then Longworth picked up the guitar himself. We found it hanging on his living room wall next to a signed Eddie Van Halen Stratocaster. Who knows, maybe Soloff planned on stealing it back once he got paid."

Paloma nodded to Ellis to continue the story. "Yeah, he was selling it, not giving him the guitar. For a million cash. Was supposed to get paid after the fourth. Not happening."

Ralston and Benny stood still, looking between Ellis and Paloma. Maggie was shaking her head. There was no love lost between her and Soloff.

"And you believe this shit? This Mona?" was all that Ralston could say.

"Got you your guitar back, right? Sure we believe her. You can call her," Ellis said, holding out an FAQ card with her number on the back that she had stuck in the guitar case. "Just got off the phone. Tells a great story."

"Chat with Gary when he comes in. He's got a good handle on this," Ellis added.

Ellis felt for Gary. It wasn't easy being the guy who worked his ass off for a rock star only to be taken for granted and overlooked. Who knows, maybe now he will get his own office.

"Benny, find Soloff. Where is he? Hospitality? I want to hear his side of this crazy story."

Benny called Soloff. A phone started ringing in the shower part of the locker room. They looked at each other, then to the doorway.

Neely, Leon and the Thorazine Kid, with huge, stoned grins, rolled Soloff in from the shower room, gaffers taped to a desk chair, a piece of tape covering his mouth. To say Soloff was furious was an understatement.

"What in the wide, wide world of sports is goin' on here?" Benny said, merrily echoing a famous line from Dr. Strangelove. Tour pranks were legendary. Ralston and Maggie just said, "what the fuck?" Then Ralston burst into laughter.

"Dude, what's uuup!" he said, approaching Soloff. Leaning towards him. Soloff strained against the tape.

"Hey, Benny, remember when we first met Soloff on tour and Walsh had hot glued him into his room? That funky hotel on Hegenberger Road in Oakland? He spent most of the day-off looking out the window at us by the pool with those bikini girls from the club. What did you call that look? Forlorn?"

They laughed. Amazingly, no one seemed in a hurry to untape him. Soloff made loud, muffled noises, shouting through the tape. His face was beet red.

"We just heard one crazy story. These guys say you're the one who had the guitar stolen and set up Gary to take the fall. What's that about? And then you sold it to some rich guy so you could get his business? Ye of little faith," Ralston said, raising his hands to the sky.

Soloff struggled against the tape and made angry, pleading sounds.

Gary walked in with the guitar in the case. Seeing Soloff taped up, he looked at Paloma and Ellis, who smiled. He then turned to Ralston, who smiled and gave him a military-style salute, Ralston's ultimate sign of respect. Gary was relieved and thrilled. He gave a smart salute back.

Paloma grabbed the bottle of expensive wine and led Ellis and the guys out of the room, then stopped and turned.

"Oh yeah, two things. It was a dick move to send Mountain Moran and his pal to our office and the hospital. You said you would stay out of it."

Ralston looked at Maggie, then Paloma, and shrugged.

"Guess my enthusiasm got the best of me," he said flatly.

Ellis and Paloma shared a look. He was a dick.

"Then two, you should check out the property records for

that cul-de-sac out in Chatsworth. Seems like a few of your houses may have been stolen," she added, leading the motley parade out the door.

Neely powered the car up Prairie, heading back to the west side.

"You think he can talk his way out of it?" Neely asked.

"Jeez, you roasted that guy," the Kid said.

"I kinda don't care. I'm just glad to be done working for people like that," Paloma said.

"You mean rock n' rollers?" the Kid, blasted on weed, half shouted.

"I was leaning more towards assholes, but I guess we take what walks in the door."

"What was that about stolen houses?" Neely asked as they drove back to Venice.

"Just a little gasoline on the fire. Ralston had bragged about owning and renting out houses on cul-de-sacs in the valley. Out at Paul's, there were two houses and three empty lots. Duffy checked at the hall of records and found permits had been pulled to build, but they never were. His guess is the guy was faking the rents and using Ralston's money as capital for "other investment purposes," of course with the intent to pay it back. Probably with other clients as well. Who knows, maybe he has a gambling jones. Given the climate with Covid, maybe his other investments went south. Those kinds of things never end well."

Heading to Venice, Neely asked, "Should I stop at Longworth's so the Kid can give him his money back?"

Everyone burst out laughing.

"Not 'til we get paid," Ellis said, giving Paloma and Leon a high-five.

"Oh shit, Neighbor Dave is still babysitting the idiots," Paloma exclaimed. "Call him."

Dave reported everything was now calm; Michael had stopped cursing out Henry, and he might have fallen asleep. When Ellis tried to add Longworth to the call, Mona answered, saying that the apps were back to normal speed, so he had taken an Ambien and passed out. Ellis thanked her again for the real story and asked her to have Longworth call the office tomorrow.

The dilemma was what to do with Michael and Henry. They had their IDs, knew who they were and after they spread their faces around the tech community, doubted another "honey pot" cyberattack from them. Plus, the partnership between the two was over. Then there was them tied up in the car. If the police were involved, it could get messy.

After taking photos of their licenses, credit cards, whatever, Neely and Ellis untied them, being cursed out the entire time. They would circulate her photo, both red hair and blonde, on tech talk websites. Michael saved her abuse for Paloma, who refrained from some informal surfer's code of punching her out. After all, they had retrieved the cash and the correct ransomware code. Why they hadn't just given Longworth the real code at the beginning was a mystery to Michael as well. Henry inspected the wreckage of his drone and threatened to sue.

Thinking this behavior rude, The Kid stabbed their two back tires. They could get new ones when Costco opened.

18

Chapter 18

July 5

Having been awake for almost two days, Ellis and Paloma slept into the early afternoon. The celebratory tequila shots, after all the cars had been collected, aided that sleep. Today, Venice was in full summer mode, with people on the streets and in the shops.

As much as she wanted to surf, Paloma chose to rest. There were bruises to heal. News reports of a new, more deadly "Delta" strain sweeping the Indian subcontinent was the cloud hanging over everyone who was out enjoying a beautiful summer afternoon at the beach. The whole pandemic thing had become tiring.

Sitting at a card table in the yard both houses shared, they wolfed down the huevos rancheros that Neighbor Dave cooked up as a late breakfast. Prewash lay by Paloma's feet. Neighbors waved as they walked by—one of the great things about this neighborhood.

The rumble of the motorcycles interrupted the stillness of the afternoon. Eddy pulled up, followed by Cindy on a Grant's Harley, then Rosato and Jim-O. Taking off his helmet, Eddy was animated.

"Incredible Malibu fireworks last night. Like the Boston Esplanade, without the cannons. They had three barges going up the coast."

Eddy loved fireworks.

Paloma ran over and hugged Cindy. Neighbor Dave and Ellis dragged a bench and some chairs across the yard as Jim-O and Rosato opened a few beers. Paloma nodded her head to something Cindy said.

"Hey, big congrats on finding the guitar. Sounds like a wild night!" Rosato said.

"Understatement" was all Paloma said.

19

Chapter 19

Coda

Near golden hour, Paloma was finally in the water. Ellis watched from the shore as she surfed the incoming tide. Riding low on her board, pushing the waves, daring them to wipe her out, she was free and alive. Her quick moves and cuts had others on the beach watching as well. Covid couldn't stop her from surfing, hadn't robbed her of that part of her life.

Ellis reveled in her freedom on the water. He compared it to the freedom he felt on tour, moving from city to city, with great music and wild crowds. After more than a year, his life of concerts and touring started to feel like the past. He wondered if this was what getting older felt like, that large life changes just happened, without planning them.

She rode her last wave up to the beach, landing where he was standing knee deep in the water. Getting the board up on the sand, she took Ellis' hand and watched the sunset.

"We got lucky and kinda stumbled onto the guitar, didn't we?

Feels weird how we found it by accident," Ellis said, dragging his foot in the sand.

"That's right. Sometimes luck enters into things. Leon really gave us the first clue when he recognized them at his restaurant."

"Yeah, but—"

"Hey, first year. We'll get better with more reps, more cases."

"Glad you are optimistic."

"Yes, you too," she said, leaning into him.

"Johnny Cristo offered me a tour today. I told him Neely's ready to move up."

"Really? See, you are optimistic," Paloma said, still looking at the sun.

"Yeah, like Duffy says, 'FAQ all the way.' Now, that's what I do. What we do. Yeah?"

"Sure, as long as there is time to surf," she replied with a smile." And pizza."

The wispy high clouds were turning a pale pink.

"So, I'm kinda curious. What did Cindy say to you?"

"Nothing special."

"She and Eddy are getting married, right?"

"Nope."

The waves crashed. They watched the sunset.

Paloma looked at him. "You really want to know?"

"Something about the look you shared after. Not the smiles I expected."

Paloma was silent. The sun was a sliver on the horizon. She pulled him close, squeezed his arm and whispered in his ear.

"Delta Covid's gonna suck, and my mom's getting out of jail, early."

Afterword

Author's Note.

Paloma, Ellis, and the Irregulars were so much fun that I wanted to keep hanging around with them while Covid became a huge player in everyone's lives. June of 2021 was "the great awakening", before the Delta variant raised new trouble. I wanted to tell this story then, where for a few sunny months, there was a joyous sense of relief when we all hoped the worst had passed.

Thanks to some of my early readers: Rob Lippincott, Dennis White, Mark Gauthier, David Sloop, Laura Ambler, and Di Rosenblum. Your encouragement helps.

Thanks to my wife Beth, who encouraged and edited me with honest feedback and always has my back. She been my rock for so many years. Thanks to my adult children, Nicky and Rosy, who have supported this endeavor, giving me room, advice, and criticism along the way, and my art director extraordinaire, Kira Klaas.

Thanks to my long-time college pal and terrific writer Bill Finkelstein, who opened the door for my television career. For that I will forever be grateful. I've worked with some incredible screenwriters who showed me, I hope, how to tell a story. Thanks to Steven Bochco, David Milch, Shawn Ryan, David Shore, and David Mamet.

In memory of:

Northwest Sound's finest; "Fast Eddie" Wynne, David "Snake" Reynolds, Bob Sterne, and Stanley Johnston.

Ronald Perfit; "Elton Ron", road manager, avid postcard writer, tour newsletter editor (*The Pittsburgh Perspirer*, a classic) and one of the smartest, funniest people I've known.

Brian Murphy and Terry Bassett, West coast rock and roll promoters of the highest caliber and good friends. They could promote a tour on a handshake.

About the Author

Steven DePaul spent two decades touring the world with rock bands, including Eagles, Joni Mitchell, Rod Stewart, Crosby, Stills and Nash, The Grateful Dead, The Cars, Boston and Bruce Springsteen. He is an Emmy-winning producer, and director for episodic television shows, including NYPD Blue, The Good Doctor, Bones, Grim, NCIS-LA and others. *Frequently Asked Questions* is his second book in the Rock and Roll Confidential Mystery series.